SMOOTH SAILING
ANCHORED IN TEMPTATION

For those who were told they were too much—
May you find love among those who know you were always enough.

Author's Note

This story is a contemporary romance where love and hope prevails, but some topics might be troubling to some readers, such as gambling addiction, financial fraud, trust and abandonment issues, and a car accident. Readers who may be sensitive to these topics, please take note.

Contents

Chapter One	1
Chapter Two	6
Chapter Three	13
Chapter Four	20
Chapter Five	25
Chapter Six	30
Chapter Seven	37
Chapter Eight	45
Chapter Nine	57
Chapter Ten	63
Chapter Eleven	69
Chapter Twelve	77
Chapter Thirteen	85
Chapter Fourteen	96
Chapter Fifteen	100
Chapter Sixteen	109
Chapter Seventeen	118
Chapter Eighteen	125

Chapter Nineteen	130
Chapter Twenty	139
Chapter Twenty-one	148
Chapter Twenty-Two	153
Chapter Twenty-Three	160
Chapter Twenty-Four	168
Chapter Twenty-Five	177
Chapter Twenty-Six	185
Chapter Twenty-Seven	195
Chapter Twenty-Eight	203
Chapter Twenty-Nine	209
Chapter Thirty	218
Chapter Thirty-One	225
Chapter Thirty-Two	229
Chapter Thirty-Three	237
Chapter Thirty-Four	246
Chapter Thirty-Five	254
Chapter Thirty-Six	260
Chapter Thirty-Seven	270
Epilogue	282
Bonus	288
Dear Reader	289
Stormy Waters	290
About The Author	303

Chapter One

July 12th, 12:15 a.m.

The willowy woman with short red hair stalked toward the entrance of The Hill and yanked the door open. Deep, sensual vocals from a local band filled the night air as the door of the restaurant-turned-nightclub opened. When it shut, the crickets and frogs took over singing. Neither calmed Paloma Wagner's boiling anger.

She whirled back to the man she was in a situationship with and pointed over her shoulder to his pretty neighbor. "Are you sleeping with Lilith?"

Asher wasn't her boyfriend, but Paloma had insisted at the start of their orgasm arrangement that they'd tell each other if they wanted more. Or less. And yes, lately, a tiny part of her had hoped he'd eventually want more. But above all, she wanted honesty.

"No." His voice was firm, but he looked away as if guilt made her gaze too heavy to hold.

She was so damn tired of men lying to her.

Heat spread from her chest, down her arms, and to her fingers that curled into fists. The warmth had little to do with the muggy Michigan night, and all to do with blooming disappointment. She shook her head. "Then what the hell is going on?"

He crossed his arms. "Nothing. I'm just worried about my neighbor."

"Because she's with me?" A man snarled.

Paloma jolted, forgetting Asher's friend Max was in the parking lot with them. He'd been leaving with Lilith. It seemed Lilith was in hot demand. Scorching jealousy flared in Paloma, but she smothered it, refusing to let it burn her.

"Fuck," Asher sighed and shoved his hands in his pockets. "Listen, man, I'm sorry. You know how I get with crowds, especially when there's drinking. I saw her leave, and I panicked. I wasn't thinking clearly."

"No shit," Max grumbled, but his tense stance fell away. "But listen, if it'll ease your mind and she doesn't mind, you give her a ride home instead of me."

His acquiescence annoyed the shit out of Paloma. Asher shouldn't get a free pass because his past made him an overprotective ass.

"It would, but swear, it's nothing against you," Asher said.

"Whatever, man. I'm going back inside." Max turned, heading toward The Hill.

She'd always found him handsome with his broad shoulders and lean, ropey muscles, even better looking than Asher. But Max was a nice guy—like a real one, not the assholes who pretend to be decent men.

And true good guys always found her to be too much.

Her jaw clenched and her gaze snapped back to Asher, who was still avoiding eye contact. He wasn't the love of her life, not even close, so it wasn't that he might be interested in Lilith that truly bothered her. It was the lying that got under her skin.

She'd dealt with enough deception to last a lifetime. And here was Asher, a man she'd trusted enough to let into her bed, into her life, lying to her. Pretending he wasn't into his neighbor when it was painfully obvious.

The anger that had been simmering now threatened to boil over. But beneath it was a sharp sting of hurt. Why couldn't he just be honest with her? Did he think she was too fragile to handle the truth? Or did he simply not respect her enough to give it to her straight?

She took a deep breath, refusing to let him see how much this affected her. Instead, she focused on the lie. The betrayal of trust cut deeper than any potential attraction to another woman.

"This isn't about your normal controlling tendencies—"

"I'm not controlling." He had the nerve to sound offended.

"Fine. We'll call it your hero complex. I see the way you watch her. You don't look at her like she's a friend." She took a small step away from him. "Don't be that guy who wants to fuck someone else but is too much of a ball sack to 'fess up."

"I swear that's not what I'm doing." He ran his fingers through his hair, pulled at the ends, then let his hands fall to his side. "But we should take a break."

"And you're telling me this has nothing to do with your neighbor?" she asked, relieved her voice didn't shake.

"It has to do with you wanting more than I can give you," Asher said.

Paloma crossed her arms, pressing against the gentle throbbing in her heart. She was an idiot. Asher wasn't even her boyfriend. Hell, that's why she'd first hit on him—because he didn't have girlfriends.

But of course, her dumb ass had to go and catch feelings for him. They might be small, but it still stung.

"Like I said before, I'm not in a position to be in a relationship," he finished.

Ah, yes, his daughter. Maybe there was some truth to it, but she was also his excuse.

"You use Raven as a shield. A justification not to get close to any woman because you're afraid of getting hurt."

"No, I don't."

She held up a hand. "It's true. I do feel more than simple lust for you, so it's better to break it off now if you don't feel the same. I'm not interested in being with a guy who can't give me what I need."

"You deserve more than I can give you," he repeated.

"Saying it once was enough, thanks," she snapped.

His words were a cop-out and total bullshit. But she should be used to it. She was always too much. Or not enough. She straightened her shoulders and lifted her chin high enough that the sting in her eyes couldn't spill over.

Kissing his cheek, she curved her lips into the smile she'd perfected after a lifetime of goodbyes. "I'll see you around."

She sauntered toward The Hill, refusing to look back. One foot in front of the other, away from another failed relationship. Forward was the only direction that mattered.

Her steps slowed. But what if there was nothing to look forward to in her future?

She rolled her shoulders and shook out her hands. It was time to stop with her pity pary for one. Dating wasn't everything. She was rebuilding her career and was almost out of the red. And Asher? It was her own damn fault for thinking those lazy Sunday mornings and midnight tacos meant anything more than convenience. Hell, she'd been the one to suggest keeping it casual. She'd practically bragged about her no-strings philosophy. Turns out she was just another woman who couldn't keep sex from getting complicated.

Pulling open the door to The Hill, music washed over her, a gentle caress on her sore heart. The daytime dinner tables were shoved against the wall, and gyrating bodies filled the makeshift dance floor with the usual last call hopefuls lining the outskirts and bar. The crowd parted for half a second, and she spotted two friends in a booth on the far side of the restaurant. They were chatting and nursing martinis. She'd grab a drink and join them.

Heading that way, she sighed. The bar was as packed as the dance floor. A man on a stool stood. Finally, a sliver of luck. She rushed forward and slid into the empty seat, nodding a thank you and signaling the bartender.

She glanced at the man on the adjacent stool and smiled. It was none other than sweet and sexy Max. Although right now, he looked more sour than sweet. No surprise. They'd both expected their nights to go very differently. She thought Asher would be coming home with her, and Max had probably assumed he was spending the night with Lilith. Instead, those two were riding off into the night together toward their happily ever after. Jerks.

Sitting straight, she ran a palm down her fitted red dress, subtly adjusting the plunging neckline. She and Max could use each other to forget about the night's disappointments. As the wise adage said, "The best way to get over a man is to get under another one."

CHAPTER TWO

July 12th, 12:35 a.m.

Max London tapped his glass on the bartop and raised a hand at the bartender. Although, he should slow down or he'd be staggering home.

"Let me get your next drink," came a sultry voice he recognized. The last time he'd heard it, it was laden with anger. Now it dripped with desire.

He turned to face Paloma. She crossed her legs and leaned against the bar, the silk of her dress pulling taut in all the right places. And damn, the woman looked really good in red. Asher was a fool to let her walk away.

"How about I get yours?" she asked, oozing confidence and sex. Was it hiding sadness underneath? She had to see the way Asher looked at his neighbor.

Before she told Brian her order, a pretty pink drink was set in front of her. Had she even ordered one? "Did you have a lager, Max?" the bartender asked.

"IPA," he ground out. Couldn't Brian, who was the regular weekend bartender for over a year, remember it? He didn't seem to have the same problem with Paloma.

Fuck, he was as bitter as his drink. It was time to go home. "Add her drink to my tab, then close it." Max downed his beer. It was time to sleep off his shitty mood.

He'd enjoyed dancing with Lilith, but there hadn't been a spark between them. His only plan was to drop her off on his way home, and he hadn't appreciated his friend's insinuations and attitude. Asshole.

"Don't leave so soon," Paloma purred, resting a hand on his knee.

The words were clear enough. It was their meaning that had his mind spinning. Her palm slid higher on his leg, and his gaze darted between her hand and her face, to those hot, red cupid lips. They curved into a smile that sent his pulse racing. Her fingers traced even higher on his thigh, and his confusion vanished. Oh. *Oh.*

"What about Asher?" he asked.

"Honey." She leaned closer. "I don't wait around for any man who looks at another woman the way he looks at her."

Every impulse in his body screamed to say yes. Which is exactly why he shifted his leg from her touch. Paloma was hotter than the July sun, but his first instincts were usually his worst—and right now, every single one of them was begging him to accept.

She shrugged and reached for her drink. He couldn't help watching her full red lips press against the glass as the amber liquid slipped down her throat.

Wait. Amber?

He glanced at his drink. It was pink. He raised his brows at her.

"Sorry." She didn't sound it and he couldn't help grinning. He liked her sass. "Brian thinks he's cute giving me that drink. It has grapefruit in it. I hate grapefruit." She took another sip of his drink.

He wrinkled his nose. He couldn't blame her for the theft. At all. "Grapefruit is nasty. Why does he make it for you?"

She pointed at the cocktail. "It's called a Paloma."

"You're named after a drink?"

"Yup. According to my parents, I was conceived on a wild vacation in Mexico when my mom discovered the drink."

Max chuckled. "I thought it was after Pablo Picasso's daughter."

"Why?"

"I don't know. Figured maybe your parents were into art. Back in high school, our senior year, you were in my art class. And way more talented than me."

"Thanks." She smiled, and he was positive it was the first genuine one during their conversation. It was beautiful. "Not that I've drawn or painted for fun in years."

"But your job is creative. You're an interior designer, right?"

She tilted her head. "How'd you know?"

When she and Asher first got together, he'd mentioned they'd met while he'd been building a house she was designing. But for some reason, Max didn't want his friend in his conversation with Paloma.

"We live in a small town," Max said. "Isn't it a prerequisite to know everyone's business?"

She groaned. "Ugh. It is." Picking up his drink, she swirled it, then took a sip. Setting it down, she said, "You, um, I don't know what it's called, but you design landscapes."

Warmth spread through his chest that she knew what he did for a living, but even so, he couldn't hold in a grin. "Landscape architect. Yup, for homes and businesses."

She stared at him for a full three seconds or so, then blinked and said, "Wow, you have a really nice smile."

He dropped his gaze to his stolen drink. "Oh, uh, thanks." He rubbed the back of his neck.

"Don't tell me the guy who designs million dollar gardens gets flustered over a simple compliment," she teased

"I don't—" He fiddled with the paper umbrella in his glass of her old drink. "They're not million dollar gardens."

She took another sip of his drink, peering at him over the rim. "So half million then? And you're still avoiding the compliment part."

His face burned hot enough to match her dress. "I design functional outdoor spaces that—" He caught her raised eyebrow and stopped himself. "I'm doing it again, aren't I?"

"Hiding behind work talk? Yup." She nudged his shoulder with hers. "But it's kind of adorable."

A laugh escaped his recently clenched jaw. When had his dark mood slipped away?

"And your work *is* outstanding," she finished.

He sat up taller. "Oh, and how do you know?"

"I decorated one of Asher's builds. During our final walk-through with the client, the landscaping was finished. Later, when I saw Asher I mentioned how impressed I was with the design. He told me your company had done the work."

Forget his chest warming—it was damn near swelling with pride. "Thanks." He swirled his new pink drink and took a small sip. He grunted as the sweet and sour flavors hit his tongue. "This isn't too bad. The tequila masks most of the grapefruit taste."

When she didn't reply, he glanced at her. Her red fingernails tapped on the bar top as she stared at nothing. He waved a hand in front of her, and she blinked. Her eyes held a bright gleam, though different from the earlier flirtatiousness.

"Could I hire you?" she asked.

Had he read her wrong? Was she hitting on him again? If so, this was by far the oddest pickup line.

Max scratched his cheek. "I'm not following . . ."

"I have a super swanky client. It's a couple with a gorgeous home in Brighton on Woodland Lake with lots of windows. They want a year-round garden in their house. And I don't mean a few potted plants, but something lush and hardy that blends with the vibe of the indoor decor."

Oh, she actually wanted to hire him for a job. And his dumb ass was a little disappointed.

And also intrigued. An inside garden would be an interesting challenge, and he admitted as much to her. He ran his finger along the rim of the drink in front of him. "I already have a lot of jobs scheduled."

"I understand you're busy, but this isn't just any job. It's a chance to create something truly unique—a living, breathing work of art that seamlessly integrates with high-end interior design. We're talking about transforming an entire section of their home into an oasis that changes with the seasons, right alongside Woodland Lake's stunning views. It's not just landscaping; it's sculpting an ecosystem. Plus, the budget . . . let's just say it reflects the caliber of the project."

He balanced the possibilities in his mind, absently running his thumb over the worn edge of the bar top. "I've already got a full schedule. I'm not sure my company is the right fit."

Taking on another project would eat up the sliver of free summer he had, and he didn't need the business or the money. But the concept tugged at him like a loose thread he couldn't help but pull. This wasn't just another job—it was the kind of innovative challenge that could transform and grow his company.

His gaze flickered to Paloma as the bass thrummed through his chest, matching his quickened heartbeat. Turning her down had been the right thing to do, even if every sip of his new drink seemed to taste of regret.

"I've seen your previous work. You can do this."

Her certainty got under his skin. For a moment, he saw himself through her eyes: not as the screw-up in his family who made too many impulsive choices. Yes, he saw the irony in taking on an impulsive project to prove he wasn't impulsive, but something about it—and her—had him intrigued.

"Walk me through the concept one more time." The smile that crossed her face told him she'd known all along he'd say yes.

The attraction hit him like gravity, but beneath it lurked a nagging voice. Her relationship with Asher was barely history before she'd turned those siren eyes his way.

It didn't matter. This was about work. He'd keep it about work.

"How about you come with me to their place tomorrow?" she said. "I'll show you my plans for the house and what they're looking for with an interior garden."

He could fit it in, so why not at least look? "Sure. What's the address?"

She gave him another brilliant, genuine smile, and his pulse raced, his heart smacking against his ribs. Shit. Good thing he'd managed to hold in his impulsiveness and had turned her down before they'd started talking. The more he got to know her, the more he liked her. He could already tell he'd have wanted more than a night with her. And all she wanted him for was to get over another man.

Working together was the smarter choice. They shook hands and he ignored how he liked the feel of her soft skin against his callused palm.

Chapter Three

July 16th, 9:09 a.m.

Paloma pressed a hand to her stomach, staring at the printer. Excitement battled with anxiety, making her regret the small bowl of oatmeal she'd eaten for breakfast. With a final whirl and quiet hiss, the sheet with Max's contract slid from the printer.

She picked up the warm paper, her fingers tracing over the blank signature line. Who would have thought a failed pickup at The Hill would lead to this? She shook her head, still amazed at how quickly their conversation had shifted from awkward flirtation to professional excitement.

Before they'd met at the Thompsons' house two days ago, she'd researched his business. It was a small but premier landscape design firm that handled major commercial and residential projects. It was a coup that he was willing to take on this specialized portion of her project even with his packed schedule. Still, her expectations needed to remain low. She'd tried partnerships in the past and they'd failed miserably.

Her phone dinged with an incoming call at the same time her doorbell rang. Her cell was face up on the desk and her dad's name flashed on the screen. They hadn't talked in over a month, and it was five in the morning in California.

Her stomach clenched, and she picked up the phone. "Dad? Everything okay?"

"Everything's fine. I wanted to catch you before my day got started."

The bell chimed again. She crossed to the door and opened it, the phone pressed to her ear. "Oh, good. I was worried because it's so early."

Max stood on her porch in a faded green t-shirt and equally faded jeans. Her breath halted somewhere in her chest. Some women loved men in designer suits. Others got hot for guys with calluses on their hands. Hers was the latter. Even his scuffed brown work boots were sexy. But it didn't matter. He might soon be her work partner. She waved him in, motioning toward her office.

"Could I call you back? I'm meeting with a potential business partner." She led Max to her office and handed him the contracts to read.

"Oh?" Her father's voice carried that familiar note of concern that always made her shoulders tense. "What kind of partnership?"

"A landscape architect. Max London. I've been hired by a couple for a full house redesign, including an indoor garden. We'll be working together to make sure his design matches mine. It's innovative. He's got great technical knowledge of environmental systems and plant life, and combined with my understanding of interior spaces, we could create something really special." The words tumbled out faster than she intended, already defensive. She had to clamp her mouth shut to keep from babbling.

"Interesting concept." Her father paused. "It's good to see you taking initiative again, especially after . . . well, after Richard."

The reminder hit like a punch to her confidence. She turned away from Max, who was thankfully still absorbed in reading the paperwork, and left the office. "Dad, that was almost two years ago. I've learned from my mistakes."

"I hope so."

Her fingers tightened around the phone, and she paced the hallway. "I'm a smart businesswoman, Dad. I've done my research." Sure, she'd proposed the collaboration impulsively, but her gut had been right about him. "Max's company is successful, his reputation is excellent, and this partnership could be incredibly profitable for both of us."

"I know you're smart. I just worry—"

"I have to go, Dad. Max is waiting." She ended the call before he could respond. Smoothing her silk sleeveless blouse, she squared her shoulders. She was done letting her past dictate her future.

She stepped back into her office, and Max looked up from the contract, concern flickering across his features. "Everything okay?"

The smile she gave him was genuine. Something about his steady presence helped ground her. "Perfect. My dad was just checking in."

And she'd prove her father wrong. Show him she wasn't the same naive woman who'd trusted her ex-fiancé with her company's finances, only to discover he'd been draining her accounts. Never again. This partnership with Max was different. They were temporary, but true business partners, sharing both risks and rewards. And this time she'd done her due diligence and planned to establish clear financial controls, where every damn transaction would go through her hands first.

"So," she said, tapping the contract. "What do you think?"

"That you're efficient." His voice was neutral. That was a good sign.

Coming around the desk, she tapped her mouse, and her computer screen blinked to life. She pulled up the designs they'd talked about while at the Thompsons' house. "I hope—"

Max had wandered to her office door and was looking into the main part of her house. "You have a nice place," he said.

"I'd hope so since I'm an interior designer." She bit her lower lip, secretly pleased. Moving beside him, she took in her favorite part of her home: the large glass doors that made up the far wall, the patio stretching the length, and beyond, the lake. "Although I think the beauty comes from the view more than my talent at interior design."

"It's a combination. Your furniture and decorations accentuate instead of competing with the view. I love doing the same with landscape designs. Focus on the client's personality and favorite features of their home and subtly highlight both." He rubbed the back of his neck. "Sorry, I'm babbling."

"Are you kidding me? It's so nice to talk to someone who loves design. Most of my friends' eyes glaze over." She sucked in a happy breath and her body hummed.

They were close enough that his scent teased her on the heavy inhale. The man smelled good, like outdoors in summer. She switched to breathing through her mouth. It didn't help. She swore she could taste him. And he was delicious.

Forcing herself to focus on business, she gestured back toward her desk. "But we should go over those designs we talked about at the Thompsons'."

He nodded and returned to the desk. Taking his time to look through the photos, he asked intelligent questions. Straightening, he picked up the contract and leaned against the nearest wall, crossing his feet at the ankles. His large hands turned the pages of the contract, the same hands that had sketched out brilliant design concepts at the Thompsons' house. They were steady and confident, suggesting he knew his craft.

Her gaze dropped to his belt, practical brown leather worn down from job sites. Unlike her ex's polished designer accessories, everything about Max radiated an earthy magnetism that made her breath catch. What would those calloused hands would feel like against her skin?

Shit. What was wrong with her? Her father's warning about Richard still stung, yet here she was imagining Max's strong fingers tracing patterns on her body instead of focusing on the contract that could revitalize her bruised business reputation. She'd promised herself that work would come before men and lust, but she hadn't counted on his quiet intensity being quite so . . . distracting.

"I'm good with presenting the job as one entity," he said. "This'll be different from my usual corporate indoor gardens. More intimate spaces, working with your residential design vision . . ." His shoulders relaxed as he leaned forward, the corner of his mouth lifting in that way that made her stomach flip. "I like that we'll be creating something completely new here."

"Me too." She couldn't keep the enthusiasm from her voice, didn't even try. Her mind raced with the way his gardens could transform her design concepts, elevate them into something unique in the industry.

"Who'll do all the paperwork?" he asked. "The billing, contacting the clients for payment? That stuff?"

His question popped her excitement. "I'd like to handle it." Her chin lifted slightly as she met his eyes, her heart picking up speed while she waited for him to push back.

"I'll do it," he said.

A heaviness filled her body, her shoulders sagging. "I'm perfectly capable of handling admin work."

"I meant, I'll take the job."

She shuffled back a step. "That's it. Just like that? You haven't even met the clients. They could be difficult."

And mysterious. Elodie Thompson had spent twenty minutes describing her vision for "intimate spaces for entertaining," her eyes sparkling with excitement while her husband kept adding specific requests about sight lines and "private gathering areas."

Max raised an eyebrow. "Why do I get the feeling there's a story here?"

"Let's just say they have—" She searched for a diplomatic way to describe their enthusiastic but cryptic consultation. "—very particular ideas about entertainment spaces. And they're passionate about weekend gatherings."

His mouth twitched. "Sounds intriguing. But I don't need to meet them. The project is interesting. And my office manager will be happy to not have to balance another project." He grinned. "And while I love designing and creating, I hate the back and forth with clients. I do my damnedest to pass that part off to my lead designer, Grace."

"I'm tempted to make you sign the contract right now. In blood," Paloma joked. "Partnering with you on this project will be fantastic for my business, and honestly, I like running the part you despise. Although, you have to at least meet with the clients. They want to make sure you understand their vision."

"You promised I didn't have to deal with them," he play-whined before giving her one of those gorgeous, heart-stopping grins.

She forced herself to focus on the practical details. "The timeline's tight. We're looking at three to four months from start to finish. Think you can handle working that closely with me for that long?"

The words were out before she could stop them. Too flirtatious, especially after she promised herself to keep things professional. But

Max only nodded, still wearing that smile that was definitely going to be a problem.

Chapter Four

July 22, 12:09 p.m.

Paloma pulled up to the Thompsons' lakeside property, her car gliding smoothly over the pristine cobblestone driveway. The afternoon summer sun bathed the front of the house in a warm glow, highlighting the elegant architecture and casting long shadows across the manicured lawn. She spotted an unfamiliar dark green truck parked near the three-car garage. Parking next to it, she read the company's name and grinned at the wordplay—MaxScape Designs.

Stepping out of her car, a cool breeze carried the faint scent of lake water from behind the house, reminding her of the hidden beauty just out of sight. In the distance, a loon's haunting call echoed across the water. She grabbed her portfolio and tablet from the passenger seat. The grand front door swung open, and Max emerged with a state-of-the-art laser measure in hand and a camera around his neck.

"Afternoon!" he called, the word carried on a rush of eager breath. "I hope you don't mind I got here early to start the site analysis."

"Not at all," she replied. Her stomach did that maddening flip-flop thing it had started doing around him. She forced her gaze away from his faded jeans that hugged his thighs, to the worn patch on his knee that somehow made him look more rugged rather than shabby. At least he'd made it clear that night at The Hill he wasn't interested in her. This one-sided attraction wouldn't go anywhere. But it didn't hurt to look. "Eager to get started?"

His eyes crinkled at the corners in the most adorable way. "I've been tracking the sun patterns since dawn," he said, clicking on his camera and showing the time-stamped photos. Then, he pulled a notepad from his back pocket. It was filled with detailed sketches. Small arrows marked the changing shadows across his precise drawings "The eastern exposure is intense—we'll need to coordinate on window treatments that protect both your interior finishes and my plantings."

"Could you show me?" she asked.

"Of course."

Their footsteps echoed in the cavernous entryway, and Paloma matched his quick stride. She pulled up her documentation app, capturing the intricate crown molding while he talked about light patterns. He moved on to shadow studies, and she cut in, "Wait—did you account for the seasonal changes? The sun angle shifts dramatically here in winter."

"Already modeled it," he said, setting down his camera and notepad on the stairs, trading them for his tablet. "Look at how the light moves across this space in December versus June."

Paloma stepped closer, studying the rendering. "This is brilliant," she murmured, mentally rearranging her furniture placement. She pulled up her preliminary designs. "If we shift the seating area two feet east . . ." Her fingers flew across her tablet, adjusting the layout. "See how it creates better flow around your garden space?"

"And leaves room for larger specimens in the corners," he finished her thought, adding potential plant locations to the shared render. His shoulder brushed hers, sending warmth through her.

Moving under the massive stairs, he said, "Let me show you the lighting issue." His fingers danced across the screen, bringing up a 3D rendering. "See this area, facing the street?"

She leaned in, her arm pressing against his as she peered at the screen. The brief contact sent a small shiver through her, and Max sucked in a breath. She glanced at him, catching a flicker of something in his eyes. Before she could name it, he quickly refocused on the tablet.

"Yes," she said, a touch softer than she'd intended, almost sounding breathy. "Will it be difficult for plants to thrive in that dark space?"

He nodded. "It could be, but I might have found a solution. Take a look at this simulation I've run." He tapped the screen, shifting, and the movement made her hyper-aware of his presence beside her. His cologne was amazing—a sophisticated blend of cedar and amber brightened with citrus notes. The way it mingled with his natural warmth created something magnetic, intensifying every time he moved close.

"The windows here create an interesting light pattern. If we install a series of reflective surfaces here and here," he pointed, tracing the path with his finger, "I can incorporate some hearty vines that thrive under low light, creating a dynamic, welcoming entrance."

"That's clever," Paloma said, her mind shifting to the job, and racing with ideas. She reached out, her hand hovering over the screen. "I planned on replacing outdated railings. You could help me pick ones that complement your vision."

He nodded, a small smile playing at the corners of his mouth. "I'd be happy to help," he said, his voice low and warm. "We could explore some designs that not only complement the lighting but also add to the overall aesthetic."

He zoomed in on the 3D rendering, his fingers brushing against hers as he adjusted the view. "Maybe something with a subtle metallic sheen to enhance the light reflection? Or we could go for a more organic look to tie in with the vines."

She leaned in, her bare arm pressing into his forearm. His grip tightened on his tablet, making his muscles bunch and flex. It was hard to look away, but she managed. Barely. "What if we combined those ideas? Perhaps a material with an organic texture but a faint metallic undertone. It could catch the light in intriguing ways while still harmonizing with the natural elements," she suggested, her excitement at the idea building.

He nodded. "That's . . . wow. It's like you've peered into my thoughts and then woven them into something even better." His gaze lingered on her, eyebrows raised slightly. He rocked forward on the balls of his feet, then tilted his head. "You have such a knack for this. What made you get into this?"

She paused, considering. It was a simple question, but something in his tone made her want to give a real answer. "I guess I've always been fascinated by how spaces affect people. How the right design can change not just how a room looks, but how it feels."

They continued talking through their designs, and electric sparks danced through her veins with each interaction, not only from working together, but from the accidental touches and wafts of his delicious scent

"I like it." She shifted to face him, finding his gaze already on her. There was a spark in his eyes that went beyond professional admiration, a glimmer of something that knocked her off-balance.

For a heartbeat, the world beyond their shared tablet ceased to exist. The air between them seemed to hum with potential, like the moment before a summer storm breaks.

Max swallowed, his Adam's apple bobbing. His gaze darted between Paloma's eyes and lips before he seemed to catch himself. "We, uh . . . we work well together," he said as if reminding himself of work.

"We do," she agreed, surprised by the husky quality of her voice. She took a small step back, grounding herself in the familiar territory of professionalism. "Your ideas complement mine perfectly. The Thompsons will love what we can create."

Wrapping up their consultation, she couldn't shake the lingering awareness of him—the way he moved through the space, how his enthusiasm for the project matched hers, the natural rhythm they'd already fallen into. Their professional chemistry was undeniable, but there was something else simmering beneath the surface, something that made every accidental touch feel like a spark threatening to ignite.

Walking back to her car, she took a deep breath of lake-scented air. The Thompson project was too important to complicate with attraction, no matter how magnetic. She'd have to find a way to channel this energy into their work.

Chapter Five

July 30th, 2:12 p.m.

Paloma flipped the grilled cheese sandwiches, inhaling the comforting scent of melting butter and sharp cheddar. Max hunched over his tablet at her kitchen table, scrolling through photos from their nursery visit. Her leather binder rested next to him. She'd invited herself along to ensure the plants would enhance her design vision for the space. The trip had been a lot more fun than she'd expected.

How his face lit up when he talked about the different plants stirred something low in her chest. The echo of his deep laughter through the greenhouse when she'd jumped at a garden hose she'd mistaken for a snake still played on repeat. Then, there was the flex of his shoulders as he'd lifted pot after pot, showing her different options for the tricky spot under the stairs.

She'd learned more about plants in three hours than her in years of design work. But mostly, she'd learned Max's enthusiasm was infectious, his knowledge ran deep, and the way he ran his finger along his bottom full lip when he was thinking should be illegal.

A sharp, bitter stench pulled her from her reverie. She glanced at the pan. "Shit! I did it again," she muttered. Tendrils of smoke snuck out from the underside of the sandwiches.

"Everything okay?" Max asked, not looking away from his photos.

"Yup, everything's great." She slid the three grilled cheeses from the griddle, flipping the burnt sides down. They would probably taste fine. She'd added extra cheese and butter.

The afternoon sunlight slanted across the sleek leather seats of the kitchen nook, warming her thighs. She sat across from Max, setting the plates in front of them, then cracked the window that ran along the table.

"Thanks," he said before taking a huge bite of his grilled cheese. His eyes widened, and something that might have been panic flickered across his face. He chewed and swallowed with obvious struggle. "It's . . . interesting."

A laugh bubbled up in her chest. "Good thing I made you two."

He nodded, his panicked look growing. He took another bite. His commitment to the charade was impressive.

She tried hers, and bitter ash assaulted her tongue, leaving behind a chemical-like tang. "Oh, that's disgusting."

"Oh, come on. It's, um, unique."

She collapsed into the back of her chair, shoulders shaking with laughter. "Stop, please."

His answering grin made her heart skip. "The char adds character."

"Character is not what I'd call it." She shook her head, still chuckling. "But speaking of character, what do you think about climbing roses? Are those possible for the garden? In yellow."

He ran his thumb along his bottom lip, and she tracked the movement. "Oh, Golden Shower roses could work. I'll have to install a grow light and manage humidity, but they're put on quite a show. The blooms start tight but slowly open up, getting more and more excited until they're completely exposed. The heady fragrance is almost too much. And once they get going, they're absolutely insatiable. Their blooms just keep coming and coming—"

"Max!" she said between bursts of laughter.

A crease formed between his brows. "What?"

"You're messing with me, aren't you?" He had to be.

"No . . ."

"There's an actual flower called the Golden Shower?"

His eyes widened and snapped shut for a split second before he snorted. "Yeah, I'll make sure to name it *Cassia fistula* in case the Thompsons have the same middle school sense of humor as their interior designer," he teased.

"Don't give me that shit. You were totally playing it up," she said. He tilted his head. "Come on. 'The blooms start tight but slowly open up, getting more and more excited until they're completely exposed.' And 'And once they get going, they're absolutely insatiable.'" She tilted her chin down. "'Their blooms just keep coming and coming.'"

"What can I say? Plants are my passion." He winked, and she didn't think anyone but a book boyfriend could pull that move off, but Max proved her wrong. "I guess all this time playing in the dirt has given me a dirty mind."

"I believe it. You turned a garden consultation into soft-core plant porn. I'll never look at roses the same way again." His answering smile lit up his whole face, and she had to look away. Opening her stuffed binders, she pulled out paint samples, saying, "After your vivid descriptions, these paint selections for the Thompsons feel a bit . . . sterile. I might swing by the paint store."

"Do you want a second opinion? I could come with you," he said.

She'd love it. He had a great eye. And if she was honest, she didn't want him to leave. A warning bell rang in her head, the same one that had gone off when her ex-fiancé had suggested he manage the financial side of her business. That lull of comfort, of companionship. No. This was different. Professional. "Don't you have another job to head to?" He'd mentioned a client in Ann Arbor.

He waved a hand. "I'll go after. I've got time."

"If you don't mind. I'd appreciate your input, especially since the living room is where the garden will be a focal point." She met his gaze and poked one of his uneaten grilled cheeses, "I'll buy you a real sandwich so you don't have to pretend to like mine."

He pushed away his plate. "Deal."

A gust of wind rustled through the open window, scattering crumbs and her paint samples. They reached to catch them, their hands touching, sending a tingle of awareness up her arm. She pulled back first, busying herself with gathering the swatches.

"Ready to go?" he asked, his voice softer than before.

She scooped up her purse and binder and fell in step beside him. "Lead the way, plant whisperer," she teased, giving him a playful nudge with her elbow. "But could you possibly keep the horticultural erotica to a minimum at the paint store?"

His laugh followed her to the door, deep and genuine. "No promises. Have you heard about the sensual unfurling of the bird of paradise flowers?"

She groaned, shoving his shoulder, pushing him out her front door. "You're impossible."

"Impossibly charming," he corrected with another wink.

They walked side by side to his truck. She cataloged the little things, like the way his t-shirt sleeves hugged his biceps, how his fingers drummed against his thigh as he walked, that crooked smile when he caught her watching.

Damn it, she was rebuilding her career. Creating perfect spaces, knowing exactly where everything belonged. But this thing with Max—the way he made her feel, the way their work sparked off each other—it didn't fit in any of her carefully designed boxes. She'd learned the hard way that mixing business and pleasure was the fastest way to lose both.

She'd hired him to help with the Thompson garden, not to make her question every professional boundary she'd set. Yet here she was, looking forward to picking paint colors because he'd be there. Heaven help her if he started describing more flowers.

Chapter Six

August 13th, 5:02 p.m.

Max drummed his fingers on the steering wheel, matching the steady folk rhythm flowing through his speakers. The acoustic guitar and raw vocals carried a wistful melody that matched his mood—light and full of possibility. Working on the indoor garden for the Thompson house was the part he most looked forward to each day. Some of it was the challenges the job presented, but mostly it was Paloma. They didn't work side by side or even see each other every day, but catching glimpses of her dark hair swinging as she bent over design boards, or hearing her laugh echo through the half-finished rooms had become the highlights of his over-packed schedule.

Earlier that morning, she'd stopped by his office with a question and coffee—fixed exactly how he liked it. They'd talked and tweaked their design vision, making it even stronger. Then somehow, they'd gotten on the topic of music and learned they had the same taste.

He turned up the volume of a band they both loved. Would she want to go to a concert, or was that crossing some professional line?

He turned into his driveway, stopping next to a sleek black Mercedes that didn't dare have a speck of dirt on it. Shit, had he forgotten Drake was in town? He opened his glovebox and retrieved his phone. There were a few missed calls and text messages from his brother.

Drake: Why do you even have a phone?

I'm in town for work

Used the hidden key to get inside your place

Max: Says the brother who doesn't bother calling until he's on his way and just expects me to be at home waiting for him.

Honestly, he was happy. It had been nearly a month since his brother had visited.

Drake: Good point

Right below that message was a new one from Paloma.

Paloma: I figured out the Thompsons. They're swingers. I'm 90% sure.

He laughed, getting out of his truck. It wouldn't surprise him, given some of the things he'd seen in the home.

Max: Why

Paloma: Their new door knocker.

A photo of an upside-down pineapple appeared under the message.

Uh-oh. He laughed under his breath.

Max: You're right

How do you know about the pineapple

Paloma: Urban Dictionary. How do you know about it?

Instead of answering the question, he typed.

Max: They also asked for a lot of pampas in the garden...

Paloma: So?

Max: Keep googling

"Drake?" he called.

"I'm in the kitchen."

Taking off his work boots, he cut through the spacious living room, passed the formal dining room with its layer of dust, and through the open repurposed barn doors. Drake sat at the round table. Besides his blue eyes, they didn't look much like brothers. He took after their mom with blonde hair and slightly thinner lips. Not to mention, he wore a tailor-made suit. Nothing in Max's closet was custom-made.

Drake was tapping away on his laptop, drinking Max's last ginger beer. Papers, a laptop, and a portable printer covered every bit of space on the table.

"Dude, make yourself at home," Max griped, even as his smile widened and they hugged. It had been too long.

"What?" Drake shrugged. "You weren't home. And it was either get some work done or snoop. I figured I wouldn't find anything exciting, so I went with work."

"Says the workaholic." Max opened the fridge. "How long are you staying?" His phone dinged, and he pulled it from his pocket. Leaning against the counter, he read it.

Paloma: Shit. I have pampas grass and a cute gnome on my back porch

He laughed. The three dots danced on the bottom of his screen. Disappeared. Just as he was about to return his phone to his pocket another text appeared.

Paloma: Why do you know so much about the swinging lifestyle?

This conversation was already veering out of work-appropriate topics. This wasn't the first time. There'd been nothing sexual, just joking and teasing, but more like flirty friends than acquaintances and work partners. Still...

Max: TV and books

Paloma: I don't believe you.

He grinned, even knowing they were blurring lines.

Max: I don't want to get in trouble with HR

Paloma: We don't work for the same company. And there is no HR. Spill, London

He hesitated for half a second, then answered.

Max: I had an interesting girlfriend from Chicago a few years back

Paloma: My mind just exploded. Nice guys aren't supposed to have swinging girlfriends.

Max: I'm a nice guy?

Paloma: Yup. But don't change the subject. Did you try it?

Max tapped the heel of his socked foot. This was way out of business partner territory . . .

Paloma: Spill Maxwell

Paloma: Did I ever tell you my nephew's name is Maxwell?

Max: Nope

Max: But I'm Maximilian - not Maxwell

Paloma: Are you kidding???? That's your name???

Max stared at his phone. What was the big deal?

Max: Yeah. I'm named after my grandpa

Paloma: I read on Urban Dictionary the name means big penis in Russian

He choked on a sip of water. Laughing, he shook his head.

Max: It's good to know Urban Dictionary has factual information

Paloma: Your new nickname is Big P

He snorted. Taking a sip of water, he swallowed it and his grin.

Max: Absolutely not

Max: And I'm telling HR

Paloma: We still don't have HR. And you aren't my employees or vice versa

Paloma: Now stop changing the subject

Paloma: Big P

Paloma: Did you swing?

He rubbed his forehead with this palm. This conversation had spiraled way out of professional territory. No since stopping now.

Max: Once

Paloma: My mind just exploded!

Paloma: Again.

Max: Don't worry, I moved back into my nice guy lane.

Max: I like experimenting, but it wasn't for me. It was a one-time thing.

"Are you dating someone?" Drake asked.

"Huh?" Max looked from his phone. He'd forgotten about his brother. "No. Why?"

"Because whoever you're texting is making you smitten smile."

"'Smitten smile,'" Max muttered, sliding his phone into his pocket. "No. I was chatting with a business partner of sorts."

"Of sorts?"

"It's temporary. A single job."

"Explain," his brother said.

He told him about Paloma and the Thompson project. Drake took a long pull from his glass bottle, hooking an arm over the back of his chair. "She, huh? Interesting . . ."

"That's all you heard?" He pushed off from the counter and opened a cupboard, grabbing a glass. "Anyway, what has you leaving Detroit and working out here?"

"I already told you this," Drake sighed. "But you were too busy ignoring me and sexting your *business* partner. A company from overseas is expanding to Michigan. I'll be here for a week but will be returning on and off for the next few months until the job's completed." He tapped his index and middle finger on the table then stopped, seeming to notice his nervous tic. "I thought while I was in the area, I could stay with you."

"You don't want to stay with Mom?"

"I'd rather visit with my little brother. Or do you not want me here because your—" he made air quotes— "'work partner' might visit you late at night."

Max snorted. "The better question is, are *you* dating someone and that's why you want to stay with me?"

Drake rolled his eyes, his corporate veneer slipping a little. "No." Then he grinned. "But I might want to make a few trips down memory lane with my favorites."

"Fine. If you'll be coming and going, just take the key you used to get inside." He took another drink of his water. "I wish you'd told me late last week you'd be spending most of the summer here. I wouldn't have accepted Paloma's offer."

"Oh, Paloma. Is that your w—"

He'd started with the air quotes again and Max swatted his brother's hands. "Asshole, we're work partners." Although, the more time he spent with her, the less he liked the title.

"Fine, I believe you," Drake said, sounding the opposite.

Max's cell buzzed in his pocket, and he checked it. The message was from Paloma, reminding him she was on her way over. "Shit, I need to get in the shower. I'm going to the tree farm with Paloma."

Drake dipped his chin, looking at Max. "And you need to shower? Won't you just get dirty again?"

"I've been outside all day." He ran a palm down his sweaty, dirt-streaked shirt. "I probably stink."

His brother tilted his head. "Is she hot?"

"Why does that matter?"

"That means yes."

"Again, what does that matter? We're working together. Not sleeping together."

"Would you shower if you and I were going to the tree farm?"

No.

"Yes. I'm covered in grime." Max turned to go.

"It's a smart move not to mix business with pleasure. Glad to see you're taking this new venture seriously."

Leaving the kitchen, Max waved a hand but didn't answer. What could he say? He wasn't sure what was the right move: stay professional friends or explore the obvious chemistry. The impulse was to explore, but he'd learned the hard way that impulses led to consequences that rippled far beyond himself. And sometimes, they shattered everything that was solid.

His phone buzzed again, but this time he ignored it.

Chapter Seven

August 13th, 6:15 p.m.

Hot water cascaded over Max's shoulders, loosening the sore muscles from a morning at his desk hunched over drafting plans, the afternoon at the Thompson house setting up some of the garden, and ending his workday helping his crew remove old shrubs at a revamped condo complex. He was up before the sun, needing to get a head start on his day so he could meet up with Paloma in the evening.

Closing his eyes, memories of her flooded his mind like spring rain. Not just that first night at the bar in that red dress—though the image still haunted him—but all the moments since then that had transformed simple attraction into something more.

The way she leaned over his shoulder yesterday, pointing out how the living wall should frame the antique mirror she found. Her perfume had mixed with the earthy scent of the soil samples he'd been reviewing, creating an intoxicating blend that stroked his desire. She'd been so excited about their shared vision, her eyes bright with possibilities. He wanted to turn his head and taste the spot where her neck met her shoulder.

With a groan, he tipped his head back under the spray, letting the water stream down his face. Reaching for the soap, he worked it into a lather, the slickness gliding over his skin as his hand traveled across his chest and down his torso.

Everything about her turned him on. From the way her mind worked—how she could take his technical solutions and transform them into something beautiful—to the sound of her laugh. Or the brush of her fingers against his when she handed him coffee fixed exactly how he liked it.

His grip tightened, and he skimmed his hand lower, unable to resist the memory of her stretched across his desk last week, barefoot and completely unselfconscious as she sketched out her vision for the Thompsons' entertainment space. The hem of her skirt had ridden up just enough to reveal the curve of her calf, and he'd lost the thread of their conversation entirely.

"Three months," he muttered, wrapping a hand around his rock-hard dick. Three months until the project was finished. Three months fighting his growing attraction.

"Getting off to my business partner is a slippery . . . slope." The self-deprecating edge did little to stem the need pooling in his gut.

He redirected his thoughts, conjuring a more "appropriate" distraction—one involving a celebrity crush. But even that betrayed him because her gown shimmered red, and when it slipped to the floor, it wasn't his imaginary muse joining him in the shower. It was her.

Paloma.

Her mischievous dark eyes glimmered as the water beaded on her smooth skin, her lips curving into a wicked smile. She leaned in, pressing a hot kiss to his neck, the trail of her lips igniting a path down his chest. She sank to her knees before him, and he swore he could feel the warmth of her breath against him.

His hand moved faster, the tension coiling tighter with every stroke. Short, uneven breaths echoed in the steam-filled room, each edged with desperation.

In his fantasy, he looked down, and there she was—her plump, red lips wrapped around him, her gaze locked on his as she took him deeper. The image unraveled him.

With a violent jerk and a guttural groan, he came, his release shuddering through him. With his free hand, he braced himself against the slick tiles. The water continued to pour over him, washing away the evidence but doing nothing to erase Paloma from his mind.

"Fuck. So much for keeping it professional," he muttered, stepping from the shower.

He'd left his bedroom door open, and from across the house, an indistinct conversation drifted down the hallway. His brother's familiar baritone, mixing with another softer voice that was like dark honey—rich and sensual. Those husky inflections, that smoky timbre … after a month, he'd already memorized every sultry note of Paloma's laugh, every seductive rise and fall of her speech.

After drying off and brushing his teeth, he quickly dressed. Before leaving his ensuite bathroom, his hand hovered over the cologne bottle. Why bother? This was a business outing, not a damn date.

"I am ridiculous." Still, he sprayed a little on his neck. The sharp, woody scent filled his nostrils, contrasting the lingering humidity from his shower. Then he swished another helping of mouthwash, all the while hearing his brother's sardonic laughter in his head.

Leaving his bedroom and crossing through the great room, he saw Paloma sitting at the kitchen table with Drake next to her. They were so close their shoulders almost touched, and whatever he was telling her held all her attention. A twinge of something uncomfortably like jealousy twisted in his gut.

He swallowed the bitter taste climbing up his throat. "Sorry, if I'd known you'd get here so quickly, I'd have skipped the shower," Max said.

Paloma's gaze lingered on him, pausing on areas that had him recalling his fantasy of her in his shower. Then she pulled her attention to Drake's laptop screen, saying, "No worries. Your brother was giving me a few tips for my business." She pointed at a sheet of paper with notes scribbled on it, then asked, "Do we have a couple minutes, or does the lighting gallery close soon?"

"It's open late tonight, so we're good. I'll grab a quick bite while you read." He walked to the fridge. "Do either of you want anything?"

Drake turned his chair, facing Max. "I raided your kitchen before you got home. That strawberry chicken salad was delish. And the blueberry pie. I swear, what I miss the most since moving to Detroit is your cooking."

"You cook?" she asked, the edge of her mouth curving up.

He shrugged. "A little. Are you hungry?"

"Guess we know who'll be making the grilled cheese during our next impromptu lunch."

He nodded vigorously. "One hundred percent, most definitely."

"Hey," she laughed, tossing a pen at him. "And no, I'm not hungry. I ate before I got here, but you go ahead." Paloma turned to Drake. "Would you mind going back to that first website you showed me?"

"Sure," he said. The soft tapping of keys filled the momentary silence. Then he pushed the laptop toward her.

Finding the spicy miso ramen from the other day, Max removed the lid and leaned against the counter. Paloma was focused on the screen, twirling a strand of hair around her finger. He was mesmerized by the simple gesture, needing to know if her locks were as soft as they looked and how it'd feel to run his hands through her hair.

He squared his shoulders, forcing his wandering mind to heel. Her unwavering commitment to the job deserved his professional admiration, not this . . . distraction. Yet, he couldn't look away, his gaze tracing the cascade of her raven hair, the elegant column of her neck.

Drake tipped his nose in the air, then smirked. "You smell divine, brother. Are you wearing cologne?"

Max narrowed his eyes and mouthed, "Fuck you."

Drake laughed, and Max couldn't help doing the same. The sound seemed to pull Paloma from whatever she was reading. Her gaze jumped to him and stayed. "You do smell nice." She pulled that delectable bottom lip between her teeth.

Drake cleared his throat and muttered something about sexual tension. Paloma dropped her gaze from Max to his brother. "If you have time while visiting, could I show you my social media branding? I'd like to see if it's on point." She rested a hand on his arm. "I'll pay you for your time."

"For a friend of Max, I'll do it for free." There was a flirt in his voice. He gave her that smile that made women and men swoon. Some days Max really disliked his perfect brother.

He twisted around, staring out the window over the sink, finishing his food, the tangy flavors as hot as his irritation. He shouldn't care, but did his brother have to flirt with Paloma?

"You charged Jackson," Max said, looking past his porch, lawn, and empty road to the dense forest.

Drake snorted. "One, he wanted the full package: help with advertising, website, and branding for all five of his hardware stores. That's a lot more work than looking at a few socials. Two . . ." When he didn't continue, Max turned, raising an eyebrow. "I should've been quarterback of the football team. I was two damn grades above. The jerk stole it from me."

Max laughed. "Did you charge him resentment tax?"

"I'd never do that!" He tugged on the cuffs of his button-up, then winked. "But I thought about it."

"So, you were a senior when Max as a sophomore?" Paloma asked Drake.

"Yup."

"No wonder we've never met. I was a year under him and Jackson in high school."

"I figured. Because I *definitely* would have remembered you." Drake's signature smile widened, and Max's hand tightened on the edge of the counter, knuckles whitening.

Paloma's lips twitched. "Aren't you a charmer."

"Yeah, of snakes," Max muttered, dropping the empty food container in the sink.

"Did you know my sister, Emmeline?" Paloma asked. "She was in your grade."

Drake tapped his chin. "Emma?"

"Yeah, but recently she's going by her full name. Emmeline."

"Did she drop that asshat she was dating back then too? Henry Foster?"

"Like the nickname, recently. She's divorcing the asshat."

Drake chuckled. "Not a fan?"

"Nope. He cheated on my sister with some guy."

Drake tilted his head and asked, "Do I sense judgment?" The question was asked without heat, but there was a tightening in his brother's shoulders.

"Maybe a little," she replied. Disappointment filled Max. He hoped she wasn't closed-minded.

"I'm bi," Drake said flatly.

Paloma held up her hands. "I'm not judging Henry for sleeping with men. I feel bad for him. His dad's awful. He's a pray-out-the-gay kind of guy. But I am angry at Henry for hurting my sister, for pulling her into his lie. Now, at thirty-five, she's starting over with a toddler. Meanwhile, he left the state, abandoning his son."

Max nodded, absorbing her words. The three sat in silence for a moment, the weight of the conversation settling around them.

Paloma sighed and glanced at her watch. "What time does Lighting Design close?"

"At 9:30, but we should get moving in case it takes us a while to decide," Max replied.

Paloma stood up. "Okay, let me get my tablet from my car. I'll meet you at yours. Nice meeting you, Drake."

"Wow," Drake breathed, his eyes following her retreating figure. He leaned in his chair, a slow smile spreading across his face. "I like your *business* partner."

All the ease and humor drained from Max. He turned to his brother. "Stick to visiting those in your memory lane."

"Do I sense jealousy? A bit of possessiveness?" Drake drummed his fingers once against his empty glass, then folded his hands like a therapist settling in for a breakthrough session. "And why? You said you're not interested in her. Are you lying to me or yourself?" The corner of Drake's mouth quirked, and Max recognized that familiar look—his brother baiting the hook, waiting for Max to bite. The annoying part was that he couldn't entirely dismiss the question.

The floorboards creaked, and he turned. Paloma stepped into the kitchen. "I forgot my purse," she said, reaching past him.

Drake tracked her movements with that practiced charm, and something primitive stirred in Max's chest, and he shifted, angling between them. Their shoulders brushed as Paloma retrieved her purse, the brief contact sending a current through him that had nothing to do with static electricity.

"Sorry," she murmured, but her eyes held his a moment longer than necessary.

Clarity struck him like summer lightning. All his half-assed rationalizations about keeping things professional crumbled. He didn't want a business partner; he wanted the way she bit her lip when she was thinking, the sound of her laugh when he said something ridiculous, and the spark in her eyes when they shared the same vision for a project. He wanted all of her.

Chapter Eight

August 13th, 6:10 p.m.

They walked into the lighting showroom, Max rehearsing his speech one final time. Working together for nearly a month had only intensified his feelings, and he was done pretending otherwise.

"Paloma—"

"Let's start with the new display lighting." She glanced at him. "Sorry, you were going to say something."

Looking into her questioning eyes, his courage evaporated. "I was going to suggest the same."

They made their way to the lighting showroom's ceiling fixture section, where dozens of chandeliers, pendant lights, and flush mounts created a glittering canopy overhead. He welcomed the distraction. He spotted a sleek pendant light on display among the forest of display models. His fingers found the metal frame overhead, but the fixture was ungainly and tilted in his grip. He grunted as the weight distribution caught him off guard.

Paloma stepped forward, her hands landing on the metal frame next to his. "Here," she murmured, her arm sliding across his chest as she shifted the angle.

Her sensual scent heated his blood. The showroom became too warm, too small. She looked up at him, her eyes wide, pupils dilated, the blue nearly disappearing in the dim light. A strand of hair had escaped her pristine updo, and his fingers itched to brush it back. The fixture wobbled slightly as his grip loosened.

"Careful," she whispered, shifting closer, steadying the light.

Her lips parted slightly, and he leaned in, drawn by her magnetic pull. "I think we should—"

The sharp clatter of the specification sheets hitting the floor snagged her attention. She jumped back, cheeks flushed, and let out a shaky breath. She bent, gathering the scattered papers, but her usual grace was gone, her movements jerky and uncertain.

"It's a good thing we didn't hook up that night at The Hill," she said suddenly, then tilted her head. "Oh, sorry. You were saying . . ."

A startled laugh escaped him, a quick punch to the solar plexus. Damn. Had he been that off base with her signals these past weeks? He stumbled to find an acceptable ending to his sentence that wouldn't make him look like an ass. "Um. I think we should, um, be looking at those pendant hybrids instead. I'd like to find something functional and aesthetically pleasing. Elodie told me they had a lot of parties, and that combination is important."

Paloma grinned. "And did she invite you to said parties? That would definitely answer our question about them being swingers."

He chuckled. "Sorry, no invite."

"I bet it'll come when this project is over. I see the way she *and* Bill look at you."

Was that jealousy he heard mixed in her teasing? They moved toward the modern lighting display. Halfway through the showroom, he had to ask, "But you're not interested?"

"In swinging?" She sucked in the side of her top lip. "In theory, it sounds like fun. But I don't think so."

"No. I meant interested in me? You said you're glad we didn't hook up." He smiled and hoped his disappointment didn't show. "Has spending more time with me made you like me less?"

"God no," she said with a soft laugh. "That's why I'm glad nothing happened. You're . . ." Her gaze lingered on his mouth before she looked away. "You're dangerous."

"Dangerous?" He set the light fixture down next to a sleek display of LED strip lighting and straightened, looking at her.

"I'm taking a break from men, focusing on my career."

"Because of Asher?" A sucker-punch of jealousy caught him off guard—not at its presence but its intensity. He didn't have a right to be territorial about her past, especially when he was the one who'd turned her down that night at The Hill. Still, knowing she might be hung up on Asher made his chest tight.

"No," she replied.

"Then why the break?" he asked gently.

She slouched onto a nearby stepping ladder. "It's not about Asher. He was just . . . a distraction, really. From something bigger." She twisted her hands in her lap. "I was in a long relationship before him. Richard and I, we were engaged . . . and I made the mistake of mixing business with my personal life."

"What happened?" Max asked, his chest tightening at the pain in her voice.

"He was this hotshot business consultant who specialized in startups. He convinced me to let him help with my business." Her voice softened slightly. "I think he meant well at first. He was always talking about building this amazing future for us, how he wanted to make sure I had everything I wanted."

"But something changed?"

"The gambling. God, I didn't know about it until everything fell apart. He kept it completely separate from our life together. Until he couldn't." She wrapped her arms around herself. "He'd go on these 'business trips' to meet clients, but in reality, most of the time he was hitting casinos in Detroit, Vegas, and Atlantic City. High-stakes poker, mostly. Started small, but then he got in deep with some dangerous people."

"How'd you find out?"

"Pure luck. One of my supplier's checks bounced, so I went to the bank in person. The teller mentioned something about a wire transfer I'd never authorized." She shook her head. "When I started digging, I found this whole separate life he'd been hiding. He had a system, funneling money from my business through fake vendors, making it look like legitimate expenses. Then he'd use that money to pay off gambling debts or buy into bigger games."

"Jesus," Max muttered.

"When I confronted him . . ." Her voice cracked slightly. "That's what kills me. He broke down completely. Said he'd been trying to fix it before the wedding, that he had these systems that couldn't fail. He kept saying he needed one big win to put all the money back, make everything right." She shook her head. "He'd even been going to Gamblers Anonymous meetings in secret, trying to get clean. But then he'd relapse, lose more, and have to cover it up with more stolen money."

"Sounds like he was living a double life."

"Exactly. And he was good at it. In our regular life, he was this amazing fiancé. Remembered every anniversary, planned the sweetest dates, talked about our future home and the family we'd have." She wiped at her eyes quickly, glancing around. Thankfully, their section of the store was empty. "Meanwhile, he's up at 3 a.m. doctoring bank statements and moving money around to hide his losses. The FBI found spreadsheets on his laptop—he tracked every lie he told me so he wouldn't slip up."

"How much did he take?"

"Almost half a million. But you know what's crazy? He blamed me. Said it was because I wanted too much. How I wanted to be the number one interior designer in Michigan, to have the best showcase home. My incessant wants were why he gambled, to keep up with my dreams."

Anger flared in Max's chest. He'd seen her work ethic firsthand, watched her pour herself into the Thompson project. The idea that someone would use her drive and passion against her, twist it into an excuse for their failures was vile.

His hands curled into fists, then forced them to relax. His rage wouldn't change Paloma's past. He took her hand and squeezed it. "You know that's absolute bullshit, right?"

"Sure." Her gaze dropped from his, telling him the truth.

"That's rough," Max said softly. "I'm sorry."

She wrapped her arms around herself. "After him, I was a mess. Felt like I couldn't trust my own judgment anymore. That's when the really bad decisions started." A harsh laugh escaped her. "Like taking home a man who ended up stealing from me."

His jaw clenched. He'd like to bury these men under some of his current landscaping projects.

"Indeed, but my brother has a shady friend who helped find that douchebag." She shook her head, then added quietly, "You'd think I'd have learned my lesson, but no. Next came the weekender—a married guy. He rented. Well, I thought he was a renter. Turned out to be another liar, just a different kind."

Max's lip curled. "Some people are shits."

She grinned. "At least I got back at the shitty cheater. He invited me over again, after I learned he was married, I brought over some *toys*." She waggled her brows in a way that suggested these items wouldn't be in any kid's toybox. "I hid them in odd places that would lead to so uncomfortable conversations with his wife."

Max straightened. "Holy shit! That was you." Asher had told him the story of Lilith's kitchen clogged with a butt plug. He'd figured it had something to do with Lilith's douche-bag ex-husband, Marshall. But, damn, knowing Paloma was who had hidden kinky toys all over in an act of revenge. He belly-laughed. "Oh, damn. I have to tell Asher. He'd laugh his ass off."

"Me and my big mouth," Paloma muttered, then gripped his forearm. "Please don't tell him I put the toys in the house."

"Wait. Are you telling me there's more?" His admiration grew. She didn't get mad and sulk. She got even. "How many are we talking?"

"That's not the point. The point is, you can't tell anyone."

"I think it's hilarious." But hearing the slight panic in her voice, he said. "I won't tell anyone."

"Thank you, I'd rather she didn't know I was with her ex-husband while they were still together."

"Technically, they're still married. She served him papers, but he's refusing to sign them."

"Why? He seems like a guy that'd love to be single?"

Max shrugged. "Got me. I only know what Asher told me the first time I met her." He grinned. "I bet you two would make great friends. You already have something in common . . ."

Her lips twitched. "What's that?"

"Similar taste in men."

She picked up a small pendant light from the display, pretending to aim it at him. "Shut up." Setting it back among the rows of artistic fixtures, she glanced over his shoulder at the wall of options. "How did we even get on this topic?"

"You saying you're glad we didn't sleep together." He gestured toward another section of pendant lights. "What about these hybrid ones for the indoor garden?"

She nodded, walking toward them. "Ah, yes. Your refusal was another ego-popping moment."

"Believe me, anyone there would have taken you home. You were hot as sin in that red dress."

She picked up two similar pendants. Putting them down, she looked at him. "Anyone but you."

He put his hands in his pockets. "I'm not into being someone's consolation prize."

"How are you a consolation prize?"

"You were there for my friend. But when that was over, you came to me . . ."

She blinked, then looked away, sucking the side of her bottom lip. "Damn, that was shitty of me. Sorry."

People said that word easily, but her apology held true remorse. He appreciated it, but didn't want to linger on that night—the memory of how badly he'd wanted to say yes still made his skin prickle with heat. Shrugging it off with a smile and nod, he moved toward a display of modern fixtures.

She stopped him with a hand on his arm, and he stilled. "Really, I wasn't thinking along those lines at all. More like. 'Well, that's over with Asher . . . but on the positive side, this guy is hot.'"

He searched her eyes, and the sincere focus on him made his pulse race while soothing his ego. His gaze moved to her plump red lips, and she licked them. She probably tasted like cherries and desire. And what would desire taste like? Paloma.

"But this is better." She sighed, and he swore he heard longing in her exhale. "I have a feeling one night with you wouldn't be enough. And I need these projects to be a success."

He tilted his head. "Projects? There's only this one job."

Would she be interested in the possibility of more after they completed the Thompson house? Business was over, and they could focus on the pleasure.

She grinned, jumping up and down, doing a little dance between the aisles. "With the possibility of many more. Sorry, I got sidetracked telling you about my pathetic dating life. But that's *why* we're better off as business partners instead of sex partners." Pulling her phone from a hidden pocket in her dress, she opened an app and turned the screen to him. "I might be a fuck-up when it comes to relationships, but not in business. Yesterday, I shared the progress of your garden on social media. This morning, five clients called me wanting something similar. And one of them is Roy Sterling."

Max stilled. "Of Bloom and Heart?" Not only was Roy from old-Michigan money but also owned the top home and garden magazine.

"Yup, him," She trilled. "He and his wife bought a house on Grand Traverse Bay. They'd like us to submit a proposal. They want the interior, exterior remodeled—including a conservatory."

"This year?"

She nodded. "If they hired us, we'd start next month. I'd have to shuffle around some clients, and the hours will be long . . . but it's the Sterlings."

He was already doing that for the Thompson project, but he hadn't minded much because he liked the challenge of creating indoor gardens. And spending more time with Paloma was a definite bonus. But he wasn't sure if he could take on another client, especially one that was out of town. That would stretch him and his employees too thin.

She came closer and took his hands. Her eyes were big and pleading. He couldn't look away. "Please, tell me you're interested. A job like that could change our lives. Take our careers to the next level."

He was fine professionally. He had more than enough money and work. Yet, refusing her made his heart ache. He was torn between his contentment and her ambition.

Seeing Paloma happy and excited filled him with joy. Her enthusiasm was infectious, and he wanted to be a part of whatever made her eyes light up like that. It was becoming harder to separate his professional admiration from his growing personal feelings.

"I . . ." he began, voice faltering. Could he balance his needs with hers? The weight of the decision pressed down on him, and then he buried his worry under the hope in her eyes and caved. "I'll do it."

She lunged, hugging him so tight his breath whooshed from him. "Thank you. Thank you," she squealed. "We are a fantastic team."

His hands instinctively found her waist, and his body came alive at the contact. Her hair tickled his chin, her curves pressed against him, and his heart hammered so hard she could probably feel it. The scent of her shampoo made him dizzy, and he had to force his fingers not to flex against her hips.

Pulling away, their gazes met, and for a moment, neither moved. The warmth of her body, her light perfume wrapped around him. He found himself wanting to pull her close again, to feel her in his arms for just a little longer.

She seemed to realize how close they were standing and took a small step back, clearing her throat. "So, um, in conclusion," she began, her voice slightly unsteady, "it's a good thing we didn't sleep together. Mixing business with pleasure usually ends in disaster."

Her gaze lingered on Max's lips for a moment too long. "Usually," he said, "but not always."

"It does for me," she whispered, almost pleadingly.

He heard what she asking. For now, he'd be her business partner and friend.

"You know what I noticed today?" she asked rhetorically.

"What's that?"

"When I saw the post from the Sterlings, you were the first person I wanted to tell." She fiddled with a price tag. "Not my brother, not my friends or family. You."

"Makes sense it's a team project."

"No, that wasn't it. In this short time, you've become my go-to friend. You're important to me."

The simple admission hit him harder than any flirtation could have. "Yeah?"

"Yeah." She leaned against a display table, playing absently with a collection of vintage-style bulbs. "And that's . . ." She shook her head, laughing softly. "That's kind of terrifying."

"Why?"

"Because important people always leave." She met his eyes. "And the Sterling project could change everything for us."

He caught her subtle emphasis on 'us.' "Professionally," he said, testing the waters.

"Right." She picked up another pendant light, then set it down without looking at it. "Though sometimes I wonder . . ."

"Yeah?" His throat went dry at the vulnerability in her expression.

"If I'm being smart or just scared." She gestured to the collection lights and LED strips they'd spent the last hour examining. "The thing is, Max, any other time in my life, I would've already . . ." She gestured between them, leaving the rest unsaid.

"I would've let you." The admission cost him, but she deserved his honesty. "Hell, I nearly did when I thought I was the consolation prize."

"But I think some risks aren't worth taking." She met his gaze. "No matter how tempting they might be."

Max studied her face, recalling her story about the fiancé, about trust broken and dreams shattered. She was more than a spark or desire to chase.

And there was more to it. He wanted to be someone's first choice, not their safe option after a string of bad decisions.

"I agree.." He took a step back, giving them both space to breathe. "These projects could transform both our business."

She stared at him for a long moment, then looked to the wall of fixtures. "Now, about these hybrids for the conservatory . . ."

He let her change the subject, watching her eyes light up when she mentioned another detail about the Sterling project. They'd made the right choice. He'd rather be her partner in building something lasting than another chapter in her book of regrets.

"Max?" She was holding up two different fixtures. "Which one?"

He focused on the lights in her hands, committing to being her business partner and friend. It was the right choice.

So why did doing the right thing feel so wrong?

Chapter Nine

August 19th, 9:45 a.m.

Paloma clutched her leather portfolio and settled into a corner table at the Coffee Bean with her latte. She and Max worked on their Sterling house proposal for nearly two weeks, and the meeting with them had finally arrived. She spread out her work, adjusting the order of her sketches while watching the parking lot through the storefront windows for his truck.

Her phone buzzed. Mom again. Her thumb hovered over the red voicemail button, but needing a distraction, she answered, saying, "Sorry, I didn't make it to family dinner yesterday. I'm meeting with an important client today and had to finish the proposal."

A heavy sigh carried over the phone. "Honey, your dad was home this weekend. Emmeline made the drive with my adorable grandson from Ann Arbor. And Felix came all the way from Traverse City. I miss seeing everyone together."

Maybe spiraling worry and self-doubt was preferable. "So glad you called to serve up a heaping side of guilt to go with my morning coffee?" Paloma half-joked.

Her mother's laugh was a mix of amusement and exasperation. "That's not my intent. Well, okay, maybe a smidge. You're practically next door, and yet . . ." She sighed again. "Is it really too much to ask for a family dinner once a month?"

"You're right." She shifted in her seat, the phone pressed tightly to her ear. Reaching for her coffee, she paused midair, retreating to fidget with a sugar packet. "I'll be there next time."

"Thank you, honey."

Spotting Max exiting his truck, she said, "Mom, I have to go. Max is here."

"Who's Max? A new man you're seeing?" Her voice carried too much hope. She was that mom who wanted twenty grandkids.

"Sorry to disappoint again. He's a business partner. Love you, and we'll talk later."

Max crossed the parking lot in the busy shopping center, his long strides eating up the distance. He paused to help an elderly woman with her bags, his broad shoulders flexing beneath his crisp blue shirt as he unloaded her cart. The genuine warmth in his smile as he chatted with the woman made him irresistible. No. Focus. This meeting was business, not pleasure.

He entered the café, and after getting a coffee, he sat across from Paloma and asked, "Ready to wow our future clients?"

Their gazes met over the papers, and for a moment, the café's bustle dissolved into a distant hum. She willed herself to stay professional. "Absolutely. My interior designs for the kitchen leading to your conservatory garden will complement each other perfectly."

"They also want a small living wall," Max said.

"Like our pineapple couple?" Paloma asked.

He laughed, the sound deep and rich, like a sensual caress. "We should stop calling them that so we don't slip and say it in front of them. But, yeah, kind of, but different. The Sterlings want wall art, circular pieces in different sizes and mosses. The swingers want shelves mixed of plants, herbs, and fruits."

She grinned. "I bet one is a pineapple."

He chuckled. "Funny you should say that. They did request pineapples, but those are shrubs and too big for the wall. Instead, they'll be in pots throughout the house. I need to give you the measurements so you can pick containers that match your design dimensions."

She leaned forward. "We could *swing* by after this meeting. You could show me where they want them."

"Sounds good. And I'm sure whatever you pick will knock their socks off." He waggled his brows. "Just be sure to only knock off their socks."

"Forget our collaboration of interior and exterior design. We can hone in on a niche. Our business name will be Fruit Forward Designs. We will cater to all your tropical . . . needs." She sipped her latte, the creamy bitterness a pleasant contrast to the spiciness of their banter.

His bark of laughter caught the attention of a nearby table of women. Their appreciative glances went unnoticed by Max. Paloma moved to his side of the table—to talk business and not to stake a claim she didn't have on him. At least, that's the story she told herself.

"As much as I'd love to continue planning our risqué fruit-themed empire," she said, glancing at her watch, "we should probably get ready for the Sterlings. They'll be here any minute."

Max nodded. "And I wanted to run a change by you before they arrive."

She listened to his idea but was distracted by the deep timbre of his voice and how he rolled the sleeve of his shirt, showcasing his lovely forearms. His movements exuded confidence, something she was lacking at the moment and, therefore, all the more captivating.

"What do you think?" he asked.

"Um . . ." Shit. She was too busy looking at him to hear him. This was why they couldn't have business and pleasure.

He quirked an eyebrow, a playful smile tugging at his lips. "Daydreaming about me again?"

"Only in your dreams," she shot back, taking a quick sip from her mug, hoping he thought her heating cheeks were from the coffee and not from being caught out. "Actually, I was thinking about ordering a muffin."

"Want me to grab us some?"

"Maybe after. I'm nervous, and my stomach's in knots," she admitted. "Please explain. I promise I'm listening this time."

He dipped his chin in acknowledgment and re-explained his change. She leaned into her chair, impressed. His idea was good—great, actually.

"Wow, Max. I love it."

The door to the coffee shop dinged, opening. In strolled an older couple she recognized: the Sterlings. She and Max stood. He moved around the table to stand next to her.

"We apologize for being late," Linda Sterling said, sinking into the plush chair across from them. "You wouldn't believe the traffic!"

"Could I see the designs for the second level before the conservatory?" Roy Sterling asked though it sounded more like a demand.

Paloma nodded, keeping her professional smile in place. Not that it mattered since Roy was looking at Max. It seemed Roy was the kind of guy who assumed the man was always in charge.

Max shifted slightly toward Paloma. "You'll have to talk to Ms. Wagner."

Roy's brow furrowed, creating deep lines that spoke of years of skepticism. "She doesn't work for you?"

"We have separate companies," Max explained. "But with these joint projects, like yours, she's the lead, not me. I work for her."

A flutter rippled through Paloma's stomach. Damn, why did he have to say it like that? So confident, so unapologetic. She forced her gaze back to the Sterlings, needing to focus on the clients and business, not the inexplicably sexy way her partner made himself her subordinate.

Roy waved a hand like he was swatting away a fly. "I'm listening."

Paloma took the lead, confident they'd win over Roy. She presented her vision for the interior spaces, giving them the minimalist beach-vibe, they requested. Then, with a graceful segue, she handed the floor to Max.

His eyes lit up as he gestured toward the blueprints spread across the table. "See how the conservatory flows flawlessly to Ms. Wagner's design for the rest of the main floor?" He traced a finger along the lines. "It's not just about aesthetics—it's about functionality."

"And here," he pointed at the deck overlooking Grand Traverse Bay, "we'll incorporate native plants to support local pollinators."

"We'll deliver a home that honors both the natural landscape and your vision," she said, gathering the blueprints with practiced care and meeting Roy's gaze. "The real gem won't be only the house—it'll be how it transforms your everyday living."

Max nodded, adding, "Each element, from Ms. Wagner's interior flow to my sustainable conservatory design, works in harmony. Like the bay sculpting the shore, your home will feel like nature herself designed it."

Linda Sterling straightened in her chair, her earlier fatigue forgotten. "Roy," she touched her husband's arm, "did you see how they incorporated all your gardening spaces without sacrificing the water views?"

"I noticed," he said, his skepticism finally giving way to something that looked remarkably like approval. "Send over the contracts first thing tomorrow."

Her expression was coolly professional, but inside, she was doing cartwheels—they'd landed the biggest project of her career. The fact that Max had backed her play so perfectly only added to the victory's sweetness.

"We will," they replied at the same time.

Linda beamed at them. "You two are such a cute couple."

Her heart skipped a beat. "Oh, we're business partners and friends."

Linda looked between them. "Maybe you should be more."

Roy harrumphed, standing. "Wait until our house is finished. I don't want romance drama messing up my place."

"Our place," his wife corrected.

"You don't have to worry. We're professionals," Max said.

After the Sterlings left, she turned to Max and asked, "So, tell me, are we too professional to delay their project? Or too professional to mess around with each other while working on their house?"

He stepped closer. Her breath caught as his fingers grazed her cheek, his eyes never leaving hers. "You tell me."

Chapter Ten

August 19th, 11:05 a.m.

The crowded coffee shop buzzed with the hum of conversation and the hiss of espresso machines, but all Max could focus on was Paloma's flirtatious question and the desire in her eyes. He leaned closer, instinctive as a river finding its path downstream. He couldn't seem to move his hand resting on her cheek. Her skin was silk under his fingers, and every nerve ending screamed for him to pull her closer, to finally taste those lips that had been driving him wild.

"Professional," he murmured, his thumb brushing the corner of her mouth, "is the last thing I want to be right now."

Someone bumped his back, knocking him forward half a step. "Sorry," said a woman whose voice was vaguely familiar. He turned to Asher's neighbor, Lilith.

Her auburn hair swept back in a wide headband, and she wore a light blue sundress. "Oh, Max. Hi." Her gaze darted around, never settling on his face for more than a second.

The door dinged with a new customer, and Asher called, "Lil, grab the table by the—" he skidded to a stop. He looked from Max to Paloma. Her blue eyes turned artic, and the warmth of their earlier moment evaporated like coffee steam. "Hey, guys. What a . . . surprise," he finished.

"Yeah, small world," Asher replied, shifting his weight from one foot to the other.

Paloma's smile was tight. "So, how are you finding *our* small town?" she asked in a way that said Lilith was and would always be an outsider. It also shouted that she wasn't over Asher. Both reminded Max that all he'd ever be to her was a distraction until she got over or got back the man she really wanted.

"Friendly," Lilith replied. Then, dropping her gaze, she added, "Mostly."

"It's a pretty welcoming place once you get past the small-town bullshit," Asher said, his tone gentle but firm. He met Paloma's eyes with quiet challenge. "Lilith's been a great addition to the neighborhood." He turned to Max. "Hope tells me you won't be taking any landscape design projects from our construction company this summer. We're disappointed. I'd rather have you than our backup designer. They're decent, but let's face it, not nearly as talented as you. What gives?"

"We . . . Paloma and I are exploring some new opportunities," he said, his voice betraying a hint of uncertainty. "We're working on a few joint projects together." Even as he spoke, the weight of his existing clients and projects pressed down on him.

He genuinely enjoyed working with her, their minds often in sync, creating designs that neither could have conceived alone. But witnessing her reaction to Asher now, he wasn't sure. Had he let his attraction cloud his judgment? Had he been too impulsive? Again.

Asher's gaze moved between them. A hint of understanding seemed to dawn in his eyes. "I see," he said slowly. "Well, I hope you know what you're doing."

Max's irritation shifted a little toward his friend. He wanted to explain, to justify his decision. But how could he when he suddenly wasn't all that sure?

"It's an exciting venture," Paloma chimed in, her voice carrying a forced cheerfulness that grated on his nerves. A heavy, awkward silence hummed between them, somehow louder than the noise around them.

"I love what they've done with the café. The artwork is lovely," Lilith chirped, probably hoping to brighten the mood.

"It's not new," Paloma said flatly. "It's been here for years."

"Right," Lilith mumbled, her cheeks flushing deeper.

"We need to get our coffee to go," Asher said flatly. "The girls will be finishing their horseback riding lessons shortly.

Paloma's jaw clenched, then loosened. "That's great that Lilith gets to meet your daughter."

"Our daughters are best friends." Asher rubbed the back of his neck, looking toward the door. He was probably debating if he should turn around and leave. Max couldn't blame him.

Another tense silence fell between them. Lilith broke it, saying, "We should go. The girls..."

"See you around," Asher muttered.

They left, but the awkwardness lingered like a storm cloud. A tangle of emotions Max couldn't quite unravel twisted around him.

After the door shut behind them, Paloma mimicked in a deep voice, "My neighbor, Lilith." Then said in her normal tone, "Asshole."

A flare of irritation bloomed in Max, not only at Paloma's spite but at himself for caring. Why did it bother him that she was still hung up on Asher? It's not like they were a couple. And yet, the thought of being nothing more than a placeholder twisted his insides.

"They are neighbors," he snapped, immediately regretting his sharp tone but too annoyed to apologize.

"That's not all they are," she clapped back.

Asher wasn't the kind of man to fool around on someone, even in a casual relationship. If he was interested in another, even slightly, he'd have broken things off first. "Then it's good he ended it with you," Max reasoned, hating how his voice caught on the words.

"Sure, fine. Defend him. Them."

"He's my friend." And what exactly was Paloma to him? More than a friend, less than a lover, and apparently still into someone else. Did all their shared moments mean nothing to her beyond convenient comfort?

"And I'm not your friend?" she retorted.

"You are," he said with false ease. And she'd stay in that lane, pining after Asher, while Max played the role of supportive friend, swallowing wants he couldn't voice. "Who he's dating isn't our business." Needing to focus on something besides his disappointment, besides the ache of being second choice, he pointed to the work proposal on the table. "What is, is our clients." The familiar territory beckoned like a sanctuary. At least there, he knew exactly where he stood.

There was a quick flash of pain in her eyes before she shuddered her expression. "Good point. Work is all that matters to me."

They sat. "So, uh, where were we before . . . all that?" he asked, waving at the scattered papers on the table.

Paloma blinked as if coming out of a daze. "Right. The Sterling account."

"Yes, the Sterling account," Max echoed, staring blankly at the documents. His thoughts were an untethered boat, drifting to his other accounts to Paloma's unresolved feelings for Asher.

"Okay, let's go over their changes," he said with forced enthusiasm.

"Changes?" Paloma frowned, then nodded. "Oh, yes. Roy wanted minimalist. And Linda wants a beach vibe. I was thinking of a few tweaks in the conservatory."

Max leaned forward, willing himself to focus. "And?"

"And, um." Her gaze drifted to the door Asher and Lilith had exited through.

Max sighed. "Paloma, if you're not up for this right now—"

"No, no," she said quickly, snapping her attention back to him. "I'm here. I'm focused."

She took a deep breath. "Okay, so the idea was to use contrasting imagery. Something that juxtaposes edgy elements with softer, more approachable ones."

Max nodded slowly, attempting to be engaged. "That could work. Like, darker, sharper furniture with more flowering plants."

"Exactly!" Paloma said, a hint of her usual enthusiasm returning. "Or we could—"

His phone buzzed, cutting her off. He glanced at it and sighed. Asher was a good guy, but right about now, a little distance would be nice.

"Everything okay?" she asked.

Max hesitated, then said, "It's nothing. Asher texted. Apologizing for the awkwardness."

Her shoulders tightened. "Such a nice guy," she muttered.

"Let's just . . ." He paused, exhaling slowly to control his rising frustration. "Can we get through this without commentary?"

"Okay," she agreed, pulling her laptop closer like a shield. "Let's push through."

They bent over the paperwork again, but the earlier easy rapport had vanished, replaced by stilted conversation and long, uncomfortable pauses. He kept reading the same line over and over.

His gaze drifted to his phone, where voicemails and texts from his other projects sat urgent and unread. A tightness crept into his shoulders at the mounting workload. This partnership with Paloma, while exciting, was stretching him thin. Late nights and early mornings had already become the norm with the pineapple house. The Sterling project would make everything more difficult.

He glanced at Paloma, watching as she twirled a pen between her fingers. Her passion and creativity were undeniable, but right now, he was drowning in doubt. Was all this added stress and work truly worth it?

With a quiet sigh, he forced his attention back to the paperwork. Only time would tell if he'd made the right choice, but for now, all he could do was push forward and hope that the promise of their partnership would outweigh the complications of their personal lives.

CHAPTER ELEVEN

September 6th, 12:15 a.m.

Paloma wrapped her thin cardigan around her, shivering as the cool night air caressed her skin. She stared at the line of light on the water created by the nearly full moon. The gentle water lapping against Hope's dock was a soothing rhythm, punctuated by the occasional creak of wood beneath their feet.

Although her friend seemed the opposite of relaxed, her posture was rigid, and she gripped her wine goblet tight enough to shatter it.

"What's wrong?" Paloma asked. "Did I piss you off?"

"No, why do you think that?" Hope replied.

She'd had her monthly sunset cruise on her pontoon with friends. Lilith was naturally among them since they lived in a small town, and Asher was Hope's twin. Paloma might have been a tad standoffish.

"For nettling Asher's *neighbor*," she said, "I should have kept my petty jabs to myself."

"You. Petty, never." Hope shook her head theatrically.

"Shut up, asshole." Paloma pinched her friend's arm playfully. "I'm not that bad."

Hope snorted. "I recall in high school when Tammy forgot to add you to the group text for her Halloween party. The next day in homeroom, you dressed up as a ghost, telling everyone you were invisible to certain friends. After she apologized and made a new group text, you came to the party as a vampire and stood on her porch until she specifically asked you to come inside."

"I was making sure. We all know vampires can't enter a home without being invited in." They laughed at the memory, and when the sound drifted off on the night air, she turned to Hope, the old glider they shared squeaking like a mouse. "But I should have left Lilith alone and not called her out. That was a bitch move. My dad called on the way over to your place. I was taking my annoyance out on her."

"But you weren't wrong." Hope's brows furrowed. "Wait, what happened with your dad?"

"What wasn't I wrong about?" Paloma asked.

"Forget it. Tell me about your dad."

"No way." She wagged a finger. "I'd much rather hear about me being right."

Hope smiled but turned toward the lake, her jaw tightening. "Maybe not this time."

In the silence, Paloma studied her friend, replaying the evening. Hope had been in high spirits on the boat, but afterward, she'd gone quiet. When had that happened? Ah, when she had walked Lilith to her car.

"She admitted it finally," Paloma said. "That's she's with your brother?"

Hope nodded. "We argued. Me and Lilith."

"Would it help to talk about it?" She didn't want to talk about Asher, who was part of her past. But Hope was a good friend, so Paloma would listen if needed.

"I'm good. I said my piece. She will do what she wants with it." Hope waved a hand as if brushing aside the topic. "Tell me about your dad. What did he want?"

"He wanted to lecture me on not screwing up my big chance." She hated the edge of self-doubt in her voice.

"Oh? What big chance?"

"I bid on a new kind of project with Max London." She smiled, a little firework going off in her chest. "We landed it."

"So that's why he's bailing on Crowley Construction. To play with Pretty Paloma," Hope teased. "And congratulations. Is the project local?"

"No, Traverse City. It's one of the homes of Roy and Linda Sterling."

Hope straightened. "The Sterlings? No way!"

Paloma's grin widened. "Yup, them."

"That's amazing. Congrats to you and Max."

"Thanks," she sighed. "I wish my dad had reacted the same. He spent the whole drive lecturing me on how not to screw this up, how I need to watch Max like a hawk because partnerships can go south fast." She gulped her wine, hoping to swallow the burn of humiliation crawling up her throat. "Like I hadn't learned that lesson the hard way."

"I don't think you have to worry about Max. He's hardworking and honest."

"We do work together well. And he's got a great eye for detail." The issue wasn't his work ethic but her attraction to him. She had the keep her eye on the prize, and not Max's ass. Lust was temporary; careers were not.

"That's cool," Hope said, swirling the wine in her glass. The moonlight glinted off the surface, casting a faint red glow on her hand. A cool breeze rustled through the trees behind them, carrying the scent of pine and lake water.

"I needed this," Paloma sighed. "A quiet moment with my friend, good wine, and this view. It's like hitting a reset button on the week's stress."

Hope hummed in agreement, then said, "You know, I've always thought you and Max would be great together. As a couple."

Hit by Hope's out-of-left-field comment, Paloma nearly choked on her wine. "What? Why would you think that?" she sputtered, her pulse quickening. A warm flush crept up her neck, and she hoped the moonlight wouldn't betray her reaction.

Max had crossed her mind numerous times, usually late at night when her defenses were down—or when he was near, smelling like someone she wanted to lick. Or when he gave her his sunshine smile.

Yet, she couldn't ignore the persistent ache in her chest, the longing for something more. Working with Max pleased, scared, thrilled, and confused her.

Hope chuckled, setting her glass down on the small table between them. "You're both creative and passionate about your work. Like Max, you're playful and sexy. You two would be hot in bed."

Picturing Max naked, sweaty, and pressed against her, whispering all the ways he'd make her come had heat plummeting south. Pushing that tantalizing treat aside, she smirked. "Are you asking to watch?" She wiggled her brows. "I always suspected you were kinky."

"Definitely," Hope agreed. "And I'm also right. You two should mix business with pleasure."

For a moment, she allowed herself to imagine it—not just the sex but the intimacy. Max's warm smile directed at her, not as a colleague but as someone more. His strong hands holding her instead of soil and plants. But then she shook her head, pushing the fantasy away.

"Fine, I admit it; I'm attracted to him. I'm certain he feels it too. Or at least he had." Paloma stared at her wine. Professional distance replaced his usual warmth since they'd taken on the Sterling project. "But we agreed that keeping things professional is the smart move. This partnership is working so well for both of us. Why risk that for a fleeting physical attraction?"

"Is it fleeting? You seem to admire him. Or at least respect him," Hope pressed.

"As a work partner," Paloma clarified. "That doesn't mean he wants to put up with me as a girlfriend."

"What's this, 'put up with me'? You are a catch. Hot. Driven –"

"Too driven."

"That's your ex talking, not you."

"Maybe," she conceded. "But I'm not willing to risk losing an amazing business partner for lust."

"Can't it be just that, lust?"

That was tempting, but Max wouldn't go for it, and she wouldn't risk losing a business partner and her heart when he tired of her. "I'd suggested that before we started working together. He turned me down."

Hope flinched. "Ouch."

Paloma shrugged. "He had his reasons. And while those reasons are gone, I get the vibe he isn't one for no-strings sex before it was my pride that was hurt. What if I suggest it now and I offend him? It'd make working together weird. And again, I don't see the point of messing with a perfect working relationship for lust. I've got toys to take care of that. I can't find another business partner like Max."

"Honey, if your vibrator is better company than a man who keeps up with your ambitions, I need the brand because mine just lie there taking up space like the men I date."

Paloma laughed, tempted to point out that all of Hope's exes disappointed her because she avoided dating the man she truly wanted—her best friend, Jackson. But since she had her own hard-earned trust issues with men she didn't want to poke at, she kept her observation to herself.

She stood. "It's getting late. I should get home."

"Are you okay to drive?" Hope asked. "You're welcome to stay here."

"This is my second glass all evening, and I've been nursing it for the last hour."

Hope rose from the glider. "I'll walk with you to your car."

Leaving behind the lake, they walked along the side of Hope's house toward Paloma's car. "I can't believe how fast summer flew by," she said.

"I know. But I am excited for the cider mills. I've been craving apple cinnamon donuts since last year." Hope smacked her lips and rubbed her stomach.

"And don't forget the harvest festival," Paloma grinned. "This time, I'm taking home that blue ribbon for the coolest carved pumpkin."

Her phone buzzed in her pocket, and she fished it out, expecting another call from her father. Instead, it was Max asking if leaving early for Traverse City on Friday still worked for her.

The thought of it made her stomach dip. She could see it clearly—her fiddling with the radio, searching for the perfect playlist to fill any awkward silences. And Max, his gorgeous profile, staring wordlessly out the car window. Three hours, possibly more, confined in the car with his cologne mixing with the stilted conversation.

She took a deep breath, but the butterflies continued to twirl and dip. Exhaling, she couldn't help smiling. Despite her nerves, she couldn't deny the spark of joy that ignited in her chest at the prospect of spending time with Max. Her thumb hovered over the reply button, alternating between tapping out a flirty and fun response or one that was all business. She went with boring.

Paloma: Works for me

Max: Great. Will pick you up at 7.

She stared at the message, so different from his usual warm texts with their playful emojis and casual banter. She'd have close to four hours trapped in a car with this new, distant version of Max.

"Earth to Paloma." Hope waved a hand in front of her face. "You've been staring at your phone like it offended you."

"It's Max."

"And that brief response has you frowning because . . .?"

"He's been different lately. Withdrawn." Paloma leaned against the porch railing. "Ever since the initial meeting with the Sterlings, he's built a wall between us. I'd thought he was annoyed with my bitchiness when we ran into your brother and Lilith at the Coffee Bean. I was a touch," she held two fingers wide apart, "rude. But it's been almost a week, and the easy conversations, the inside jokes, that spark when our eyes meet—it's all gone."

"Did you ask him why?"

"No. Work has been crazy busy for us; we've barely seen each other. And why bother?" She stood and hugged her friend. "It's for the best. Like I said, mixing business with pleasure is asking for trouble."

"But you two would be soooo hot together," Hope teased.

She wiggled her shoulders. "Girl, I'm hot with anyone."

"That's true. Drive careful and text me when you get home."

Paloma nodded, getting into her car. Her phone buzzed again.

Max: I'll bring the site plans.

Short and curt. Professional, distant words that shouldn't make her heart ache, but did.

She pressed her forehead against the cool metal of her car, cursing. The end of the week would rush toward her, and then the ride to Traverse City would crawl to a standstill. It'll be an eternity—three hours of carefully measured words and avoided glances. Three hours of pretending she didn't miss his sunshine smile or how he leaned close when she spoke, like he wanted to take in every word.

Three hours of wondering what changed and if she should try to fix what she must have broken.

CHAPTER TWELVE

September 13th, 1:15 p.m.

"Hey, Sleeping Beauty, you alive?" asked the sultry voice that visited Max's hottest fantasies often.

Opening his eyes, his heartbeat quickened, and warmth spread through him. Paloma stood a few feet from him on his porch in a summer dress in her signature red that he couldn't help admiring. The color was stunning on her.

He shook his head. She's a business partner, not a daydream.

The comfortable rocker squeaked as he stood. He stepped toward her before catching himself and moving back, and grabbing his duffle. "Shit, sorry. I know you wanted to get on the road to beat the rush hour traffic. My plan was to wait here and be ready as soon as you pulled up." A yawn overtook him, and he covered his mouth, his jaw cracking.

Her brows rose. "Seems like you needed a catnap."

More like he needed to hibernate. For the last week, he'd been getting up before the sun and working until it set to carve out time for this overnight trip to the Sterling house in Traverse City.

"I'm good," he lied. "Ready?"

She nodded and stepped off the porch, walking toward her red car. He slid into the passenger seat and rubbed his eyes, debating whether sleeping the three-hour trip would be rude. He was exhausted, and things between them had shifted since the run-in with Asher. The easy camaraderie they once shared had given way to an uncomfortable formality, leaving an almost palpable tension in its wake. Yet underneath it all, the constant current of attraction was a struggle to ignore.

The only time things weren't strained was when they talked about work—which was for the best. And that's what he'd focus on. "Since they've asked me to design the landscaping as well, I've been thinking about the garden layout. How do you feel about bringing some of the outdoor elements inside? Like extending the natural stone from the patio into the living room."

"Oh, I love it," she exclaimed. "Blending the actual outdoors with the interior space would create such a beautiful flow. Can you imagine how stunning it would look, especially with the right lighting?"

Her eyes sparkled with excitement, causing a warmth spread through his chest. Damn, she was beautiful. But she wasn't his to admire. She was hung up on Asher. The reminder was a bucket of cold water, dousing the spark of desire that had flared in his chest.

"I'm glad you like the idea," he said, his voice carefully neutral despite his internal conflict. He turned his gaze to the road ahead, hoping the passing landscape would distract him. Silence settled between them, heavy with unspoken words. Or maybe all this angst was one-sided, and she didn't notice his mood shifts.

The hum of tires on asphalt filled the car, punctuated by the rhythmic click of the turn signal as Paloma merged onto the highway. His eyelids grew heavy, but her voice cut through the white noise. "You know, you've got that same faraway look my dad used to get on long drives."

His sleepy brain jolted awake, curiosity piercing through the fog of fatigue. Dad? She'd mention her mom and siblings but never talk about her dad. He shifted in his seat, turning toward her. The sunlight between the trees cast fleeting shadows across her profile, kissing her cheeks and lips in a hypnotic pattern. "Were you a road-tripping family?"

"No. We were the kind who traveled first class, vacationing where my dad worked."

"What's he do?"

"He's a hospitality design architect," Paloma said. "He designs luxury hotels and resorts all over the world, creating lavish, one-of-a-kind spaces. His projects took months, sometimes even years. That's why we'd always vacation where he was working."

He raised an eyebrow, intrigued by this glimpse into her family life. "That sounds interesting. Did you enjoy it?"

"Mom called it 'mixing business with pleasure,' but I think it was more about keeping the family together."

There wasn't a change in her body language or facial expression, but he caught a hint of something in her voice—a subtle undercurrent of melancholy that tugged at his heart. The lavish vacations and worldly experiences suddenly seemed less glamorous, tinged with longing. A pang of sympathy tapped at his heart.

A thoughtful silence settled between them, broken only by the steady hum of the engine and the occasional whoosh of a passing car. She merged onto the fast lane and then glanced at him. "What about you?" she asked, her voice quieter, almost hesitant. "What are your parents like?"

That familiar tightness banded around his chest. Images flashed through his mind: his father's smile, the sound of his laughter in the kitchen, the screaming beep of machines in his hospital room. He swallowed hard, pushing the memories away. How could he possibly explain the weight he carried, the guilt that gnawed at him every time he thought about his family?

Moreover, what were they to each other? Colleagues? Friends? Their attraction was undeniable, but he wasn't sure if it went beyond physical desire. The thought of baring his soul, of sharing his pain with someone passing through his life, had him hesitating. His dad wasn't a casual anecdote to chase away boredom during a long car ride.

"They're . . . my mom and Drake, they . . . we're all trying to navigate things the best we can. It's not always easy, but we manage." He sighed, then said, "It's complicated. They worry a lot. Especially about me."

"And your dad?" Paloma asked, her voice gentle, tinged with curiosity and concern.

His gaze remained fixed on the passing landscape, his jaw tightening. After a moment, he replied, "He . . . he's not with us anymore."

Her quiet gasp filled the car, and a moment later, her small hand covered his. He turned his and squeezed before letting go, even though he wanted to keep holding her. He was ridiculous—into a woman who wasn't interested in him.

"What happened?" she asked.

"Heart failure." The words dropped like stones. His fingers drummed once, twice on the steering wheel. He couldn't bring himself to unpack all those memories, not here, not now. "It was a long time ago. I was a freshman in high school."

"That's when you moved to our town, right?"

"Yup, second semester. I met Asher through Jackson in Biology. He's the reason I got into landscape architecture. Sort of. He got me a job working at his family's construction company, but I was more interested in the designing the outside than inside. I spent my free time sketching landscape ideas for the sites we were working on."

He paused, a faint smile tugging at his lips, recalling those early days with Jeff. "It started with doodles, but then a landscape architect the homeowners had hired came across one and loved it. He hired me, then mentored me, and later, sold his business to me when he retired."

She turned in her seat. "His name was also Max?"

The question caught him off guard like he'd missed a step. "No . . . his name's Jeff."

"But your company is MaxScape Designs."

A chuckle escaped him. "Oh, well it was kind of a pain to change names, but the inner kid in me couldn't resist."

She grinned. "It is perfect."

His shoulders relaxed as he continued, more comfortable with this topic. "What about you? How'd you end up in your field?"

As she shared her career journey, the miles slipped by unnoticed. Their conversation flowed easily from one topic to the next, with professional anecdotes giving way to more personal stories and shared laughter. The tension that had lingered between them since the start of their trip slowly dissipated, replaced by a growing sense of camaraderie.

Lost in their discussion, he almost missed the "Welcome to Traverse City" sign as it came into view. The long drive had passed in a blink. He glanced at her relaxed smile. The carefully maintained professional boundary he'd been so aware of at the start of their trip had softened without him noticing.

Her smile faltered, and she twisted in her seat, glancing at the welcome sign. "Oh, shit. I was supposed to call him when I was a half hour from his place." She said then asked the Bluetooth in her car to call Felix. Her brother answered on the second ring, and Paloma said in a rush, "Sorry, Flea. I'm ten minutes from your house."

"Perfect," came a deep male voice for the speakers. "Fence would *love* to see you."

Max glanced at Paloma and caught her rolling her eyes. He asked, "Who's that?"

She shook her head and said quietly. "I'll tell you later." Then said louder, "Seriously, Felix, hanging out with criminals? What does Abigail think about that? Or your customers?"

"One," her brother began, but another guy with an even deeper voice cut in, "Darling, you wound me."

"Ugh, Flea, take me off speaker," Paloma demanded.

"One, he was an alleged criminal," her brother began again. "He was never arrested." Another pause and murmurs rose, then Felix amended, "Okay, never convicted. Two. Abigail suggested I hire him to help him toward a different career path. He's no longer selling stuff that fell off the back of the truck. He drives the truck. He's my luxury courier. I've needed someone like Fence since I connected with a guy in Detroit who rebuilds and refurbishes large antique pieces. His items are in high demand with a lot of my clients."

Paloma's brow furrowed. "Is that code for something, luxury courier? You're not doing anything illegal, are you?"

Felix laughed, "Sister, I'm offended."

"And my family would murder him. They'd bury him next to Hoffa," interjected a woman with the polished cadence of a prep school education.

"That's true," Paloma muttered, then said, "Anyway, I could drop Max off at his friend's first, then come over. That should give you time to finish whatever you're doing."

"Oh, he's still with you?" her brother asked. "Bring him. We're playing cards and need even numbers."

"Or," rumbled another man—probably the criminal Max was growing to dislike. "Drop him off. I'll sit out the game. I'd much rather get caught up with you, pretty lady"

Max bristled at the man's blatant flirting. Turning to Paloma, he blurted out, "You know, I love cards." The words tumbled out before he could stop them. Sure, he hadn't touched a deck in years, but that was beside the point.

"Great, see you in a few. Love you, sis." Felix hung up.

Not wanting to look closely at why he threw his plans with Jamie out the car window, he asked, "Why do you call your brother Flea?"

"To annoy him. When he was little, I convinced him he was named after mom's scrawny cat from her childhood, who always had fleas. He threw a fit, tears and screaming, all of it. Mom thought it was funny. Dad was less amused since I told Felix the story during an unveiling of one of his resorts." She shrugged. "Since then, I've called him Flea."

Max snorted. "He must love that."

She grinned, and the devil behind it was adorable. "I think he hated his high school nickname more."

"Which was?"

"Alley Cat because he was a bit of a slut," she said with a hint of fondness in her voice. Max burst out laughing. "He grew out of that in college. And now he's blind to anyone who isn't Abigail. You'll see how he looks at her—like she hung the moon and stars. He's so completely, utterly in love with his girlfriend that it's almost sickening how sweet they are together. But mostly, it's just beautiful to see him so happy and devoted. You'll get to meet her this evening." Paloma's fingers tightened on the steering wheel. The car slowed as her foot eased off the accelerator. "Speaking of tonight, are you sure about coming over? Your friend won't mind?"

He avoided the question, asking his own. "Who's Fence?"

She sighed, facing the street. "Remember when I told you about the guy I took home who stole from me?"

"Yeah . . ." He forced his voice to stay even though the mention of another man getting to touch Paloma and then hurting and humiliating her made him want to do violence.

"Fence is his nickname. I don't actually know his real name," Paloma admitted. "Well, with his contacts, he helped me get back what was stolen."

"Ah," Max said. Well damn, now he couldn't hate the man. "As for my friend, Jamie and I don't have a set time." That was a lie. He was expected in the next hour or so. But there was no way he was leaving Paloma with her knight in tarnished armor.

Chapter Thirteen

Paloma's car swung left onto Front Street, tires crunching over loose gravel. Max rolled down his window, taking in the faint freshwater scent from nearby Grand Traverse Bay. It was mixed with the subtle fragrance of hanging baskets and planters that decorate the street. The combination was Michigan magic.

The sugar maples lining the street were beginning to hint at autumn, with a few leaves starting to blush gold at the edges. The design was perfect for the bustling city. Their still-full canopies provided a beautiful backdrop and ample shade for pedestrians strolling along the sidewalks enjoying ice cream and the sunset.

She made another turn, and the busy main street faded away like the last whisper of summer. She parked in front of her brother's house, a beautiful two-story building with burnt red siding and white trim. Max had a soft spot for homes with front porches, and Felix's lined the front of his. A mature sugar maple dominated the small yard, its canopy a vibrant palette of reds and golds that seemed to capture the essence of a Michigan autumn.

"Nice place," Max said, retrieving Paloma's small roller bag from the trunk and walking her to the porch.

The front door swung open before she'd even knocked, and in the entryway stood a taller, masculine version of Paloma. The same black hair, azure eyes, and wide, full mouth regarded her with a huge grin.

He pulled her into a bear hug. "Sis! It's been too long."

"It has." She squeezed him tight.

A woman with light brown hair who looked like her last name should be Kennedy or Rockefeller glided around Felix. Her green eyes crinkled with genuine delight as she enveloped Paloma in a tender embrace. "How are you?" she asked, her voice rich and melodious, each word enunciated with the polish of a finishing school education.

Paloma beamed, pulling away from the hug. "Max, this is my brother, Felix, and his girlfriend, Abigail."

"Nice to meet you," Felix said, ushering them inside. "I'd give you a tour of the whole house, but the upstairs is going through a major renovation, and anyway, all the fun is downstairs.

Crossing the threshold, Max was enveloped in the warmth and the intoxicating aroma of spiced rum. Through the foyer, they stepped into laughter and clinking glasses. The house was filled with people.

"Welcome to card night. Poker's in the dining room," Felix announced. "To the right, in the dining room, is poker." Max glimpsed a long cherrywood table, every seat filled. Then, they moved to a large, open family room and kitchen. Groups of four sat around a coffee table, another at a high top. "In here is euchre. At the breakfast nook is Texas hold 'em.

"What do you say?" Abigail asked, pulling out two bar stools at the kitchen's island. "Play a little euchre?"

"Euchre?" he echoed, punched in the heart by nostalgia. During his second semester at his new high school, he'd been paired with Jackson for an assignment. They'd gotten along, and Max had been invited for cards. There, he met Asher and other people who were still his friends today. They taught him the game, but more importantly, it had been the first time he'd truly felt like he belonged in his new home. "I'd love to," Max said, his voice thick with memory.

Felix mixed drinks as they settled into their seats. The familiar rhythm of shuffling and dealing filled the air. Max was instantly at ease, swept up in the friendly competition and banter.

The hours slipped by, and the next time he looked out the window, the moon and stars were out, and he was three or five old-fashioneds deep into what was shaping up to be an unforgettable night. His cheeks ached from laughter, and his mind buzzed pleasantly with liquor. Across from him sat Paloma, his partner against Felix and Abigail. Fence and a woman whose name he couldn't quite recall—was it Bella?—were sipping their drinks and watching the action.

"Alright, last hand," Felix announced, shuffling the cards. "We're all neck and neck, so this is for all the marbles."

Max picked up his hand, glancing briefly at Paloma before he assessed his cards. He had the Jack of hearts, nine of hearts, King of clubs, ace of spades, and Queen of diamonds. The up card was the ten of spades. Across the table, Abigail shuffled her cards while Felix looked at his hand thoughtfully.

"Pass," Max said, his eyes flicking to Paloma. She met his gaze, her brow knitting slightly, and he caught the faintest tilt of her head. He'd learned that meant she had a plan.

"Pass," said Abigail.

"Pass," Felix echoed, scanning the table.

Paloma hesitated for a fraction of a second before saying, "Pick it up," to Felix, her tone steady. He noted how her fingers tapped lightly on the table, a subtle signal that she had a strategy in mind.

He grinned, scooping up the ten of spades. "Spades it is, then."

His focus remained on Paloma as he led with the ace of spades. She played the nine of spades, and he noticed the slight tightening in her shoulders. She was taking a calculated risk, and he had to support it.

Abigail played the King of spades, and seeing no spades in his hand, Max discarded his nine of hearts. He caught Paloma's gaze, and she gave a nearly imperceptible nod—a sign that they were still on the same page. Felix threw in the ten of hearts, clearly biding his time.

Abigail led the next trick with the Queen of spades. Paloma played low, clearly setting something up, and Felix took the trick with the Jack of spades. Anticipation built in Max, he nudged Paloma's ankle under the table. She tapped back, a jolt of warmth spreading through him at the simple touch. It was all the confirmation he needed—they were in perfect sync, reading each other's intentions without a word.

"Come on, babe," Felix crowed. "One more, and we've got this."

Abigail led with the ace of diamonds. Paloma played another low card, holding back, and Felix followed suit. Max didn't hesitate; he confidently laid down his Queen of diamonds, taking the trick. Paloma's gaze was on him, and he swore it was warm with approval.

It was his turn to lead. He looked at Paloma, searching her expression for a hint of what she might be holding. She met his eyes, her lips curving in a small, confident smile, and that was all he needed. He played his Jack of hearts—the left bower in a Spades hand.

Her beautiful face lit up as she laid down her ace of hearts, and a thrill ran through Max. Groans echoed around the table. "Last trick, Paloma," he said, his voice low and sure. "Bring it home."

Without hesitation, she played the Jack of spades—the right bower—sealing their victory. The room buzzed with the energy of their triumph, but Max was only aware of her smile, the way it matched his own.

"Yes!" he exclaimed, reaching across the table to high-five her. Their hands lingered, fingers brushing, thrill shot through him. He held her gaze, and the electricity between them was palpable—a shared spark of victory and something more unspoken.

Felix shook his head. "Unbelievable. How did you know she had the right bower, Max?"

He shrugged, still grinning at Paloma. "I didn't know for sure. But something told me she had a plan, and it'd be a good one."

The corner of Paloma's mouth twitched—that telltale sign she was holding back a full-blown smile. The warmth from the bourbon made him a little looser and his grin a bit wider. His foot nudged hers under the table again. Her gaze met his, a glimmer of mischief dancing in her eyes.

"Pretty good, huh?" she said, her voice a little slower, leaning back in her chair as if she'd won a marathon instead of a card game. She stretched her arms overhead, the movement exaggerated, and let out a satisfied sigh. "I mean, I practically carried the team."

He snorted, recognizing her playful jab for what it was. "Oh please," he retorted, "I was the mastermind behind this operation."

She quirked an eyebrow, a challenge clear in her expression. "Is that so? And here I thought I was partnered with a guy who wears his heart on his sleeve. Or should I say, his cards on his face?"

Before he could fire back, his phone buzzed in his pocket. He fumbled for it, glancing at the screen through tipsy eyes. He caught the time and muttered, "Oh shit," as he answered, with a slight slur, saying "Jamie, shit, sorry. I lost track of time."

"It also sounds like you lost track of the drinks you've drunk," his friend laughed.

"Yeah, I'll definitely be getting an Uber to your place. I'll call now." He stood, and thankfully, the room only tilted instead of spinning.

"Don't worry about it. I'll come get you. Front Street isn't far from me."

Max gasped. "How do you know where I am at?"

Jamie snorted. "You told me when you texted to tell me you'd be a little late. This was back when you were sober."

"I'm sob—" He cut off that lie. "I'm buzzed, not drunk."

"Whatever, man. I'll be there in a few." Jamie hung up, still laughing.

Maybe it was time for water. Max pulled up short. The woman who'd been standing next to Fence blocked his path.

"Bella?" Her name was a question along with why she was in his way.

"Isabella," she corrected, her voice soft and playful. She rested her hand on his bicep, her touch lingering as she gave his arm a gentle squeeze. "I couldn't help but notice your game earlier. You've got quite the intuition."

He nodded, a little uncomfortable with the attention. "Thanks. Paloma and I seem to click when it comes to Euchre."

"She's your work partner, right?"

He nodded, and she leaned closer, her breath warm against his cheek. "Oh, good, because I wasn't just talking about the cards." She leaned in, her voice dropping to a conspiratorial whisper. "I've been watching you all night. The way you read people, the way you . . . connect. It's impressive."

A flicker of surprise pinged through him, followed by a twinge of discomfort. Her gaze was intense, almost hungry, and he leaned back slightly. He was a little flattered, but mostly he didn't like that a woman who wasn't Paloma was in his personal space.

"You know," she said, her fingers tracing a small pattern on his skin, "I'd love to see how that intuition of yours translates to other . . . situations."

His brows shot up, and his mind raced, struggling for an appropriate response.

"Max!" Paloma's voice cut through the moment like a knife. He turned, and she was striding toward them, her eyes flashing with an emotion he couldn't quite place. Her easy smile was replaced by a taut line, her posture rigid. "I thought we were going to, um . . . discuss that thing."

"What thing?" he asked.

She moved closer, her shoulder brushing against his arm, effectively creating a barrier between him and Isabella, causing her hand to slip from his bicep. She took a small step back, the self-assurance draining from her features as she glanced briefly at the floor.

"You know, the . . . thing. About the . . . project." Paloma turned to Isabella, her smile not quite reaching her eyes. "Sorry, inside joke. You know how it is with . . . partners."

He couldn't help but notice that she left out the "business" before "partners." Was it intentional?

"Right," Isabella said, glancing between them. "Well, it was nice meeting you, Max." She picked up her drink from the kitchen's island and walked toward Fence.

Paloma visibly relaxed, leaning slightly into Max. "I need some air. Come with me?"

Hell yes, he was going to follow her. He needed clarification on that bewildering exchange.

Once outside, her eyelids fell closed, and the cool air ruffled her hair. "Much better," she murmured.

"What was that all about?" he asked.

Opening her eyes, she looked at him. "What do you mean?"

"Come on, Paloma." His words cut through the night air. "That whole scene back there. The 'thing' about the 'project'? The way you practically shoved yourself between me and Isabella?"

Her cheeks blazed crimson as she averted her gaze. "I don't know what you're talking about."

"Really?" he pressed. "Because it seemed an awful lot like you were jealous."

Her head whipped around. "Jealous? Me? That's ridiculous!"

He leaned in, and the scent of her perfume clouded his senses, stoking his frustration. "Is it? From where I'm standing, it looks like you couldn't handle seeing another woman flirting with me." Aggravation simmered beneath his skin, warring with a burning curiosity. He forced a laugh, but it sounded hollow. "What, you don't like anyone hitting on your backup plan?"

The words hung between them, charged with unspoken tension. He hadn't meant to let that slip, but there it was—the ugly truth neither of them wanted to face.

She took a half-step back, her head tilting. "What are you talking about?"

"Asher," he replied, done tiptoeing around the other man's shadow looming between them.

"What about him?" she snapped.

Tightness gripped his jaw. "You're going to make me spell it out."

She slammed her hands on her hips. "I've already apologized for coming on to you that night at the bar. It was a shitty thing to do, but that was months ago!"

"But you're still hung up on him," he stated matter-of-factly.

Stepping toward him, she poked him in the chest. "For fuck's sake, Max!" Her eyes narrowed. "Who the hell do you think you are? You don't get to make assumptions about my feelings!"

He jutted out his chin. "I saw you at the coffee house."

"Another emotionally stunted male," she muttered. "I wasn't pining after Asher. I was being a petty bitch. There's a huge difference. I was pissed at the way he discarded me." She dropped her hand and shrugged. "Which is dumb because we didn't have anything special. And he was right to break it off since he's obviously interested in Lilith. But . . ."

"But what?" Max asked.

"But I did text him and apologize." She shrugged again and smiled. "I'm petty but not stupid. He's good for my business. I'm on speed dial for him and Hope when any of their clients need a home designer."

The ground tilted under him. He'd read the situation completely wrong. "I'm sorry for jumping to conclusions. I should have known you better than that. It's just . . . when I saw you at the coffee house, I thought . . ." He shook his head, stepping down two of the porch steps. "Never mind. You're right; I shouldn't make assumptions about your feelings."

The tension seemed to drain from her body. She moved in front of him. Still on the porch, they were now eye level. "It's okay," she said softly. "I get it. It probably looked bad from the outside."

They stood there, the air between them thick with unspoken desires and lingering tension. His gaze dropped to her lips, and he swallowed hard, suddenly very aware of how close they were standing.

"Paloma, I . . ." His pulse thundered in his ears, and he leaned in, her lips tantalizingly close. The world had narrowed to this single, perfect moment—her warmth, scent, the promise of a kiss hanging between them like a gossamer thread.

He leaned in, intending to close the final distance between them. Then, the bass from a car boomed, shattering the delicate silence.

His stomach lurched as if the ground had liquefied beneath his feet. Reality crashed between them with brutal force, leaving him reeling. Headlights, harsh and unforgiving, pierced the darkness, pulling alongside Felix's house.

Shit. Jamie.

He stepped onto the sidewalk, the space between them suddenly vast and aching. A cold emptiness settled in his chest where anticipation had burned mere seconds ago. He summoned a smile that was probably more like a grimace, hyper-aware of Paloma's proximity, of the moment slipping away like water through cupped hands.

They walked to Jamie's car, and Max introduced Paloma. His skin prickled with frustration, desire thwarted and unresolved. "Give me a second to grab my duffle," he told his friend.

He turned to Paloma. Her body language was closed off. "I guess this is goodnight then," she said, her tone neutral. Her car was parked a little farther down the street, and they walked toward it.

"Yeah, I guess so," Max replied, searching her face for any hint of the connection they'd shared moments ago. "Thanks for inviting me tonight. It was . . . fun."

She nodded, her expression guarded. "It was. I'm glad you met my brother and Abigail."

He hesitated, wanting to address what had almost happened between them. "Paloma, about what—"

"We got caught up in the moment." Her gaze focused on her car, now a few feet away.

A pang twisted in his chest. "Right," he said, failing to keep the disappointment out of his voice.

He went to the back of the car to grab his bag. The trunk popped open, and their gazes snagged over the hood. A spark of electricity passed between them.

"Max, I—" Paloma started, then stopped, shaking her head slightly.

"What is it?" he asked, his hand pausing on the handle of his bag.

She opened her mouth, then closed it again, clearly struggling with what to say. Finally, she managed, "Have a good night. I'll . . . I'll pick you up tomorrow morning on the way to the Sterling house."

He pulled out his bag and closed the trunk with a soft thud. "Yeah, see you tomorrow." All the way to Jamie's car, the weight of Paloma's gaze followed him. Hand on the passenger door, he turned and caught a glimpse of conflict in her eyes before she quickly looked away.

Climbing into Jamie's car, Max tossed his bag in the back seat, his mind whirling with unanswered questions and unresolved tension. As they pulled away from the curb, he watched Paloma in the side mirror. She stood rooted to the spot, her expression unreadable in the dim streetlight.

"Everything okay, man?" Jamie asked.

Max tore his gaze from the mirror. "Yeah, everything's fine. Just . . . complicated."

CHAPTER FOURTEEN

September 14th, 10:15 a.m.

Max held open the massive wooden front door, still reeling from the two-hour client meeting with the Sterlings that had upended all his conservatory design plans. Paloma stepped past him, the faint scent of her perfume teasing him.

They stepped onto the circular drive. Through the trees, waves crashed against the rocky shore below, their rhythm blending with the rustle of maple leaves that were turning from green to orange. Zipping up his jacket against the morning chill, he adjusted the strap of his messenger bag.

He shook his head. "Wow, Roy is something. He is particular in what he wants."

Paloma ran a hand over her sleek updo and let out a strangled laugh. "Until his wife makes a suggestion."

Max snorted. "Then he pauses and says the same thing—"

"And they both pretend it was his idea." She threw up her hands. "I nearly bit through my tongue when he spent fifteen minutes explaining why they absolutely had to have the exact light fixtures his wife mentioned two minutes earlier."

"Well, at least we know the real approval process now." Max grinned, checking his watch. "Do you want to grab breakfast?"

"Yesss." The word sounded like a deflating balloon. "I overslept and was too nervous to eat anyway. Felix says there's a great breakfast place if we made a left instead of right when leaving the peninsula."

Max snuck glances at Paloma's profile as she navigated the coastal road. The almost-kiss from last night replayed in his mind: the desire in her eyes, the way she'd tilted her head and body toward him, and how his heart had nearly burst from his chest before Jamie's terrible timing. Now, she was strictly business, detailing her vision for the house like nothing had happened. Maybe that was her way of telling him to back off.

She parked at the corner of a small strip mall in front of a weathered diner with blue trim and windows facing the harbor. Inside, they slid into a booth, and the waiter handed them menus, asking if they wanted coffee. They did, and after he left to retrieve the carafe, Max couldn't hold back anymore. "Do you regret last night?"

"Hell yes!" she groaned, her fervor making his stomach drop. "Why did I drink so many of those fancy martinis Abigail made? And then stayed up talking with her and Felix until three in the morning before one of the biggest client meetings of my life."

Right. She was choosing to pretend the almost-kiss hadn't happened. He should follow her lead, but his mouth had other ideas. "I meant, do you regret that we almost kissed? Or regret that we didn't?"

Her fingers stilled on the menu, a faint blush creeping up her neck. "A little bit of both."

The waiter interrupted with coffee and a chipper, "Ready to order?" They went through the motions of choosing breakfast, though his stomach was twisted in knots, waiting to see if that was all Paloma would say.

After the waiter left, she stared out the window, watching the cars on the road between them and the harbor. Maybe that's all she'd say. He sipped his coffee, doing his damnedest to swallow his impatience and impulsiveness.

She met his eyes, and the pain there made his chest ache. "Look, I want you, but we need to keep things professional. I've worked too hard rebuilding my reputation after my ex nearly destroyed it and my business. These projects with you—the Thompsons, the Sterlings—are my chance to prove myself. To show everyone who whispered behind my back that I'm not some lovesick fool who's too dumb to manage her business."

"I'm not asking you to give up your career," he said softly, fighting the urge to reach for her hand. "We're in this together. All I'm asking is we explore this attraction."

"I can't."

"Why?" The question burst out before he could stop it. Typical. He kept pushing when he should have backed off.

"Honestly? Because nice guys like you scare me more than the obvious jerks. With them, I know the score. But men like you . . . it's different. I don't know what I'm getting into, and I don't know how to trust what I feel." She blinked rapidly. "I still wake up some nights in a cold sweat, wondering if I'll ever trust my judgment again. I can't risk messing up what we have professionally. I'm good at casual. I'm not good at," she gestured between them, "whatever this could become."

Her words were a physical weight on his heart. Everything in him wanted to promise he'd never hurt her, but empty promises weren't what she needed. "What about after?" he asked quietly, his usual impulsiveness giving way to something more careful, more deliberate

She traced the rim of her coffee cup, not meeting his eyes. "The project is going to take three to four months. You'll be sick of me by December."

The words hit him like a punch to the gut. Sick of her? Did she think so little of herself? For once, his usual impulsiveness stilled. She needed patience, not his typical headlong rush. "And if I'm not?"

She shrugged. "Fine. After the final walk-through with the Sterlings, I'll take you to dinner at Trattoria Stella if you aren't ready to run in the other direction."

"I'd be happy going to Don't Drive-in as long as it's with you."

"So would I. Their patty melt with jalapeños is amazing," she joked.

The waiter balanced two heavy white plates. The scent of maple syrup and salsa had his stomach growling. He slid a towering stack of banana-stuffed French toast drowned in maple syrup in front of Max, followed by a massive breakfast burrito for Paloma that leaked green salsa onto the plate.

"Hot sauce?" the waiter asked, already reaching into his apron.

"Yes, please!" Paloma's eyes lit up as he set down Tabasco and Sriracha. She dumped both liberally over her eggs. She caught him staring and grinned. "What? I love my food spicy, full of flavor."

"I'm just making mental notes for December," he said, cutting into his French toast. "When I cook you dinner after our first official date."

She rolled her eyes, but her smile lingered. "Pretty confident for someone who has to wait three, maybe four months."

"I am." He leaned back, picking up his coffee. "Some things are worth waiting for."

CHAPTER FIFTEEN

September 23st, 4:05 p.m.

Paloma pulled up the long driveway of the colonial revival home. The late afternoon sun glinted off Woodland Lake, casting a golden glow across the weathered shingles and wrap-around porch. She parked next to a large motorcycle, eyeing it. She had to search to remember the actual names of the pineapple couple, ah, yes, the Thompsons. Her little inside joke with Max had almost erased their actual names. She shook her head. The Thompsons had told her they wouldn't be at the house and to leave everything in the library. But the motorcycle said that might have changed their minds.

Her gaze shifted to the trees surrounding the property. Touches of autumn appeared in the sporadic leaves, turning yellow and pale orange at their edges. She closed her eyes, savoring the quiet: the rhythmic lapping of waves against the shore and the occasional cry of a wheeling gull. With a deep breath, she opened her eyes.

Okay, get moving. Time to get to work. She'd drop off the updated floor plans and check out the changes made to the main bedroom.

And she couldn't wait to see Max's progress on the indoor garden: the soft rustle of ornamental grasses, the soothing trickle of the wall fountain, the lush scent of moss and ferns.

She stepped out of her car, and the breeze danced with the hem of her knee-length skirt. Opening the rear door, she retrieved her portfolio and set off toward the house. Each footfall on the cobblestone path seemed to echo with thoughts of Max.

Their other projects and schedules hadn't lined up since returning from Traverse City, which was a relief—and torture. The physical distance helped dull the constant awareness of him, gave her space to breathe without his presence making her question their agreement to wait. But she missed him, and a week apart hadn't diminished how her body hummed at the thought of him.

"Deal with today's problems," she muttered. "Tomorrow's will come soon enough."

Rounding the car, she paused beside the motorcycle. Her fingers traced the iconic American emblem on its tank. She'd always wanted to learn to ride. Maybe next summer.

It seemed the Thompsons had more hobbies than swinging. She grinned, laughing to herself. No, she didn't have proof, but she'd bet on the odds.

Patting the motorcycle, she left it behind and approached the house. She pushed open the side door next to the garage and stepped through the mudroom. The short heels of her boots clicked along the vestibule floor. She called out, "Hello? Elodie? Bill? Anyone home?"

No reply came, but a noise drifted from the kitchen. Upon entering it, she found the room empty. Then she heard a slicing sound emanating from her favorite feature of the house: the central staircase connecting the second level and the walk-out basement.

She'd originally wanted to knock it down and move it because it ran along the large, three-story window in the front of the house. However, after Max transformed the space into a garden oasis, she was glad he'd convinced her to keep it. Its beauty competed with the view of the lake.

Stepping into the great room, she halted. Had the man she couldn't stop thinking materialized from her thoughts? Max's shirtless back was to her. His trowel sank into the rich potting soil as he leaned over the indoor planter, triceps flexing with each careful movement. Droplets of sweat caught the late afternoon sunlight filtering through the windows, turning his skin to burnished gold. Damn.

A rush of warmth flooded her. Part of it was his obvious physical appeal, but the rest was harder to pinpoint. Something was mesmerizing about the way he worked. It spoke to a deeper part of her she couldn't understand.

She was captivated by the subtle shift of his shoulder blades as he reached for a branch and the careful tilt of his head as he examined a leaf. This wasn't merely a job for him but a labor of love. Although she couldn't see his face, his focus was palpable, and his dedication was evident in every line of his body.

A surge of admiration welled inside her, surprising in its intensity. She respected his professional skills, but seeing him like this, wholly absorbed in creating beauty, revealed a depth she hadn't expected.

Her fingers twitched at her sides, fighting the sudden urge to reach out and trace the contours of his bare back, to share in this moment of creation. She was drawn to his masculinity but also the care and attention he embodied.

She shook off her fascination and called out, "Max?" When he didn't acknowledge her, she shouted, "Max!"

He started, then turned around. Her breath caught in her throat. If his back was impressive, his front was downright mesmerizing. Those biceps she'd already fallen for, but now her eyes got to feast on bare broad shoulders and a firm chest with just the right amount of hair. Her gaze followed the tantalizing trail disappearing into his jeans. Her attraction to this hardworking man surged, leaving her breathless and hungry.

He pulled a pair of sleek wireless earbuds from his ears. "Paloma," he breathed, her name falling from his lips like a caress. "What are you doing here?" His casual tone belied the intensity of his gaze.

She swallowed hard, working to find her voice. "I'm dropping off updated plans for the Thompsons," she said, tossing the leather portfolio onto the walnut coffee table. It landed with a soft thud that echoed in the spacious great room, its high ceilings and large windows filling the space with late afternoon light. "I didn't realize you'd be here."

"Surprise," he said softly, taking a step closer. The air between them seemed to crackle with unspoken tension, and memories of their almost-kiss hovered like ghosts in the space between their bodies.

She pulled her gaze from him, scanning the garden she'd grown to love. Her attention caught on the new additions, a smile tugging at the corners of her mouth.

"I like the tree," she noted, gesturing to the one he'd been tending. "And that pineapple bush," she chuckled, shaking her head, "it's ridiculous how well it fits. The Thompsons will love it."

Her fingertips brushed a petal, savoring its silken texture. She turned to face him, becoming aware of his proximity and his undeniable allure. She needed something—anything—to focus on besides him, and asked, "Is the motorcycle outside yours or theirs?"

"It's mine," he replied.

"You keep surprising me. You aren't supposed to ride a motorcycle."

"Why? Is this something to do with your nice guy stereotype again?"

She bit her lip, heat rising to her cheeks as she averted her gaze. "Maybe."

He stepped closer, bringing with him the earthy scent of freshly turned soil and clean sweat. "What do you have against nice guys?"

Confused looks and gentle letdowns—the echoes of "You're just . . . intense" and "We want different things" rang in her mind. Then Max's easy smile during their shared lunches, the warmth of his praise after a job well done. The thought of that smile fading, replaced by the same overwhelmed expression she'd seen too many times before, had her chest tightening.

"I have nothing against them." She pointed at the soil on his arms and aimed for a teasing, light tone. "You're getting into this project, aren't you?"

He glanced down and grinned. "Can't plant a garden without getting a little dirty."

Was it her, or did his tone sound suggestive? Afraid she'd see the answer in his eyes, she stared at his neck, unable to look away from a drop of sweat that trickled from his clavicle to his chest.

"You're too much of a nice guy to be so dirty," she muttered, knowing damn well her words made no sense.

"Nice guys like getting dirty too." Leaning closer, his heat reaching out to her, he said, "And if we're going to stick to stereotypes, you've forgotten the most important one about nice guys."

"And that is?" She still didn't move away but kept her gaze glued to his neck as if avoiding his eyes would save her from where this was heading.

He rested a palm on her hip, and a shiver raced up her spine, her skin tingling where his hand rested. "Nice guys finish last." He hunched forward, running his lips along the hollow of her collarbone, a spot that always ignited her desire. He paused, then did it again before moving to her ear and whispering. "Meaning you finish first . . . repeatedly."

His quiet confidence made her pulse race and her breath catch. It wasn't only the physical desire in his tone but the promise of being cared for and truly seen that heated her everywhere. There was an unspoken understanding that with him, she could let go and trust he would follow through on his promises—at least where her body was concerned.

She took in the rise and fall of his Adam's apple when he swallowed, the sound almost deafening in the electric silence. His nearness was intoxicating, every inch of him drawing her closer, tempting her to cross the line she'd sworn she wouldn't.

"We shouldn't," she whispered, but her body betrayed her resolve even as the words left her lips. The heat radiating from his skin called to her, and she leaned closer.

He stilled. "Do you want me to stop?"

Every logical thought, every hard-earned lesson warned her away—mixing business and pleasure would unravel all she'd built, thread by careful thread. But when Max looked at her with those steady blue-gray eyes, her carefully constructed walls began to crack and crumble like ancient stone.

She bit her lip, torn between desire and caution. "I . . . I don't know," she admitted, her voice barely above a whisper. Her fingers twitched at her sides, itching to reach out and touch him.

He waited, his body still except for his chest's steady rise and fall. His eyes, dark with desire, never left hers, but there was no pressure in his gaze—only patience. He wouldn't touch her again, giving her the space to decide.

Another bead of sweat trailed down his neck. She had to fight the urge to lean forward and taste it. His jaw clenched slightly, the only sign of his struggle. But he still waited. His self-control and willingness to let her set the pace only made her want him more.

Her resolve weakened with each passing second. The memory of their almost kiss, the tension that had been building for weeks, and their undeniable chemistry came crashing down on her.

With a shaky exhale, she decided. Fear and excitement mingled in her chest as she met his gaze. "No," she breathed. "No, I don't want you to stop."

The last thread of restraint snapped, and the tension between them ignited into a flame she couldn't control. With a pounding heart, she stood on tip-toes and kissed him. The touch sparked through her, creating a wildfire.

His hands wrapped around her, pulling her against him until there was no space between them. The desire she'd buried since their kiss last week surged to the surface, and she gave in completely. Running her hand up his bare back and into his hair, she gripped the strands tightly.

Heat flooded her core with his deep, guttural groan. He tilted his head, deepening the kiss, his tongue tracing the seam of her mouth with a slow, deliberate sweep. She parted her lips for him, and he claimed her, his kiss fierce and consuming, drowning out everything but the need to be closer, to feel more of him.

Her body ached with a raw, unrelenting need, and she pressed into him, her hands roaming over his body, wanting to memorize every inch, and becoming drunk on the intoxicating heat of his touch.

"More," she begged.

"Wrap your legs around me," he demanded, and she listened without hesitation.

After a few short steps, he lowered them until she sat on the cold walnut table. On his knees, he pushed open her legs and settled between them. They were eye to eye, making it easy to kiss him and keep her legs around him. She scooted closer and rocked against his torso, desperate for friction.

"Do you need more?" he asked, his breath warm and tantalizing as it ghosted over her skin. His lips traced a path along her jaw, then descended with a slow, deliberate hunger, pressing rough kisses against the exposed curve of her neck and chest.

"Y-yes." Her confession blended with the heat of his touch.

His palm skated up her thigh, stopping at her lacy underwear. "Can I taste you?" he asked.

Her hands, resting limply on his shoulders, tightened into fists. She pressed them against him to anchor herself. "Yes," she repeated, the single word carrying the weight of her surrender.

His eyes darkened, and a wicked smile curved his lips as a shudder of pleasure seemed to ripple through his body. "You have no idea how much I've wanted to hear that," he murmured, his voice thick and hungry. "Lift."

She did, and he slid her underwear down her legs slowly, all the while his hot gaze locked on hers. Only when he'd pushed up her skirt, exposing her to him, did he look away. "So fucking perfect," he said, before shifting and kissing one knee then her other.

With the same unhurried patience, he kissed a trail up her inner thigh. Reaching the apex of her center, he licked her with the flat press of his tongue and she damn near passed out. "Max," she moaned and rocked, digging her fingers into his hair.

Hearing his name on her lips seemed to ignite something primal within him. He devoured her with an intensity that made her legs tremble, her release building like waves against a breakwater. A low rumbling sound crept through the haze of her senses. She couldn't place it, her mind too clouded to process anything beyond the sensations Max was pulling from her. The noise grew louder, and a flicker of awareness bloomed in her subconscious, though it was lost when her climax overtook her. She gasped, pulling on Max's hair.

Then, he was gone.

She sat up, looking for him. "Wha—"

"Someone's here." His blue eyes were nearly black, and his pupils were blown so large, but she couldn't tell if it was desire or panic.

"Hello? Ms. Wagner," called Elodie, the click of her high heels growing louder.

CHAPTER SIXTEEN

September 21st, 5:05 p.m.

Shit. That sound. The distant mechanical groan that had barely cut through the hazy bliss of Max between her legs. A garage door.

Paloma's heart pounded, her ribs practically rattling with each beat. Max bolted upright, his warm hands vanishing from her thighs, tugging down her skirt. A whiplash of emotions coursed through her. Moments ago, she'd been lost in sensation, her world narrowing to touch, heat, and pleasure. Now, reality crashed into her, sharp and immediate.

Her mouth was desert-dry, and her gaze dropped to his erection pressing against his jeans. And damn. He was big. Not crazy scary big like the girth of a soup can and the length of a tire iron. But, the kind of substantial that made her thighs clench with possibilities. The kind of size that in skilled hands . . .

The sharp rap of footsteps on the hardwood jerked her back to the present. Two sets were getting closer, and the living room lights were suddenly far too bright.

"Get over there," she urged in a harsh whisper "And hide your dick behind a pineapple or something! Where's your shirt?" She lurched to her feet, snatched up her portfolio, and dropped it again as she whirled around, shoving cushions aside, yanking up the rug corners. Where the hell had her underwear landed?

She spied the black lace crumbled next to the coffee table's leg. Scooping them up, she tucked them in her skirt pocket like an unwanted confession. Her skin prickled, and damp dread welled inside her with each echo of Elodie Thompson's heels on the hardwood floor, each click a countdown to . . . what? Discovery? Disaster?

Max crossed the room, his hair disheveled from her fingers, his still-bare chest heaving, a smudge of dirt streaking his jawline. "Your shirt," she hissed. "Where is it?"

"I tossed it somewhere," he muttered.

"Paloma?" Elodie's voice rang out around the corner, and then she came into view. "Are you here? I thought that was your car—oh!"

Her gaze darted to Max, who had grabbed his T-shirt from a makeshift workbench and was putting it on. "I didn't realize you two were . . . hard at work already," Elodie said, her voice a touch lower, silkier than usual. Her gaze returned to Max again, lingering, and Paloma had the crazy urge to tell the woman to stop checking him out—as if either of them had a claim to him.

"Not me. Just Max. On the garden. He's working on your garden. I came—" She choked on her panic and shitty choice of words, which were coming out all wrong: too fast and much too loud. One breath in. Another out. "I arrived here a few minutes ago to drop off the main floor bedroom changes."

Bill's eyes narrowed slightly, and he glanced between them, his expression shifting from curiosity to speculative. The awkward silence stretched, thick with unspoken secrets and suspicion. His tongue darted out, wetting his lower lip. His gaze fell to the table she'd lay on with her skirt up around her waist.

Elodie followed her husband's gaze and squeaked. "What's that on my walnut slab?"

Holy Hell, no! That was *not* evidence of her orgasm on the surface. Elodie wiped her hand on the wet spot of the ten-thousand-dollar table. Paloma gasped, her heart hammering.

Max stepped forward. "I'm sorry, I set a butterfly pea flower there."

What the fuck was a pea flower? "Mrs. Thompson, I—" Paloma's voice cracked. After a solid year of re-building her business and carefully cultivating clients in Michigan's exclusive neighborhoods—poof, all gone because of one amazing orgasm.

"Do you have any idea what organic compounds can do to raw wood? This isn't sealed yet!" Elodie's voice rose sharply. She bent closer to examine the mark on the wood.

The mark—oh god, the mark that Elodie had just touched—seemed to glow like a neon sign of Paloma's indiscretion.

Bill stepped closer. "Honey—"

"Don't 'honey' me." Her voice climbed higher with each word. "This is a museum-quality piece of timber. I didn't spend three months tracking down the perfect slab to have it stained before it's even finished!"

"Mrs. Thompson, it was my fault," Max said. "I was showing Paloma the flowering specimens for the indoor garden, and I—"

"I don't care whose fault it is!" Elodie cried. "This isn't any piece of wood. It's an old-growth Indonesian walnut. Do you know how many tables I had to reject before finding one with this grain pattern?" She ran her fingers along the edge of the slab as if checking for further damage. "What if it seeps into the grain? What if it leaves a permanent mark?"

Paloma covered her mouth. The urge to throw up was all-consuming. Her carefully built professional reputation teetered on the edge. The Thompsons were important not only in Brighton but all of Michigan. One complaint about the careless handling of materials could sink Paloma faster than a stone in the harbor. And if they found out what really happened...She couldn't even think about the consequences.

"I can have a specialist look at it immediately," she offered, her professional demeanor wavering under Elodie's fury. "There are treatments we can try—"

"Treatments?" Her laugh could have frosted glass. "This isn't some mass-produced piece of furniture. This is functional art. And now it has a . . . a . . . flower stain on it!" She gestured at the mark, her perfectly highlighted hair swinging like a weapon.

Bill cleared his throat. "Honey, I'm sure it can be fixed. Remember what that specialist did for the teak when we had the water damage in Aspen?"

Elodie's shoulders lowered a fraction, but her lips remained pressed in a thin line. "That was different. That was sealed wood."

"Mrs. Thompson," Paloma said, forcing herself to maintain a steady voice despite her racing heart. "I know someone who specializes in raw timber restoration. He worked on the Guggenheim's Brazilian walnut installation. I can have him here first thing tomorrow morning."

Elodie's perfectly manicured fingers drummed against her thigh as she considered this. "A Guggenheim piece?"

"Yes." Paloma pulled out her phone with trembling hands. "I can call him right now. He owes me a favor after I sourced that rare purple heartwood for his gallery showing."

"Fine," Elodie huffed. "But if there's any hint of discoloration, any variation in the grain . . ." She left the room, her husband following, but her threat remained.

"What the hell is a butterfly pea?" Paloma hissed.

"It's a flower. Its scientific name is Clitoria ternatea." He shrugged. "I freaked out. It's the first thing that came to me."

She'd laugh if the situation wasn't so awful. The Thompsons could decimate her career, which was finally in the red.

As if reading her mind, Max whispered, "Think we're fucked?"

"I don't know." She ran her palm along her skirt, smoothing out any imperfections—but she was the imperfection. Too impulsive, to the point of recklessness.

"Hey," Max touched her arm. "Your restoration guy, is he good?"

Paloma nodded, pulling from his touch and ignoring the hurt that flashed over his face. "He is. But Elodie . . . she notices everything. If the wood isn't perfect . . ." She couldn't finish the sentence. Losing this project wouldn't only cost her money; it'd cost her reputation. In this business, reputation was everything.

Elodie's sharp voice carried through the house. "I knew we should have waited for that craftsman in Copenhagen . . ."

"El, let Paloma call her contact. We'll worry about it after." Bill's voice had the patient tone of a man well-versed in his wife's moods. "Tonight, we have that thing at the Lake Club."

"The Fall Festival? That's not until eight." Elodie sounded less irritated. "Though we should go early. Last year they put us next to the Hendersons." Her words faded, then "so vanilla" floated back, followed by Bill's muffled laughter and "I'll call the club."

A minute later, he returned to the living room. His gaze lingered on Max for a moment before turning to Paloma. "We like your idea of marble floors instead of wood in the main bedroom, but we'd like to look at the samples. Did you bring them?" he asked.

"I did," she said with a bit too much enthusiasm. They're in my car. Would you and Mrs. Thompson like to see them?"

By the time she showed them the samples, called her contact about the table, and the Thompsons were pulling out of their driveway, things were somewhat back to normal—or at least damage control seemed possible.

Paloma turned toward the house, pressing her hand to her stomach. She had to end what was happening between her and Max. She wanted Max and her career, but having both wasn't possible. And no way was she risking her career on a man. She learned her lesson with her ex-fiancé.

Her footsteps echoed in the empty foyer as she re-entered the house. Her pace slowed when she approached the living room. She hesitated for a brief moment before entering. Her gaze drawn to the coffee table. She could almost feel the phantom press of cold wood under her, and the warmth of Max between her legs. A warm flush crept up her neck, clashing with the chill that ran down her spine.

She looked away and found Max watching her from across the room. He stood in front of his lush garden, one hand resting on a potted fern. His jaw was tense, his eyes dark, and focused on her.

"I'm sor—"

"Nothing like that can happen again," she said, aware of how dry her mouth had become. "I told you I can't separate business and pleasure. They almost caught us fucking on their coffee table." Her fingers fluttered to her throat, pressing against her collarbone. "I would've been ruined."

His lips twitched. "Or they'd ask to join in."

She stared at him. How could he joke? Her career wasn't a joke. "And I don't want to have to let them, to save my damn job. This," she pointed between them, "*won't* happen again."

The slight trace of humor drained from him. "Here, in their home, was a mistake, but not us," he said.

"Yes, us. I love my career. And it's the only thing I'm good at. Not love. Not lust. Not relationships. If I have to choose, I'll pick my career."

His expression shuddered, his eyes losing their warmth, and he took a small step back as if her words had physically pushed him. "Understood," he said in a low, flat tone.

"What do you want from me?" The words burst from her like shards of glass, sharp and cutting. Do you expect me to give up my career because you made me come?" She jabbed a finger toward the coffee table. "One orgasm isn't worth my entire future, no matter how good."

Why did every man think her ambition was worthless, something to do until she fell in love—or this case, lust?

"I'm not asking or expecting you to pick. I'm asking you to give us a chance to see where things went between us. I like you—I like you a lot—but I won't push if you aren't interested." He turned toward the garden, giving her his back.

She liked him, more than was safe. But she couldn't risk her career. "I'm sorry, Max," was all she could offer.

"It's fine." His voice said the opposite. He picked up a shovel, giving her a beautiful view of his wide, muscular back. Right before he reached the garden, he turned. "But please, don't kiss me again. Don't flirt with me." He paused, his gaze locking with hers, the tension between them crisp, like the first cool breeze cutting through the lingering warmth of late summer. "Not unless you mean it."

Her throat tightened, and she opened her mouth to respond, but no sound came out. Did she mean it? Did she even know what she wanted?

"I . . ." she faltered, desperate to shift the focus back to work, away from the mess of emotions swirling inside her. "Okay."

He nodded and turned away. She should leave. That would be the smart thing to do. But watching him shut down, seeing the stiff set of his shoulders as he worked, made her chest ache.

Her smartwatch vibrated and she glanced at it, seeing her brother's name. He was probably following up about the accommodation issue they'd discussed this morning. The Sterling project . . . God, how were they supposed to handle that now?

She cleared her throat. "My brother called earlier with news about Traverse City." The words hung in the stale air between them, her attempt at normality withering like week-old flowers. She pressed on anyway. "Abigail agreed to let us use her condo while we're working on the house."

Max's hands tightened around the shovel, then turned. "Really? After what just happened, you think we should share a place?"

He wasn't wrong, but her tight budget didn't include $500 a night for two hotel rooms for two weeks or more. "The drive is over four hours away. We need accommodations with office space. Her place is close to the Sterling house. And nearly everything close to the Sterlings is booked solid for fall tourist season."

"And you can shut off this thing between us? Just like that?" He snapped his fingers.

"Yes," she lied. "The condo has two bedrooms, and it's the only option that makes sense financially and logistically. Unless you want to explain to the Sterlings why their designer and landscaper can't coordinate or keep things professional."

His jaw tightened, his muscles working. "If you're so worried about keeping things professional, maybe you should find another landscaper."

Her stomach plummeted. "Don't be ridiculous. You're the best, and I need your expertise. We just need to . . . to forget what happened here and focus on work. We're adults. We can handle sharing a condo for a few weeks without . . ." She wasn't able to finish the sentence.

"Fine, if that's what you want." He dug the shovel into the shallow dirt, turning it over with practiced precision, as though the garden was the only thing that mattered.

She lingered by the door, watching his shoulders move beneath his shirt. The same shoulders she'd gripped less than an hour ago. Her fingers tingled with the memory.

"I'll email you the Traverse City schedule," she said, her voice steadier than her heart. When he didn't respond, didn't even look up, she left. Her heels clicked against the hardwood, hollow sounds that echoed through the empty house, marking each step that took her further from him.

At her car, she caught her reflection in the window: perfect hair, crisp blazer, not a thread out of place. The consummate professional. Only the black lace still tucked in her skirt pocket told a different story.

CHAPTER SEVENTEEN

October 4th, 4:00 p.m.

Max gripped the handlebars of his motorcycle, his knuckles white beneath his gloves. In a few days, he'd be alone with Paloma for two whole weeks. Two weeks of pretending he didn't want to touch her again, to finish what they'd started in the Thompsons' house. Two weeks of trying to focus on work when all he could think about was the softness of her skin under his fingertips, her taste, the intoxicating scent of her perfume mingled with desire.

He'd promised her he wouldn't push, wouldn't flirt unless he meant it. But damn, how he wanted to. The urge to throw caution to the wind, to risk it all for another moment with her, was almost overwhelming. But he wasn't the impulsive screwup of his youth.

He turned into the parking lot of The Hill, adjusting for the uneven surface, hating his lies. His resolve was as steady as the gravel under his tires. Another man with a little more control wouldn't have taken that kind of risk at a client's house.

He parked and dismounted his bike and took a deep, centering breath. The crisp autumn air filled his nose, carrying the aroma of grilled burgers and fresh apple pie. His stomach growled in anticipation as the scents mingled with the earthy smell of fallen leaves and the faint tang of gasoline from the surrounding vehicles. He focused on the mouthwatering fragrances rather than the knot of anticipation that had taken up permanent residence in his stomach lately.

Gravel crunched under tires as Jackson and Asher pulled in next to him. A minute later, the rumble of Tate's Triumph approached, its deep purr cutting through the quiet country air. He executed an impressive tight U-turn, the bike's chrome gleaming in the late afternoon sunlight.

Max removed his helmet and asked no one in particular, "Why is Tate selling his bike? He's a great rider and seems to love it."

"He says he doesn't have time to ride and doesn't want to pay for the extra parking spot at his condo," Asher said.

Jackson tucked his helmet under his arm, lowering his voice. "You know, I met Tate's new girl last week. Katrina. I think she might be the reason."

Max raised an eyebrow. "Why?"

Jackson's mouth tightened into a grimace. "I got the feeling she wants him to be his only hobby."

"She's intense," Asher agreed.

Tate killed the engine, then removed his helmet. "The backroads out here were fucking fantastic. I swear, every time I come here, I want to quit my job and leave the city."

Jackson and Max exchanged a look but said nothing. Tate was Lilith's brother and the newest to their circle, so none of them knew him well, but Max hoped everything was okay.

"You could," Asher told Tate, nodding toward The Hill. "I heard the owners are retiring and selling the restaurant."

Tate laughed. "Funds manager turned entrepreneur, that'd be a change. Instead of managing other people's millions, I'll do it for myself. Come on, let's grab a table at my future restaurant," he joked.

"Go ahead, I'll meet you there," Max said. "I need to store my shit."

"Same," Jackson added. Asher and Tate nodded, heading toward The Hill.

Max closed and locked his saddle bag, asking Jackson, "How's it going with your newest hardware store in Grand Rapids? It's your third, right?"

"Yeah, my third. The distance makes it challenging, But once I get a good, solid manager who's local, I'll be less stressed." Jackson locked the forks on his motorcycle, then asked, "How's the new projects with Paloma going?"

"Interesting."

"I bet. What's it like working with her? She seems . . . intense." Jackson grinned. "And hot."

Max's mind flashed to that moment in the Thompsons' house—Paloma's lips on his, her skin under his fingertips, smooth as silk, warm and inviting. Her addictive taste. He shook off the memory, his chest tightening at the crushing weight of her words afterward: "I want you, but I want my career more."

"It's complicated," Max replied, aiming for nonchalance but missing by a mile.

Jackson paused to lock the steering and said, "Complicated, huh? Spill it, London."

They started toward the diner, their boots kicking up gravel. "She's brilliant," he said. "She has an amazing eye, and her business sense is waaay better than mine. And yeah, she's gorgeous, but it's more than that. She has this . . . presence."

"My friend, you sound like you're whipped."

"Shut the hell up." Max chuckled. "And okay, fine, I'm attracted to her. And it's messing with my head. We work well together, but there's this . . . tension. It makes it hard to focus sometimes," he admitted, leaving out the part about how they'd nearly been caught messing around by a client. Jackson would tease him mercilessly until they were old and gray.

His friend let out a low whistle. "Well, well, well . . . looks like our boy Max is feeling the heat! But, come on, man, you're overthinking this; mixing business with pleasure is a fucking fantastic combination."

"I disagree," he lied. "We've got two high-profile projects on the line and clients counting on us. If we mess this up, it's not just our feelings at stake—it's our reputations and our careers. I'd feel like a dick if emotions screwed things up."

"Then don't let emotions factor in. Have some fun. Release that tension. You're both adults."

Max shoved his hands in his back pockets. "I'm not sure we're on the same page. About everything."

"Oh, damn." Jackson shook his head, running a palm up his face to his short locs. "The attraction is one-sided. That sucks."

"No, it's not that. More like she's afraid it'll affect our work."

It was Jackson's turn to look confused. "Why? It's not like you'll be fucking on the table at a client's house."

Max choked on a swallow and stumbled over the gravel. He quickly regained his composure. "Right, of course not," he said, forcing a laugh that sounded strained. He picked up his pace, hoping the brisk walk would explain away the heat creeping up his neck. "That would be so unprofessional."

"Holy shit, London! What did you two do?" Jackson said to Max's back, catching up a second later.

"Noth—"

Jackson shoved Max playfully. "Don't fucking tell me nothing, you liar."

"All I'm saying is—"

"Save it." Jackson's grin widened. "Your face says everything. You kinky bastards did something, didn't you?'

Max kept walking. There was no point in denying it. "We might have gotten a little carried away." He dipped his chin and looked at his friend. "At a client's house."

Jackson's eyes widened. "Were they home? Like, watching?" He wiggled his brows. "That *is* kinky."

Max snorted. "No, you asshole. But they came home. We were nearly caught."

Jackson tilted his head to the sky and laughed. When the asshole got control of himself, he said, "And that's why you should just fuck. Get it out of your systems, then maybe it won't spill into your working hours."

"Does that even work? The whole, 'get it out of your system?'" He didn't think there was any 'getting Paloma out of his system.' He'd only grow more addicted to her.

Jackson shrugged. "It does for me."

Max fought the urge to roll his eyes. That was because Jackson was in love with Hope. He couldn't give anyone else a chance when the guy was hung up on his best friend.

"Look, man," Jackson continued. "Sometimes you've gotta take a risk. If you both feel it, why fight it? Life's too short for what ifs."

Max mulled over his friend's words. Despite Jackson's obliviousness to his own romantic situation, there was some truth to what he was saying. Maybe fighting the attraction was causing more problems than it would solve.

He could taste the freedom of giving in to their attraction, of exploring their electric connection without restraint. But the stakes were high; their professional reputation and hard-won projects could all come crashing down if things went wrong.

And yet, the thought of never knowing, of always wondering "what if," was equally unbearable. Almost as unbearable as the upcoming two-week trip to Traverse City for the Sterling project. The two of them stay in the same house away from their usual environments.

"You still with us, London?" Jackson's voice broke through his reverie.

Max blinked. He'd stopped walking. "Yeah, just thinking about that job I mentioned. Paloma and I are heading out of town for two weeks to start the groundwork."

"Two weeks, huh? Sounds like the perfect opportunity to 'release that tension.'"

"It's a work thing, man."

"Even better!" Jackson clapped Max's shoulder. "Two weeks of 'professional development,' if you know what I mean."

"Shut the fuck up," Max groan-laughed.

Jackson held up his hands in mock surrender, but his smirk said it all. "I'm just saying, two weeks is a long time to dance around each other."

"It is," Max sighed. "But we'll keep it professional. It's what needs to happen." Unless she was sure about changing things. He couldn't take the back and forth.

He pushed open the door to the diner. Two weeks in Traverse City. The ball was in her court, and he'd respect whatever she decided.

But damn if a huge part of him hoped she'd change her mind.

Chapter Eighteen

October 10th, 4:45 p.m.

Paloma twisted the key in the lock and pushed open the door to Abigail's condo. Sunlight streamed through the floor-to-ceiling windows, painting warm stripes across the polished honey-colored hardwood floors. The open-concept living area stretched before them, a study in modern elegance and comfort.

Max came up behind her and breathed, "Damn this is nice."

The condo was stunning, but the view outside demanded attention. The balcony, accessible through sliding glass doors, offered an unobstructed panorama of Grand Traverse Bay. The water stretched to the horizon, its surface a mesmerizing dance of sunlight and shadow. In the distance, the silhouettes of sailboats dotted the bay, their white sails billowing in the breeze.

"Right," Paloma agreed. "Although I shouldn't be surprised. She is a Hayek."

"No shit." Max let out a low whistle as he moved toward the gourmet kitchen, running his hand along the massive island topped with veined marble. "Don't they own a sports team?"

"Not big into sports?" she teased.

He raised his hands in mock surrender, a playful glint in his eyes. "Don't tell anyone. I don't want to lose my man card," he joked.

She ran her palm along the sleek leather couch, its unyielding surface crossing the fine line between aesthetic appeal and practical comfort. It had the former but not the latter. The failed contrast reminded her of the delicate balance she was trying to maintain with Max.

Patting the impractical couch, she left it behind to check out the kitchen. Drawing the fancy wine cabinet, she bent to examine the labels. Top-shelf stuff. She straightened, and Max's deep voice came from close behind her. "Find anything good?" he asked, his breath tickling her ear.

Her back brushed against his chest as she turned. They were mere inches apart. She could see the flecks of green in his ocean eyes and smell the faint scent of his delicious cologne. Her breath caught in her throat.

"I, uh . . . " she stammered, then cleared her throat. "I was checking what Abigail likes. For a thank you gift."

"Good idea," he said, his voice lower than usual, but he was the first to step back, turning to the fridge and opening it. "For someone who spends most of her time at your brother's, her fridge is stocked."

She moved next to him. "Do you think she'd notice if we ate all her food?"

Max snorted. "Only if you plan on replacing it with your cooking."

"Ouch," she clutched her chest dramatically, stepping back. "I burn a few grilled cheese sandwiches . . ."

"I think one of them growled at me," he teased.

"Alright, alright, I surrender. My kitchen skills are a national disaster. If there's any cooking to be done during our stay, it will be your job. Happy now?" She playfully swatted his arm. "Come on, Gordon Ramsay, let's check out the rest of the condo."

The first room in the short hallway was a bedroom converted into an office and library. Abigail was a woman after Paloma's heart. All but the wall with a window overlooking the bay had floor-to-ceiling bookshelves. She ran her fingers along the spine until they landed on a familiar title.

"I can't believe Abigail has this," she murmured, pulling out the book.

Max looked away from a different shelf. "What's that?"

She turned, about to answer, when her foot caught on the edge of a rug. She stumbled forward, the book slipping from her grasp.

Max stepped toward her. His hand caught her elbow, steadying her, while his other arm reached past her to grab the falling book. The sudden movement brought them chest to chest, faces inches apart. "Are you okay?" he asked, his voice low, with a hungry edge.

She stepped back, nearly stumbling to put distance between them, fighting her body's urge to lean into him. "Fine, I'm fine." The room was suddenly too small, too warm. She had to leave before she did something stupid, like kiss him. "I'm going to check out the rest of the house."

She nearly ran from the office, her past failed relationship chasing after her. This was exactly how it started. Desire and delusions made her think this time would be different. And then it would all come crashing down, and she'd be left picking up her broken pieces.

Five minutes later, she stood in the center of a beautiful main bedroom, her panic cresting. Max's footsteps grew louder, and then he appeared in the doorframe. "Where's my bedroom?"

"Good question."

A line appeared between his brows. "What do you mean?"

She spread her arms wide. "This is the main. We've seen the office." She pointed in the general direction of the hallway. "Down there's the bathroom. Besides the kitchen and living room, those are the only rooms."

"Fuck," he whispered.

No. No, that wouldn't be happening. "I need to call Felix."

She stepped around Max, making her way to the kitchen. Grabbing her phone from the counter, she dialed her brother's number and put it on speakerphone. After Max told her not to flirt or hit on him, the last thing she needed was for him to think she'd set this up like some rom-com.

Felix answered right before her call went to voicemail. "How was your drive, sis?" he asked.

"Fine, but you said Abigail's place had two bedrooms."

"Yeah. One, the main. The other was converted to a kick-ass office. What's the problem?"

"What's the problem?" she squeaked. "Why in the world did you think I wanted to share a room with my business partner?" She couldn't say, bedroom. The word would conjure up her recent dark dreams of the man who'd followed her into the kitchen, looking as panicky as she felt.

"You two aren't fucking?" Felix sounded truly perplexed, and Paloma wanted to sink into the pretty hardwood floors.

"No! He's my business partner."

"I thought he was both. My bad. I totally thought you had a little pleasure going with your business." He chuckled. "Well, after these two weeks of sharing a bed, you might."

"Asshole," Paloma laughed-groaned and hung up. She looked at Max. "This is my mistake. Tomorrow I'll find a hotel for myself. That way only one of us has to do the drive. I'll sleep on the couch tonight."

They glanced toward the living room. The couch looked perfect for reading a book or watching TV but not for sleeping. It was deep but not long, and the sides were impossibly high.

"We're adults. Let's share the bed," Max said. "The thing's huge. We'll be fine."

She turned away, pretending to examine the couch, but was trying to hide the flush creeping up her neck. She had to get it together. It was sleeping. In the same bed. With Max.

Images flashed unbidden through her mind: his strong arms, the way his shirt sometimes clung to his chest. Or like the notorious afternoon at the pineapple house—without his shirt. She squeezed her eyes shut, but the memory was burned into her.

She opened her eyes and turned to Max, hoping her face didn't betray the turmoil within. "You're right," she said, proud of how steady her voice sounded. "We're adults. We can handle this."

It was one night. She could handle sleeping next to him for one night. It was no big deal.

Chapter Nineteen

October 11th, 6:05 a.m.

Sleeping next to Max was a big deal.

Paloma sat on the balcony with her laptop and a cup of steaming coffee, watching the sunrise, her insides a horny mess. She had to find a hotel for one of them, or she wouldn't survive the next two weeks.

The cool morning air helped clear her head, but every time she closed her eyes, flashes of the previous night danced behind her eyelids. Max's warm body next to hers, his scent tempting her. Despite her best efforts, she drifted to the evening before, replaying the events that led to her current state of frustration.

Everything had been fine until he'd stepped from the ensuite bathroom. He'd walked out with wet hair, a worn T-shirt, and gray sweat pants—*gray sweat pants*.

"Are you kidding me?" she groaned.

He stopped walking. "What?"

"I'm wearing these." She waved a hand at her loose-fitting, navy cotton sleep pants and tank top. She'd even put on a wireless bra. "And you have on that. I should change into lingerie."

He grinned. "You won't hear me complain, but why?"

"Come on, have you scrolled any social media lately? Gray sweatpants are catnip to women." And wow, his were doing him all sorts of justice.

His grin widened. "I could take them off."

She tapped her chin. "Depends. Are you wearing old tighty-whities where the elastic's shot and there are stains?"

He snorted. "No, sorry. Boxer-briefs." He wrinkled his nose. "Without stains."

"Fine, whatever," she pouted, closing her laptop. "I'm going to shut off the light and pretend you're in an ugly onesie. Or a set of my dad's pretentious silk PJ sets."

She clicked off the light, and his deep chuckle filled the darkened room. Great, she couldn't see him, but his scent of cedar and man settled over her. What did that man bathe in, pure temptation?

"Damn it, Max. Do you have to smell amazing too?"

He full-out belly laughed. "Would you like me to fart?"

"Yes." She twisted on her side, pushing him. Her hand stilled on his muscular chest, memories of her pressed against it and kissing him rushed in. She shoved away the thought and said with forced lightness, "I'm kidding. Please don't fart."

He grabbed her hand before she could pull it away, and awareness spread through her like wildfire. Electricity seemed to crackle from the point where their skin met.

"Your hands are so soft." He brushed his thumb over her knuckles. The tender gesture sent shivers down her spine.

"I use a lot of lotion." She winced at the dumb reply and at how damn breathless she sounded. But, dammit, she was balancing on a knife's edge, torn between yanking her hand away and pressing herself against him.

"Are you trying to crush my hand?" he asked, his tone amused.

The change in atmosphere was so sudden that a startled laugh escaped her, and she released his hand. "Oh! Sorry. I was making sure you wouldn't try to make any moves on me," she joked.

"I'd never!" he gasped in mock offense. "I'll have you know I'm a perfect gentleman."

She needed him to be a gentleman but didn't *want* him to be one.

"Although . . ." He paused dramatically. "I can't promise I won't snore."

She groaned, partly in relief at the broken tension and also in frustration at the lost moment. "I'm not sure that makes up for the gray sweatpants and smelling good."

"Don't worry, early tomorrow, I'll be offering up my impeccable morning breath," he added helpfully.

"Be still my beating heart," she deadpanned, then let out a snort of laughter, even as her pulse thrummed with desire.

He chuckled along with her, but there was an undercurrent of something in his voice. "Tell you what," he said, "if I start snoring, you have my full permission to smother me with a pillow."

"Tempting," Paloma mused. She kept her tone light despite the lingering tension. "But then I'd have to explain to the cops why I murdered my business partner. Paperwork would be a bitch."

"Fair point. How about you give me a good kick instead?"

"That I can do," she agreed, grinning in the darkness, grateful for the return to their usual banter even as she mourned the loss of their heated moment.

Silence settled around them. She wouldn't call it comfortable, but it was somehow soothing.

"Hey, Paloma?"

"Yeah?" She held her breath. Would he address the constellation of 'what-ifs' twinkling between them?

"Sweet dreams. Try not to fall madly in love with me before morning, okay?"

She grabbed her pillow and smacked him with it, both of them dissolving into laughter that might be a touch too loud, too forced. As their mirth subsided, a confusing mix of relief, disappointment, and anticipation swirled within her, keeping her awake well into the night.

On the other hand, he had rolled to his side and fallen asleep in minutes. He didn't even have the decency to snore.

In the morning, she woke before the freaking sun with Max and his erection pressing into her ass. She wasn't a woman known for her impulse control and therefore deserved a damn medal for quietly leaving the bed and settling for a hot cup of coffee instead of the hot man who'd been plastered against her.

She sighed. The sun had nearly risen, painting the sky in soft pinks and golds. Taking a sip of her coffee, she grimaced. It'd gone cold.

"Time for the impossible task of finding a hotel," she muttered. Setting her mug on the small metal side table, she tapped on her laptop to reawaken it.

"Talking to the seagulls," Max asked from behind her, making her squeak and nearly drop her computer.

She twisted around, forcing herself to keep her gaze on the throw blanket wrapped around his shoulders and not check if he still had morning wood. "I should kick you," she joked.

He winced, handing her one of the two mugs of steaming coffee he held. "Shit. Did I snore?"

"No." She took a cup, wrapping her hands around the warmth and inhaling the scent of rich, dark roasted beans mingled with hints of hazelnut. "But sneaking up like that about gave me a heart attack."

He chuckled, rubbing the back of his neck. "Sorry about that. I'll work on my stealth mode." He pointed at her laptop and asked, "Up early for work?"

"No. I have everything in order. I was looking for a hotel." She stared at the screen, her distress returning. "Turns out fall and wine festivals are a big tourist draw."

Max raised an eyebrow. "No luck?"

"None." She sighed heavily, slamming her laptop shut and standing, moving to the balcony but turning to face him.

He took a long sip of his coffee, his gaze steady on her. "So . . . I guess that means we're sharing a bed for the next two weeks."

She searched his face. His expression was neutral, but blue hazel eyes fixed on her with an intensity that made her skin tingle. "I . . ." she faltered.

The logical part of her brain screamed to find an alternative, to suggest one of them sleep on the too-small couch. But the memory of his body pressed against hers that morning, the lingering scent of his skin silenced her protests.

Max set his mug on the balcony railing and took a step closer. "Unless you have a better idea?" His voice was low, almost challenging.

She swallowed hard, acutely aware of his proximity. "No. I don't have a better idea."

A slow smile spread across his face, making her heart skip a beat. "Well then," he murmured, "I suppose we'll have to make the best of it."

She shivered, unsure if it was from the chilly morning or the situation. He shrugged off the throw, wrapping it around her shoulders, closing it tight at her neck, running his knuckles along her jaw before retreating. The touch was featherlight but was like a match struck against her skin, igniting a fire that threatened to consume her. Her eyes fluttered closed, and every nerve tingled. In her desire, a new plan formed.

Her lashes lifted to find him still there, the space between them electric. He was so close that the heat radiating from his body warmed her, and the narrow space seemed to pulse with possibility.

"Max." She let his name hang in the air, biting her lip as she wrestled with what to say next—if she should say what she wanted, then cast restraint to the flames. "I want to sleep with you. And I don't mean next to you." Her cheeks flushed, her heart pounding. "But we've got this job, and it's important. I don't want to screw it up because we couldn't keep our hands off each other. Or can't stop thinking about putting them on each other."

His eyes darkened, pupils dilating as they fixed on her with an intensity that made her breath catch. He leaned forward slightly as if drawn to her, one hand gripping the balcony, knuckles white.

"So, here's what I'm thinking." She shifted to face him more fully. "We enjoy each other physically. But we don't talk about what this could mean or turn into—until after this job's done."

His gaze lingered on her. He leaned back, picked up his mug, and swirled his coffee before meeting her gaze. "You're saying . . . sleep together but keep it casual until we finish the Sterlings' house?"

She nodded, searching his face for his reaction, but couldn't get a read on him, so she continued. "Exactly. Right now, I need space from the constant 'what ifs' in my head and the . . . well, you." She gave a small laugh. "But since I can't escape you physically, maybe if we keep it simple until we're done here, I can focus on work during the day." Taking a deliberate step toward him, she murmured, "And you at night."

He set his coffee back on the railing, ran a hand through his hair, and rubbed the back of his neck. After a moment, he turned to her, his eyes searching hers. "I hear what you're saying. And I'd be lying if I said I wasn't interested." He paused, tapping his fingers against the railing. "But I think we need to be clear about what happens after this project ends."

She tilted her head. "What do you mean?"

He leaned against the balcony, crossing his arms. "I mean," he said, his voice measured, "that once we wrap up here, we need to decide. Either we explore this," he gestured between them, "for real, or we go our separate ways. I'm not interested in an indefinite casual arrangement."

"Okay. We'll talk when we get home. So, you agree to this agreement?"

He leaned closer, his scent of sleep, cedar, and something uniquely him wrapped around her. "God, yes. Because honestly, if I have to sleep next to you for two weeks and not touch you, I might lose my mind."

She blinked. His words and their decision slowly unwinding the knot in her chest. She stood on the edge of something steep, unsure whether to step forward or back. That was a lie—she was ready to jump and deal with where she landed later.

"Are you telling me what was pressing into my butt this morning when I woke wasn't run-of-the-mill morning wood?"

He groaned, rubbing his short, trimmed beard roughly. "So, me pressed up to your ass wasn't a dream?"

"Nope." She bit her lip, resisting the urge to laugh as warmth bubbled inside her. "That was one-hundred percent real."

Max shook his head and stepped closer. His hand moved under the blanket and hovered near her waist, his fingers brushing the skin between the fabric of her shirt and pants. Her pulse quickened, and her breath hitched as their gazes met. The desire reflected in his gaze matched hers. Slowly, almost hesitantly, he lowered his head toward hers, their lips mere inches apart.

Right before their mouths met, her phone shrilled, loud and insistent. She jerked back, glancing at her cell on the small table. "My alarm," she muttered, her heart pounding, and her thoughts scrambled. Cursing, she hit the snooze button.

The alarm meant one thing: work. As much as every part of her wanted to forget everything but Max's lips on hers, she couldn't afford to blur the lines they'd barely kept intact.

"We need to get to the Sterlings'," she said, her voice steadier than her body aching with need. "And speaking of that." She pulled back slightly, putting just enough space between them to breathe and regain her composure. "One more ground rule."

Max raised an eyebrow. "Okay, hit me."

"While we're working, we're that: work partners," she stated, her tone firm but gentle. "Nothing like what happened at the pineapple house can happen while we're on this job."

He picked up his mug with both hands and rested his elbows on the balcony railing. The pale light of dawn softened his features, casting a pearlescent sheen on his tousled hair.

His gaze drifted from the awakening city below to meet hers, and the corner of his mouth twitched upward, mirroring the gradual rise of the sun. "And after hours?"

She inhaled slowly, tasting the morning air tinged with the possibility of what might happen between them in the evening. "After work hours, we pick up where we left off."

Her work alarm went off again, and he reached over, silencing it. "We better get moving. But after work, you're mine." He leaned in, kissing her softly, but he pulled back when she tried to deepen it. "Already breaking your rules?" he teased.

Work. Right. She had a job to do and clients to impress. But as she gathered her laptop and empty mug, she couldn't tell if she'd just made the best decision of her life—or the worst mistake of her career.

She followed him inside, and every step was a battle between desire and duty. Time to be a professional. At least until sunset.

Chapter Twenty

October 11th, 9:00 p.m.

Paloma leaned against the elevator's wall as it glided to the top of the condo. Her feet were sore from being on them all day, but her pulse picked up with each floor she passed. Max had left the Sterling house long ago. She'd worked way later, but that was behind her, and the evening with Max spread out before her. Anticipation sank into her skin, zinging through her.

Caution whispered that craving his company and not just his body wasn't keeping things casual, but she'd worry about when this work trip ended. The elevator dinged on the top floor. Leaving it, she unlocked their door and went inside.

The scent of autumn deliciousness filled her nose. The subtle fragrance of pumpkin mixed with a woody, slightly peppery smell, all topped with a creamy goodness. It made her stomach rumble.

She followed the aroma to the kitchen and took in one of the sexiest sights in the universe—Max in a worn Henley, jeans, and stirring something on the stove. "Why does it smell like heaven in here? What are you making?"

"Pumpkin Alfredo." He offered her a spoonful of the sauce and said, "This is homemade, but sorry, not the ravioli."

A wave of toasted autumn hit her, and the herbal notes of sage danced across her tongue, followed by a subtle peppery bite that cut through the butter's richness. The sound that escaped her was damn near X-rated, but she didn't care. The sauce deserved the adoration and more.

"Keep making those sounds, and I'll cook for you every night," Max said, his voice an octave deeper than usual.

She looked at him. His focus was on her mouth, and his look of desire caused her hunger to switch from food to him. She moved closer, but an alarm interrupted them.

He twisted around to the oven. "The Brussels sprouts are done."

She wrinkled her nose as childhood memories of the mushy, bitter vegetable assaulted her. "Ugh."

He laughed. "Don't give me that until you try my dad's recipe."

Her gaze swept over the kitchen: the simmering pot, the steaming oven, the neatly chopped herbs on the cutting board. His back was to her as he reached for the oven mitts, his muscles flexing beneath the worn Henley. He was as tempting as his dinner.

"You didn't have to do all this," she said softly.

He set the tray of Brussels sprouts on the granite counter. They had a delicious scent of sweet and savory. "Trust me, it's better for both of us if I cook," he teased. He leaned in, running his nose along her neck. "This morning you mentioned focusing on me tonight."

The promise in the rumble of his voice warmed her in all the right places. "Oh, yeah?" she hummed.

"Yes." He stepped back and grinned. "And I don't want to risk your cooking killing me first."

She arched an eyebrow, the corner of her mouth twitching. "Rude. And I'd meant we could have picked up something to eat."

He shrugged. "I like cooking."

The aroma of his past filled the air, and she hoped he'd open up more and tell her the stories behind the recipe and the memories it held. A warmth spread through her chest, different from the cozy heat of the kitchen. He was sharing a piece of himself. The gesture touched her more than she'd expected.

Resting her elbows on the island, she watched him work. The view was sweet and seductive. "Did someone teach you to cook? Or are you self-taught?"

"Both my parents love to cook, but my dad was a chef. Owned a restaurant back in Chicago."

"Were you close?" she asked.

His expression softened, a hint of sadness creeping into his eyes. "As close as a teenage troublemaker could be to his dad, I guess."

Her heart ached for him. She moved closer, placing a hand on his arm. "Losing a parent is always hard, but during those years . . . it must have been especially tough. I'm so sorry, Max."

He stirred the sauce, his gaze turning distant. "It was." He paused, swallowing hard. "And the worst part is, it was my fault."

A knot formed in her stomach. She couldn't fathom how Max could blame himself for what seemed like a medical issue. "Why would you think that?" she asked gently.

He sighed, set the spoon down, and leaning against the counter, his body language spoke volumes. His shoulders were hunched as if he were carrying an invisible weight.

"Max," Paloma said gently, stepping closer and touching his arm. "Whatever it is, you can tell me. I'm here to listen, not to judge." Heaven knows she was no saint.

He met her eyes, and the pain she saw there made her heart ache. "I was a bit of a troublemaker. I loved the thrill of risk," he began hesitantly. "Anyway, my friends and I . . . we broke into this rich guy's house. It was stupid. Jack, my best friend back then, his mom worked for the guy. She mentioned one time that he never used his alarm. We thought it'd be fun to break in and swim in his indoor pool." He ran a hand through his hair, a rueful smile contrasting with his sad eyes. "We waited until it was late and scaled the fence. I remember my heart pounding so hard I thought it might burst out of my chest. But we made it inside the house without any issues. The thrill was unbelievable."

Paloma listened intently, her hand resting on Max's arm in silent support. Her heart picked up its pace a little, sensing things were about to go south in his story.

"We were having a grand time in the pool. Well, all of us except Danny, who'd been snooping through the house. He found this ornate book in one of the rooms. I can still feel the carving under my fingers," he muttered, his expression darkening. "Inside was cocaine. A lot of it."

Imagining teenage Max in such a dangerous situation made her heart skip and tumble, but she kept silent. She gave his arm a gentle squeeze, silently encouraging him to continue.

"We were such idiots. Thought we'd hit the jackpot. Snorted a few lines like we'd seen in movies." His voice was thick with regret. "We're lucky one of our dumb asses didn't OD. Anyway, that's when the lights came on. The owner was there, caught us red-handed."

"The guy gave us two choices: the cops or our parents." He let out a bitter laugh. "I realized later he was probably bluffing. He was a TV anchorman. He wouldn't have wanted anyone to find out about his little stash. Anyway, parents were called. My dad lost his shit." Max let out the saddest laugh she'd ever heard. Her eyes filled with tears. "If he were alive today, I'd still be grounded."

His gaze met her, and it was filled with a mix of shame and regret. "Instead, the next day, he was rushed to the hospital."

"Max," she said softly, her heart aching for the scared, guilty teenager he'd been. "That must have been awful. But you have to know, your dad's heart failure wasn't because of that night."

Max shrugged. "The stress I put him through. All the trouble I caused. It couldn't have helped."

She wanted to tell him it wasn't his fault, that he'd been a kid who made a stupid mistake, like most teenagers. But platitudes wouldn't erase years of guilt. Instead, she tightened her arms around him, hoping her embrace could convey what words couldn't.

"A few days later, my dad died." His voice cracked. "We had to move to Michigan after that so my mom's family could help."

She listened, holding him in silent support. She could feel the heaviness of the past bearing down on him.

"My mom never says anything outright," he continued, his voice low, "but I always feel it. This . . . expectation. Like she's holding her breath. Waiting for me to fuck up again."

Her heart ached for him. She could almost see the teenage Max, grief-stricken and guilt-ridden, trying to navigate a new life under the burden of unspoken accusations.

"Max," she said softly, choosing her words carefully. "That must have been incredibly difficult to deal with, especially while you were grieving."

He took a deep breath, his shoulders relaxing slightly as he exhaled. He shifted slightly, his arms loosening their hold on her. With a gentleness that belied his strength, he eased back, his fingers trailing lightly down her arms as he created a small space between them. His eyes met hers, a mix of vulnerability and gratitude in his gaze.

"Anyway," he said, his tone lighter but with a slight roughness that betrayed his lingering emotions, "enough about the past. Let's eat."

He turned to the stove, picked up the wooden spoon, and stirred the sauce. The familiar motion seemed to ground him, bringing him back to the present.

She was touched that he had shared such a personal, painful part of his past with her. A part of her wanted to delve deeper, to offer more comfort or understanding, but she recognized his need to step back from the heavy conversation. So, instead, she murmured, "It smells amazing. Is there anything I can do to help?"

His smile grew a bit more genuine as he glanced at her. "Actually, yeah. Could you find the plates?"

Nodding, she moved to the cabinets. The confession stayed with her, but it wasn't oppressive. Instead, it felt like a shared secret, a trust given and accepted.

She reached for the dishes, glancing at him. His shoulders were looser, less tense, as if unburdening himself had physically lightened his load. A warmth unfurled in her chest, threading itself with the pull of attraction.

After setting the plates on the counter, she touched his arm, waiting for him to meet her gaze. "Thank you for trusting me with that," she said softly.

He met her gaze, a small smile tugging at his lips. "Thanks for listening. It's . . . nice to have someone who doesn't judge."

The silence settled between them. But as their gazes held, something shifted, loosened, and then melted away. His expression transformed—the vulnerability fading as his eyes crinkled at the corners. A warm flutter replaced the weight in her chest, and she returned his smile.

Stepping away, she searched for glasses, aware of him watching her. His attention sent a thrill through her. The air between them crackled with energy, but it wasn't nervousness that made her pulse quicken—it was anticipation.

Returning to him, she briefly pressed against him. "You know," she said, her voice low and teasing, "if you keep looking at me like that, we might not make it to dessert."

His sharp intake of breath was gratifying. She continued her tasks, her movements purposeful and assured, reveling in the charged atmosphere they'd created. The heavy conversation from earlier hadn't been forgotten, but it had evolved into something else—a new level of intimacy that only heightened her attraction.

They sat at the sleek, modern dining table crafted from rich walnut wood. Its rectangular surface was the perfect size for an intimate dinner for two. The table was positioned near the floor-to-ceiling windows that dominated one living area wall, offering a panoramic view of the bay.

The October night had already settled in, wrapping the world outside in darkness. The bay was a vast expanse of inky black; the far shore was barely visible, marked by a few scattered lights from homes and small businesses.

The aroma of their meal mingled with the ambiance created by the view, making the moment feel almost surreal. She took her first bite and, again, couldn't help but moan at the explosion of flavors, the exquisite taste heightened by the equally exquisite setting. "Oh my god, Max. This is incredible," she said, savoring another bite of the ravioli.

He grinned. "Told you my cooking was better than takeout."

Between bites and conversation, she studied Max. His forearms flexed as he cut into his food. The subtle bob of his Adam's apple as he swallowed was mesmerizing. Until she noticed another huge yawn overtaking him. It was his third in a short span of time. The wall clock read a little after ten, and before heading home, he'd mentioned taking a quick nap. Thinking back, the man was always tired.

She set her fork on the table. "Do you have mono?" she asked, only half joking.

He snorted. "No. Why do you ask?"

"Well, on the drive here, when I stopped for the restroom and a snack, you were sleeping when I came out and didn't wake up until we'd arrived. You also mentioned you might take a nap today. Last week, when I swung by your office, you were hunching over some blueprints and asleep."

"I never did get that nap today. I'd spent it on the phone, checking up on my other jobs." He chuckled. "Which is probably why it seems like I have mono. I'd had a full schedule before taking on this job and the pineapple house. To keep up, I've had to forgo some of my beauty sleep," he added with a wry smile.

She tilted her head, studying him. "Why did you do it? Take this job, I mean."

"Because the challenge sounded interesting." His fingers traced the rim of his water glass, his touch light and deliberate. "And I could tell it was important to you." The sincerity in his voice melted her heart.

"That means a lot to me." She reached across the table, touching his hand, and awareness zinged through her. "But I don't want you running yourself into the ground."

He turned his palm, catching her fingers in his. The touch sent a spark through her. "Don't worry about me. I'm tougher than I look." Another yawn overtook him.

She noticed the fatigue etched in the lines around his eyes. A wave of affection washed over her. "Hey, why don't you go grab a shower? I'll clean up here."

He looked like he might protest, but another yawn escaped. "You sure? I don't mind helping."

"I'm sure," she said, standing and gathering their plates. "Go on, get some hot water on those muscles. I'll be right behind you."

The moment the words left her mouth, a spark of heat jumped between them. His gaze met hers, a flicker of interest cutting through his exhaustion. "Is that a promise?" he asked, his voice low and teasing.

She didn't hesitate and met his gaze, a slow smile spreading. "Definitely," she replied, her tone leaving no doubt about her intentions. "Consider it incentive to stay awake."

He stood, and for a moment, she thought he might close the distance between them. Instead, he stretched, his shirt riding up to reveal a tantalizing strip of skin. "In that case, I'll try not to fall asleep in the shower," he said with a wink.

"No promises on what I'll do if I find you asleep," she called after him. "I might take you up on the offer to smother you with your pillow."

His laughter echoed down the hallway, and she rushed to finish the dishes. The anticipation of what might happen when she joined Max energized her. She was done playing —they would finally act on the tension building between them.

CHAPTER TWENTY-ONE

October 12th, 6:15 p.m.

Paloma tapped her stylus on the tablet screen, adjusting the Sterlings' living room color scheme. She'd been staring at it for twenty minutes, not able to focus. The problem was her libido. To put it plainly, she was too horny to think. She glanced from her perch on the sleek bar stool, past her makeshift workstation, to the source of her problem.

Max.

He was on his knees, muscled forearms flexing as he tightened a valve on the newly installed irrigation line. A tool belt hung low on his hips, and sweat glistened on his brow. Her body hummed in anticipation. They were close to the end of the work day when they'd be alone, without any distractions.

A twinge of anxiety settled in her chest. Her craving for him was too intense, too soon. She'd been down this road before. That wasn't true. They weren't even dating, yet her feelings for him were too strong. Too intense. She looked at her left hand, where her engagement ring had briefly sat. Richard's words the night she'd confronted him about the gambling sliced through her.

"This is what I mean, Paloma. You're just... too much. Too intense. Too focused. Always pushing. You and your big dreams. What did you expect me to do?"

The memory stung, but what hurt more was how those words had echoed through other relationships. Always the same message, just packaged differently. Too demanding. Too driven. Too emotional.

Max glanced up, their gazes snagging. Instead of looking away, he held it, and a slow smile spread across his face. That smile did things to her insides, made her want to forget every cautionary tale her heart had learned.

Her phone buzzed with an incoming email from Mrs. Sterling. Grateful for the distraction, she opened it. Her stomach dropped. "Shit."

"Everything okay?" Max asked.

Not at all. "The Sterlings plan on stopping by tomorrow morning for a site visit." She shot up, her heart skittering against her rib. She scanned the room. Tools lay strewn across paint-splattered drop cloths like battlefield debris, and the half-finished irrigation system crawled along the walls in a tangled mess. The arch she'd had contractors expand gaped unfinished, mocking her. "We're not ready."

"It does seem a bit early for a site visit," He replied. "We're only a few days in."

"I guess they're eager." She snatched up loose tools, piling them together with jerky movements. The clatter of metal on metal punctuated each frantic grab. "We need to at least get this area presentable. Show some progress."

"Paloma. Breathe." She heard his amusement and didn't appreciate it. "I am breathing," she snapped, then her stomach twisted in regret. "Sorry. I just—this project needs to be perfect."

He stood, brushing dirt from his jeans. "It will be. But right now, you're spiraling."

She couldn't deny it; she was letting her fear of client disappointment take over. Letting that need to exceed expectations consume her. Something that usually exhausted others around her. "Your right. I'm sorry."

He came close, rubbing his hands up and down her arms. "No need to apologize. I love your drive, your passion."

Sure, he found it endearing now. How long until that changed?

Her phone rang again, but this time the song was her brother's. Stepping away from Max, she hit answer and speaker, saying. "Hey, Flea."

"Hey, Drunk Decision. Sorry I wasn't able to stop by with lunch, like I'd hoped. I had an emergency at the store."

"Everything okay?" she asked. The last emergency at his Traverse City store had ended with a high-profile arrest, turning him and Abigail into local crime-stopping celebrities.

"Fine. All taken care off. Anyway, want to meet up for dinner instead?"

She caught Max's gaze. He didn't speak, but his eyes said plenty. She was certain he was thinking of the same thing as her—their interrupted morning. Dinner wasn't what either of them wanted.

"No, we're beat," she said, her voice a touch breathier than usual. "We're going to grab something quick on the way to the condo."

"Sooo, how's that working out, you and London living a real-life forced proximity, one-bed romance?"

She barked a surprised laugh. Her gaze flickered to Max and then away. "How do you even know the names of romance tropes?"

"Abigail loves them and might have introduced me to a few. The spicy ones are fun to . . . read."

"Ew. Stop. I don't want to talk about my brother's kinks."

"Fine, we'll talk about yours," he teased. "You haven't mentioned finding a hotel. And it took you two an awful long time to answer the door this morning."

"Shut up, Felix. I'm hanging up."

"Wait! Just tell me one thing. Was London wearing pants when—"

She ended the call, her cheeks burning. Behind her, Max's dark laugh sent heat pooling in her belly—okay, maybe the heat was pooling a little lower. She turned to find him watching her with that intense gaze that made her forget all about maintaining professional boundaries.

"Ready to get out of here?" he asked.

"What about the Sterlings?"

"The place isn't a disaster, only a work in progress. And it shows our progress."

"True, but—"

"Paloma. Like Felix mentioned, you haven't eaten all day. Let's get you some food. And if you want we'll come here early tomorrow, well before the Sterlings and do some housekeeping."

"Okay," she relented and began gathering things, carefully placing fabric swatches and paint chips back into their labeled slots in her sample case.

His arms wrapped around her from behind, and he kissed her neck. His touch heated her everywhere, but she twisted from his grasp. Wagging a finger at him, she said, "Not during working hours. We don't want a repeat of what happened at the pineapple house.

"I don't know." He grinned. In it was all sex and promise. "You seemed to enjoy yourself."

"It was a powerful orgasm," she admitted. "But the afterglow was heart-stopping. And not in a good way."

"Speaking of that, was your contact able to fix the table?"

She nodded. "Disaster was avoided, but the paperwork was interesting. I never thought I'd have to use the phrase 'pussy plant juice'."

Max choked mid-sip from his water bottle. Once he could speak, he said, "Did you really put that on the paperwork?"

She laughed. "Hell no. I lied and told him I didn't know what it was." Turning to her workstation, she picked up her messenger bag. "Ready?"

"More than ready." He came closer, and she shot him a warning look. Thankfully, he didn't push it, only grinned and turned, gathering his tools.

All she wanted to do was press into him and feel his hands on her skin, but they had a reputation to maintain and clients who could drop by anytime—something they'd learned the hard, heart-stopping way. So, she only watched.

Picking up a metal toolbox, he walked to the front door and opened it. "Let me take you somewhere first," he said.

"Somewhere that isn't the condo?" She couldn't hide the disappointment oozing from her voice.

"Trust me." He turned around, coming so close that if she took a deep breath, her chest would touch his. "Trust me. The food first. You'll need your strength for what I have planned."

CHAPTER TWENTY-TWO

October 11th, 6:30 p.m.

Max approached the passenger side of his truck and opened the door for Paloma like a true gentleman. His fingers trailed across her lower back as she climbed in, too deliberate to be polite. Heat bloomed under her skin.

The scent of leather and his cologne filled the air inside the cozy cab. It did nothing to cool her desire.

He started the engine and drove down the long driveway of the Sterling's house. Making a left, he said, "I saw a place yesterday on the way to the condo and thought you'd love it."

"Is it a sit-down restaurant?" Yes, she was exposing her eagerness, but her need to touch and taste him was more powerful than her empty stomach.

"It's not," he answered. His focus remained on the road, but the slight curve of his lips told her he knew exactly what she was thinking. And from the way he shifted in his seat, his thoughts weren't far from hers.

"And I promise you won't be disappointed."

"Now?"She rested her hand on his knee, drawing small circles against his jeans with her thumb. His fingers tightened on the steering wheel. "Or later?" Her question dripped with intent.

He pulled into a lot and parked the truck. Then he ran his lips along her jaw to her ear and whispered, "Both." He bit gently on her lobe before backing away.

His teasing had her fighting the urge to climb onto his lap. As if reading her impulse, he said firmly, "But food first." He gestured with his chin toward the window.

She followed his gaze. Her breath caught for an entirely different reason. Through the windshield was a beach she hadn't visited since last summer. Back when she'd escaped to her brother's place after Richard's betrayal. The familiar shimmering expanse of the bay stretched before her, catching the early evening sun. The pull of it tugged in her chest alongside the lingering heat of desire.

She rolled down her window, and the unique blend of sun-warmed sand, damp earth, and something distinctly aquatic flowed into the car. It wasn't the briny smell of the ocean but a hint of fish and algae mixed with the crisp, clean aroma of fall in Northern Michigan.

"Want to eat by the water or get it to go?" he asked, his hand resting lightly on the door handle.

She wanted him naked and doing wonderful things to her body, but this stretch of bay was her sanctuary. Last summer, these waves had been her only witness as she'd pieced herself back together after Richard shattered her world.

As if Max sensed her dilemma, he said. "Let's stay. We have to eat, so why not enjoy the view?"

"We could eat and drive," she said, half-joking."

He pointed toward the food truck. "They serve street tacos. Not the best meal for a driving dinner."

"True," she agreed. "Are you sure you don't mind?"

"For you? Of course not."

This man was too good. He made it clear at the house that he was ready to get her back to the condo and under him but was willing to wait to give her this moment. If she weren't careful, she'd fall for him.

That sent a jolt of fear through her. She was already teetering on the edge of feeling she'd promised herself she wouldn't feel. And seeing that familiar look of overwhelm in his eyes made her chest tighten.

She wouldn't think of that now. They'd agreed these next few weeks were about pleasure, and that was what she'd focus on—work during the day and his body at night.

Stepping from the truck, the cool autumn air nipped at her skin. She grabbed a blanket from the cab, shook it, and started for the beach. The parking lot's asphalt was still warm from the day's heat, a stark contrast to the cooling air around her. Her steps quickened, eager to get near the water. She slipped off her shoes at the transition from pavement to sand, relishing the cool grains between her toes. The sun dipped toward the horizon, painting the sky in vibrant hues of orange and pink. Small waves lapped gently at the shore, creating a soothing rhythm.

She found the perfect spot between sand and water and sat. The beach was quiet, with only a few others dotting the shoreline. Listening to the gentle waves, she let the peaceful atmosphere wash over her.

A light breeze ruffled her hair, carrying the mingled scents of the water and distant pine trees. She opened her eyes, scanning the parking lot for Max. As if on cue, she spotted him walking toward her, carefully balancing their dinner and a couple of drinks. The sight of him, silhouetted against the colorful sky, made her heart stumble, then raced to catch up.

Reaching their blanket, he handed over her food and settled beside her. They unwrapped their tacos, and the spicy aroma filled the air. She took a bite, a satisfied moan escaping her.

"Good?" he asked, his voice low.

"Mmm, so good," she replied, licking a bit of sauce from her lower lip. His eyes darkened and followed the movement, and his breath caught slightly.

Not that she was any better. Between bites, she watched his hands—strong, capable fingers that hours ago had been building their client's garden, now delicately maneuvering a messy taco. A dollop of salsa rested on the corner of his mouth. She gently combed through his short beard to wipe it away.

Their gazes locked, and for a heartbeat, the world narrowed to just the two of them. His lips parted slightly, but before he could speak, a seagull swooped down, snatching a chip from his plate. The spell broken, they burst into laughter.

"Damn sky rats," she said, wiping her mouth and covering her food from the birds. "I'm really glad we're doing this. Not just the job, but . . . this." She gestured between them.

The corner of his mouth quirked in a gentle half-smile, and he leaned closer to her as if drawn by an invisible thread. "Me too. I've never enjoyed anyone's company quite like yours."

"Same." She squeezed his hand, letting her touch linger. "Tell me something I don't know about you."

Max looked to the sky, his thumb absently stroking the back of her hand. "I used to be terrified of the water. If I couldn't see my feet, I'd scream. Cry."

"Really? When did you grow out of it?"

"Who says I did?" he joked.

She laughed, bumping his shoulder with hers. "My bad. Sorry for assuming."

"When I was six. Thanks to my dad," he said with a fond smile. "He spent the entire summer teaching me to swim. By the end of it, I couldn't get enough of the water."

She leaned against him, picturing a young Max conquering his fears. Her heart also ached for what he'd lost. "Your dad sounds like he was amazing. I bet he'd be proud of the man you've become."

"Who knows . . . maybe."

She gave his hand another gentle squeeze. "Definitely."

They continued talking, sharing stories, and laughing as the sun sank in the sky. They finished their meal as the last rays disappeared into the water, taking the rest of the day's heat.

She shivered slightly, pulling her knees to her chest. "I guess that's our cue to head back," she said, her voice soft.

He nodded, his gaze meeting hers with an intensity that made breathing nearly impossible. "Yeah, I suppose it is," he replied, his tone low and filled with promise.

They packed up their sunset picnic, folding the blanket still warm from their bodies. The cooling sand shifted beneath her bare feet, each sinking step drawing her closer to him. His fingers found hers, calloused and warm, and her pulse quickened.

At the truck, he tucked a windblown strand of hair behind her ear. His touch lingered, trailing down her cheek. "You have a bit of sand," he murmured, his gaze never leaving hers.

She leaned into his touch. "Thanks," she whispered.

His hand lingered on her cheek, his thumb gently caressing her skin. Her breath hitched, her heart racing, wanting him. The parking lot lights flickered on, casting a soft glow around them.

"Paloma," he murmured. "You have no idea what you do to me."

She shivered, not from the cool evening air but from want. She huddled close to Max, and he banded his arms around her back. Pressing her hand on his chest, she felt the steady thrum of his heartbeat beneath her palms.

"I think I have some idea," she said, her fingers curling slightly into the fabric of his shirt. "Because you do the same to me."

His thumb grazed her cheek as he held her gaze in the soft glow of the parking lot lights. "Can I kiss you?" he asked, his voice dropping to that deep rumble that had her insides melting.

"Ye," she whispered.

He moved slowly, deliberately, as if giving her time to change her mind. Then his lips were on hers. The kiss was nothing like their first frantic encounter. That had been all heat and urgency. This started gentle, an exploration that made her toes curl in the cool sand.

She rose on her tiptoes, pressing closer as her fingers curled into his shirt. The low groan that escaped him vibrated through her body, resting between her legs. His hand slid from her cheek to tangle in her hair. The waves and the autumn breeze faded until all she could focus on was the heat building between them.

His other hand settled at her waist, his fingers flexing against her hip when she nipped at his lower lip. The kiss deepened, and he backed her against the truck door. Her pulse raced at the way his body caged hers, solid and warm against the cool metal.

He pulled back, breathing hard. "We should stop, he said, voice rough with desire, "before we forget we're in public."

The clang of the taco truck's window shuttering closed startled her. The person who'd made their dinner was getting more of a show than they'd bargained for. Max's fingers tightened on her hip before he stepped back. "Let's get you home." His words held a promise that sent heat pooling low in her belly.

Chapter Twenty-Three

October 11th, 7:45

Paloma's body hummed as she climbed into the passenger seat of Max's truck. The sound of him closing her door echoed through her. He walked around the front of the truck, his movements purposeful and controlled. When he slid into the driver's seat, the small space of the cab seemed to shrink even further, filled with the heat of his proximity and the lingering scent of his cologne.

He didn't seem the type who liked when a woman shoved her hands down his pants without foreplay or warning, so she took a subtler approach, playing with the anticipation he seemed to love. She ran her fingers along the outside seam of his jeans. Starting at the knee and stopping mid-thigh, each stroke moving higher and higher.

Switching, she traced along the inside stitching. He sucked in a breath but didn't tell her to stop. Good. And going by the way he kept shifting in his seat, and his erection was clearly defined through his jeans, he didn't mind.

But to tease him, she stilled her hand and asked, "Do you want me to stop? You really should focus on the road."

His jaw clenched and unclenched, a muscle twitched in his cheek. He shifted again, his fingers flexing on the steering wheel. "I'm focused on the damn road," he said, his voice low and rough. He swallowed hard, his Adam's apple bobbing. "Don't stop."

"Ooh, someone's bossy." And she liked it.

By the time he pulled into the underground parking lot of the condo, she had his jeans completely unzipped and her hand wrapped around his erection, stroking him.

Or she did until he swung the truck into the parking spot. Then he shut it off and pulled her onto his lap, kissing her with a feral intensity that was perfect. He moved to the hollow at the base of her throat, just above where the collarbones meet, and licked before kissing her.

She gasped, "How did you know?"

He chuckled against her skin. "I pay attention to what you like, to what makes you react." He met her eyes. "And I want to know everything about you, Paloma. Not just this."

The intensity in his gaze made her breath catch. "Everything, huh? I might be more than you bargained for."

"I'm counting on it," he murmured before capturing her lips again. "I should take my time and savor you. But I swear if you were wearing a skirt, I take you right here in this truck."

"And I'd let you," she panted. "Hell, I'm considering it. Let someone see my bare ass, as long as your hands are on it."

She'd meant every word . . . until a nearby car door slammed, followed by conversation. A grin pulled at the corners of his sexy mouth. "Still feel the same?" he asked.

"Maybe not." She slid off his lap.

"Let's get inside." He tucked himself back in his jeans and looked into his rearview mirror. "I hope we don't run into the people we just heard."

"Why?"

He motioned to the front of his pants, where his erection was *very* noticeable. She licked her lips, and he growled, pulling her gaze to his face. His eyes flamed an inferno, making her want to push him into the elevator or under the stairs and have her way with him.

Instead, she joked, "Don't worry, you can hide behind me."

"I don't think your stunning ass pressed against my dick would be a good solution right now," he replied.

Thankfully, nobody was in the elevator. Once the door closed, his gaze landed on the camera in the corner. "Fuck," he muttered, pulling a laugh from Paloma. Until now, Max had rarely sworn.

His eyes narrowed, and he pulled her to him, doing the exact thing he said they shouldn't do—holding her ass to his front. From the camera's angle, the embrace probably looked innocent, but what he was doing to her was not. He trailed kisses down her earlobe, gently nipping as he went. His teeth and tongue traced the ridges of her spine, each touch igniting sparks beneath her skin. All the while rocking subtly against her. She pressed into him, ripping a quiet, delicious moan from him.

The elevator door slid open. He roughly walked them forward, holding his hand to her waist. She loved his intensity and need, the way it matched hers.

They were inside the condo in no time. The soft glow of the city lights filtered through the sheer curtains, casting long shadows across the room. The faint hum of the heat clicking on mingled with their heavy breathing, creating a cocoon of sound around them. They stumbled toward the couch. The leather creaked softly under their weight as they sank into its deep cushions. She straddled his hips and buried her nose into his neck as he unbuttoned her top. He smelled like every fantasy she'd ever had.

"Do you want to move to the bedroom?" he asked, pushing her blouse off and kissing her shoulders.

She yanked on his shirt, and he shifted, giving her room to remove it. "Absolutely not," she breathed. The man was gorgeous. His body was naturally lean and toned, the kind of effortless fitness from an active lifestyle rather than hours at the gym. A faint trail of dark hair led enticingly down from his navel, disappearing beneath his waistband. His skin glowed golden in the dim light, marred only by a small scar below his collarbone that somehow made him even more irresistible. She leaned forward, kissing his tight nipple. On impulse, bit gently. His hips jerked, and his deep groan told her he liked it. She did it to the other side and was rewarded with the same reaction.

"We've started. We're *not* stopping," she said against his hot skin. "If the phone rings, we aren't answering. If someone knocks on the door, they're staying outside. I don't care if the damn building's on fire. We are *not* stopping."

Kissing the top of her head, he said, "Works for me."

He unclipped her bra and leaned back, his hot gaze roaming over her. "You're even more beautiful than I pictured in my fantasies."

She bit her lower lip, fighting back a grin that threatened to spread across her face. A pleasant warmth crept up her neck to her cheeks. "Oh?" she purred, arching up, loving how his eyes dilated. The blue in them was barely visible. "And just how many fantasies have you had about me?"

His gaze dipped to her lips, then chest. "Depends. Are you talking about today? Or since we met?"

"Careful, London," she teased, trailing a finger down his chest. "A girl might think you're getting attached."

His eyes softened, a smile playing at the corners of his mouth. "Would that be so bad?"

Her heart skipped a beat, but she couldn't answer him. Deflecting, she said, "Let's focus on making your fantasies a reality."

His gaze was on her face, but his hands were busy. They were sliding along her torso, his thumb stopping just below her breasts, rubbing along the undersides. Then he moved up, teasing her nipples. She always preferred attention to all of her and laid a hand over his, hoping he'd get the message.

Proving his intelligence, the man leaned in, kissing her everywhere—from collarbone to the tops of her breasts. He picked her up and switched seating positions, then slid off the couch onto his knees, his lips traced the underside of her breast, then moved to her belly, continuing downward until reaching the waist of her pants. Leaning back on his heels, his hands ran down her legs, resting at her ankles. Gently, he removed her ballet flats, his fingers caressing her instep. After being on her feet nearly all day, his touch was incredible. The plush carpet tickled her bare soles, a stark contrast to the firm pressure of his hands. The sensation was so intense that there was a possibility she could climax from that alone.

But she needed him closer. Needed his heat, needed him. With the leg he wasn't holding, she wrapped it around his back and pulled him forward.

He stumbled forward, catching himself on the couch. "Impatient," he teased.

"Maybe a little." She held her fingers an inch apart. Reconsidering, she spread her arms wide and grinned. "Maybe a lot."

He unzipped her pants. "Lift your hips."

She did as she was told, and he removed the rest of her clothes. His intense gaze conveyed his intentions, sparking a brief internal debate. Should she let him proceed with his evident plan or pull those tempting lips back to her mouth? Past experience promised one hell of a good orgasm if she chose the former. Yet the urge to have his body pressing into hers, on top of her, was overwhelming.

That desire won, and she grabbed him and kissed him hard, unprepared for how it shattered her. The touch of his lips was primitive and dangerous—no polite flutter of attraction but a wildfire that blazed through her blood. She lost herself in the sensation for a moment, surprised by how easily he could ignite this fire within her.

"I want to taste you again," he said.

"And I want you right here. It's my turn to get what I want."

He smirked. "You didn't get what you wanted last time?"

She met his gaze. "Oh, I did. But I'm a ravenous woman. I always demand more."

His eyes darkened. "Then let me give you more. Let me give you everything."

The weight of his words hung between them, and something beyond desire echoed through her. "Everything is a lot to promise, Max."

"I don't make promises I can't keep," he said softly, cupping her face.

He probably believed his words now, in the heat of passion, but when he cooled down, so would his feelings for her. She pulled away from him and his false promises but kissed his palm to show there were no hard feelings.

She smiled. "All I want is orgasms."

He quirked a brow. "Orgasms? Plural?"

She gave him a one-shoulder shrug, reaching for the zipper of his jeans. "What can I say? I'm a greedy woman."

"I love it." He slipped a hand between her legs, his palm pressing into her clit. "I'm going to be the man that makes you glutton with pleasure."

She pressed her thighs together, her need swelling. "I hope you're not all talk, London."

He captured her lips, running his tongue along the seam of her mouth before diving in. He kissed her until she was panting and rocking against his hand. He slowed his touch, becoming almost reverential. The change in pace made her wonder if he, too, was grappling with the intensity of their connection.

She hooked her fingers into the waist of his jeans. "Take them off."

He stood and unbuckled his belt, the clink of metal incredibly erotic. Then, he shoved them down and kicked them off.

Naked before her, he sparked a whirlwind of cravings. She yearned to feel him inside her, to watch him between her legs as he stroked himself, to taste him as he came apart with her mouth wrapped around him.

Her skin prickled, and her body hummed like a taut violin string. She stood, pressing into this body. Her nose reached his neck, and she inhaled him like a fine wine. His faded cologne had mixed with his natural scent—a whisper of honest exertion not sharp or acrid, but earthy and alive, like sun-warmed soil after a light rain. The combination was intoxicating and amplified her desire.

Her fingers twitched, aching to trace the scar below his collarbone, to map every inch of him. Their eyes locked, and she caught a glimmer in his gaze, making her stomach flip. There wasn't only lust but a dangerous hint of promise. It was the kind of look that could lead her down a path of heartbreak, beckoning her like a siren's call.

Could this time be different? Could she trust her feelings? Could she trust him?

The questions swirled in her mind, even as her body hummed with an answering intensity. Part of her wanted to retreat, to protect herself from the vulnerability of the moment. But a stronger part, a part she couldn't quite silence, urged her forward, whispering, "Yes."

His fingertips traced her jawline, his touch impossibly gentle despite the heat between them. "You still want this?" The tenderness in his touch belied the purely physical nature of his words.

She pulled him closer, refusing to acknowledge how that gentleness made her heart squeeze. "Yes," she breathed against his lips. "Show me exactly what you can do."

CHAPTER TWENTY-FOUR

October 11th, 8:05 p.m.

"Show me exactly what you can do," she breathed against his lips.

He leaned back, taking her in and grinning. And sweet mercy, his smile. Her knees nearly buckled as his mouth found her neck, his hands the only thing keeping her steady. Then he was on his knees before her, and holy hell—the first sweep of his tongue had her clinging to his shoulders, fighting to stay upright. Each stroke, each touch of his fingers had her climbing higher, his name falling from her lips. The tension coiled tighter and tighter until she shattered, but he didn't stop. He guided her to the couch, and damn if he didn't prove himself again and again until she could barely remember her name.

But those sounds he made—deep, primal groans that vibrated through her body as he tasted her. The way his shoulders bunched with restraint beneath her fingers. It was too much, yet she needed more. Needed to taste him, to feel him come undone against her tongue the way she had against his.

She nudged him to his feet, her body still tingling from his touch. The condo's living room was bathed in the soft glow of a single lamp, reflecting the raw hunger in his eyes. The sight of it sent a fresh wave of desire through her.

She knelt before him, her hair tickling his thighs, her breath warm against his skin. "Paloma," he begged, his voice thick as tar and just as dark.

"What, Max?" she asked before wrapping her hand around his erection and taking him into her mouth.

Words seemed to fail him. His hands raked along her scalp, roughly and oh-so-perfect. The noises he made—his groans, his demands, his murmurs of how good she was, how fucking fantastic he made her feel had her arousal dripping down her thighs.

Without warning, he stepped back. She tried to go with him, but he ground out, "No," tugging lightly on her hair.

She looked up, pushing out her bottom lip. "But I want more."

He gripped her chin. "And I'll give you more. Which is why we have to stop." The hold on her tightened slightly, and he pressed up. "Come here."

Once again, she followed his orders. No surprise. She'd do whatever he said if he kept making her feel this good.

He brought her in for another soul-searing kiss, walking her backward. When her legs hit the back of that odd-shaped couch, he turned them around and sat. She straddled his lap. Returning to his mouth to hers, he grabbed her ass and pulled her closer. The length of his erection lined up to her front, pressing into her clit as she rocked against him.

If they kept this up, she'd come. Again. He moved his lips from her mouth to her neck and mumbled into her ear. "What do you want me to do? What will make this feel better?"

"Tighter. More," she gasped, trying to explain, but unable to form the right words. Hell, she wasn't even sure if she knew what she needed.

He pressed her impossibly closer, digging his calloused fingers into her ass. The slight shift had her climax, pooling, low and tight. Then he moved his hold to her hips, gripped them tight, and rocked her along his length in a way that made her head fall back and her eyes roll shut.

He trailed his lips down her neck to her breasts, and her breath caught. Not only from the physical sensation but from the tender way his fingers intertwined with hers. In that moment, she felt seen in a way she hadn't in years—maybe ever.

"Max, please." She begged. "Don't stop."

"Take what you need," he said, returning to her lips.

His demanding kiss pushed her over the edge. Her pleasure owned her; her orgasm spread through her body. But even in its strength, she wanted more of him. "I need you," she gasped.

"You have me. All of me."

She understood he meant his body, but she pretended he truly meant all of him. Then she pushed that sappy fantasy aside for another day and said, "I want you inside me."

He lifted her off his lap. She instantly missed his warmth. "W-what? Why?" she sputtered.

"Just a second, sweetheart." He kissed her temple. "Let me get a condom."

He shifted off the couch and grabbed the leg of his jeans, pulling them closer and taking a square package from the pocket. Once he had it, he turned to her and wrapped a big hand around her ankle. He kissed his way up her until reaching the apex of her thighs. He looked at her from between her legs. Pure sin danced in his eyes. He licked along her heat, then sucked on her already overly sensitized clit.

She arched up and away, gripping his shoulders. "I c-can't take it. Give me a minute," she begged.

He kissed her belly, chuckling. "I thought you said you were greedy. A glutton. I need to make sure that you get your fill of pleasure."

The ripping of a foil packet whispered between them, and her satiated body was suddenly starving for him. His shoulder and muscles bunched and moved beautifully as he rolled on the condom.

She shifted to lay on her back, and he crawled up her body, settling between her thighs. Given the odd shape of the couch, they didn't quite fit. They should move, but she didn't want to stop and get off this ride. And he made it work, sliding slowly inside her, giving her time.

"Is this okay? Does it feel okay?" he asked.

"Yes, to both. More than okay. Closer to nirvana than okay," she replied.

"I agree." he said against her neck, but then echoed her thoughts from a second ago, "But this fucking couch is terrible."

He pulled her up and sat like they had before, except this time he was inside of her instead of gliding along her. The sensation was intense, all-consuming. He trailed his hands down her thigh, across her stomach, chest, and shoulders as if he was mapping her, finding his way.

His hands reached her hips and gripped her gently, pulling her up and sliding her down at an excruciatingly wonderful pace. The tempo was perfect, exactly what she needed to recover from her two climaxes.

"I haven't felt this way in a long time," he murmured.

Her heart dipped. "What way?"

He was quiet for a moment. "Like I don't want to let go."

He'd change his mind. They did eventually. But she wouldn't worry about that or how much she already liked him. Right now was for pleasure.

She kissed him slowly and thoroughly, his arms moving her at the same pace. She traced her hands up his torso, fascinated with the way his beautiful body flexed and moved. Recalling his pleasure point from earlier, she leaned over, flicking the tip of her tongue over his nipple.

His grip on her tightened, and his pace was much less gentle. He ground out, "Palamore."

She giggled and straightened to look at him. "Who's this Palamore?"

His eyes were hazy with lust, but his grin was adorable. "Paloma, more. Is that better?"

"No. I like my new name better. I love that I'm causing you to lose the ability to speak?"

"Forget talking. You feel so fucking good, I'm losing my damn mind." His hand slid lower, pressing into her clit, circling.

She sucked in a sharp, bliss-filled breath. Their eyes locked, and in his gaze, she swore there was more than hunger. Unwilling to look too closely, fearing it might be a lie, she circled her hips. With a gentle push, she tilted his chin upward, planting a kiss on his Adam's apple before kissing her way down his chest.

"Fuck," he muttered, all guttural groans and gravel.

The press and sweat between their bodies was the exact friction she needed. And her third orgasm began to build. "Close so close," she said against his ear.

"What do you need to be there?" he asked.

"Kiss me. Let me ride you."

He did as she demanded. His hands moved to her ass, his fingers pressing into her heated skin but not holding tight. He let her move as she needed. Her pants became sharper and higher as her growing pleasure twisted tight around her and then exploded on a shout of his name.

Her bliss nearly broke her as her ecstasy crescendoed. Slow as honey drizzled on sun-warmed skin, it receded to a languid satisfaction.

He stood, not breaking their connection, and carried a boneless body. Wrapping her legs and arms around him was a struggle. "I got you," he said, walking through the living room, down the hall, and to the bedroom.

Holding her tight, he moved them to the center of the bed. She was on her back, and he rested on his elbows on the sides of her head. He didn't move his hips. "Watching you come is the most beautiful thing I've ever seen," he told her between gentle kisses.

He was still in her and hard as granite. His heart thrummed, fast and strong, against her chest. The vein in his neck was pounding, showing how he ached for release. Yet he didn't rush as if he could keep satisfying her over and over all night long.

"And what about you?" she asked. "When will I see this with you?"

He brushed his mouth across her lips. "We'll get there. I'm enjoying myself plenty."

No doubt. She was too, but she intended to see him break apart, to lose control. She wanted him to be as addicted to her as she was becoming to him.

Bucking her hips, he let out a surprised grunt and fell to his side. She pressed on his shoulders, pushing him flat on his back, and climbed on top of him. She rose to nearly the crown of his erection, then lowered herself slowly. Once there was no space between them, she circled her hips—that last bit was for her, and a moan escaped between her lips.

His hands skated up her sides to her chest. His gaze flipped from her eyes to breasts to where they were connected as if he was trying to drink every last drop of her.

"So beautiful," he murmured.

She took him fast and hard instead of going slow. His eyes flared hot as he grabbed her waist. His roughness thrilled her. Again and again, she took him until his grip tightened enough to leave bruises. She reveled in his firm hold and the way he was losing control.

"Come here," he commanded, gripping the back of her head and bringing her to him. He kissed her with a desperation that told her he was close.

It was her turn to ask, "What do you need?

"You," he said into her mouth.

He held her waist and slammed into her with enough force that she gripped the headboard. She bared down on him; the friction and his brutal thrusts had another orgasm building.

She'd have been shocked, but her body was too busy shaking, and her brain was wiped of everything all but base need. "Shit. Fuck. I think I'm gonna come again," she gasped.

Their lips met as she rode him hard, and he matched her intensity, slamming them together. Her climax crashed through her, stealing her breath and any chance of shouting his name.

Sweaty and sated, her muscles went slack and pliant. Flipping them over, he pounded into her relentlessly, his movements erratic and his gaze locked on hers. Urging him on with her hips, she wrapped her arms tightly around him, short fingernails digging into his back.

Then he broke. His body went rigid as his mouth, resting on her neck, pressed into her with startling force. She felt the outline of his teeth against her skin as a final, resonant groan shuddered through him.

The full wonderful weight of his body landed on hers for a quick moment before he rolled onto his side. After some time, he kissed her temple and said, "Be right back."

They'd left a light on somewhere in the house, and she admired the view of him walking to the ensuite bathroom. He was probably disposing of the condom, but she missed him.

That was an alarming thought, but one to worry about tomorrow. No, even better, she'll worry about it when they leave Traverse City.

He returned to the bed, and she nestled against his chest. Her eyelids fluttered closed, and she savored the afterglow. A delicious languor spread through her limbs. Part of it was the multiple orgasms, which was rare enough, but that wasn't all of it. There was something more, an ineffable connection that thrilled and terrified her. She longed to believe it was mutual, yet a nagging doubt whispered that it might be just her imagination, a projection of her desires.

Needing to lighten her dangerous thoughts, she joked, "Damn, Max if I would've known it'd be this great between us I would've let you keep going at the pineapple house. Hell, I'd let the Thompsons take pictures, invite friends over. I. Would. Not. Have. Cared."

His deep belly laugh filled the room. She absolutely loved the sound. It was better than her favorite song.

"Does that mean I've slackened that greedy appetite of yours?" He kissed her neck. "Or do we need to go for around two?"

"Seriously?" She sat up and stared at him, trying to gauge if he was joking. "You could go for another round?"

"Maybe not right this second," he admitted. "But if you get back on top of me. Start moving that ass again, I'm sure I can get ready in no time."

"Damn, *I* need a break. I don't want you to break me."

His brows pulled tight. "Was I too rough?"

She ran her thumb over the crease. "No. You were exactly what I needed."

"Past tense?" He rested a hand on her hip.

"I definitely want more in my future," she replied.

"For the next two weeks while we're here?" he asked.

"Yes."

He began drawing circles on her hip with his fingertips. "And after?"

Her heart leaped at the possibility, but her fears screamed to be cautious. It was safer to postpone his question. She needed more time to see if she could trust him with more than her body. "Remember, we'll worry about that after we return home."

His lips flattened for a beat before his smile returned. He kissed her once, light and quick, sitting up and bringing her with him.

"Where are we going?" she asked.

"To the shower. I'm gonna clean you up and massage any parts that might be sore."

She let him carry her to the ensuite bathroom. He sat her on the counter, then turned on the shower. She started to scoot off, planning to get under the spray, but he shook his head and picked her back up.

Under the hot spray, he shampooed and conditioned her hair, giving her one of the best scalp and neck massages of her life. Then he grabbed the soap, lathered it up, and washed her. She shouldn't let him take care of her. It did things to her heart that she didn't want to happen.

She wouldn't let him in, but she could let him take care of her, at least for tonight. Tomorrow, she'd remember to pull back into that safe zone where emotions don't rule her.

CHAPTER TWENTY-FIVE

October 18th, 9:10 p.m.

Max stood at the island counter in the condo, making drinks for himself and Paloma. Water from his wet hair trickled down the side of his neck, a reminder of the recent shower fun.

Grabbing bourbon, he poured two shots into each of their glasses. He was unable to wipe the grin off of his face. The last week was fantastic. Their first time together and all the days that followed.

Like last night. They'd driven separately because her to-do list had her working outside the Sterling house. He'd missed her but had been greeted with the most glorious surprise—Paloma at the door completely naked. She'd removed his clothes in under a minute, and in less time, he had her bent over that stupid couch he was starting to love.

Today was just as fun. He'd kept it professional during the working hours, but barely. And who could blame him? She might have looked professional and proper in her ankle-length tweed skirt and camel-colored ankle boots. However, on the way to work, she'd told him she'd selected the outfit in case things got too hot in his truck again and they couldn't make it inside the condo.

Her husky voice repeated that declaration in his brain all day. He'd barely gotten anything done and kept having to correct his mistakes.

Then, finally, they were in his truck. She'd taken his hand, placing it under her skirt. He'd moved up her thighs to where her panties should have been, but instead of lace and cotton, there was her warm, wet flesh. Lust had exploded through him, and he'd pulled over the truck, determined to have her right then and there at the side of the road.

"Not yet," she chastised, her throaty laugh filled the cab, going straight to his dick. "What happened to that anticipation you love?"

"It's disappeared, alongside your panties," he grumbled but returned to the road. He'd kept one hand on the steering wheel and the other between her legs, teasing her until she was rocking against his palm.

They hadn't made it inside. When he pulled into the condo's covered lot and had the truck in park, she was on his lap, unzipping his jeans. Then they had an encore in the shower.

Glancing toward the bedroom where Paloma sat with her laptop, heat spread through his veins. Both encounters had been amazing, but that last time in the shower, when they had taken more time to explore each other . . .

He capped the bourbon and closed his eyes, recalling how the steam kissed her skin. The way after, they'd kissed for an eternity, exploring with their hands and lips. Then she went down onto her knees and took him into her mouth. She looked up at him with water dripping from her lashes and hair, and he'd damn near come. He'd silently praised all that was unholy that he hadn't because the way she had teased him with her tongue and lips until he'd come all over her chest had been a nearly divine experience.

After, he'd brought her under the water and cleaned her slowly. Then he'd turned off the shower and carried her to the bed. There, he'd feasted on her until she was shaking and gasping his name.

He shook his head; too much of his blood was rushing south. He focused on finishing their drinks. He poured Vernor's into hers. In his, a splash of water, half a lemon, and a bit of honey. With both glasses in hand, he carried them to the bedroom.

He paused in the doorway. Paloma's long, smooth legs rested on the blue comforter. And he really liked the way she looked in his gray sweatshirt. He wished they could stay forever in this bubble.

Her gaze met his, and her smile stirred something more than desire—a glimpse of possibility.

"You're staring," she said, her voice low and teasing, shifting her attention from the laptop to him to the drinks. "Oh, those looking as temping as you."

He handed her a drink and scooted next to her. Adjusting a pillow behind him, he rested against the headboard. "Working?" he asked.

"Catching up on emails." She closed her laptop and turned to him. "You like to cook, but what are your other hobbies?"

"My hobbies?" he echoed. "Why are you asking?"

"Well, you've been inside me, and you're my friend. I don't know much about you outside of work." She grinned. "Besides that you like swinging."

"One time . . ." He shook his head, pretending to be exasperated, but was touched by her interest in him.

She tsked. "That's more than ninety percent of the population."

"If you'd seen how many people were there, you might have to lower that percentage."

Her eyes widened. "Really?"

He nodded. "Yeah. I'm glad that party was in Chicago. It's less likely I'll run into any of them. I'm sure they're nice people, but it'd be awkward for everyone."

"I feel like maybe I'm missing something." He pulled her bottom lip between her teeth, then let it go. "Should we…"

"No," he said. An unexpected possessiveness held him in this grip. "I can't tell you what to do, but there'd be no 'we.' If I saw another person touch you—" His mouth pressed into a thin line. "I couldn't stand idly by. Or join in. Not with you."

"Not with you," she echoed softly. Then she looked at him and grinned. "Okay, swinging is out. So, what do you do when you have free time?"

Free time? Since taking on the Paloma Projects, there hadn't been much of it. Not that he was complaining. He might be exhausted, but he loved his time with her.

"Besides cooking?" He took a sip of his drink, loving the way she settled against him. "I ride motorcycles. I have the Pan Am you saw, as well as an older Bonneville."

"Not one, but two," she said with that same warmth she'd shown when first discovering she rode.

"You still surprised I'm a nice guy with a motorcycle?" he teased.

Her lips curved into a smile. "I'm learning there's a lot more to you than first impressions. Have you taken either on any long trips?"

"A few. Last summer, I rode with my brother in Nova Scotia. There's something about being on the open road, just you and the machine." He chuckled. "Though sometimes the maintenance can be a challenge. During that trip, all that salt air from the coast started messing with the electronics. We stopped at this little café in Peggy's Cove, and my display screen went on the fritz—numbers jumping everywhere like it was possessed. We had to backtrack to the Harley in Halifax to clean out all the connections."

"Even with the issues, it sounds like such a fun adventure," she said wistfully. "Learning to ride's always been on my bucket list."

"I'll teach you next summer." Had that come off as too presumptuous that they'd be together next year? He wouldn't mind, and maybe by then, she'd be convinced he wanted more than her body.

"Don't I have to be endorsed?" She either didn't notice the significance or was choosing to ignore it.

He rolled with it. "Yes, but they teach the basics. You'll need more practice before hitting the busy roads. I think you'll love riding. It's a great stress reliever."

"Is that your subtle way of saying I seem stressed?"

"No, that's my not-so-subtle way of trying to spend more time with you."

The admission slipped out before he could catch it, but her slow smile made him glad for the honesty. That smile did things to him, made him imagine possibilities he hadn't considered in a long time.

Her phone dinged from the nightstand, the sound sharp in their quiet bubble. Her brows furrowed as she read the text.

"What's up?" he asked. An unease he couldn't explain filled him.

"Roy Sterling wants a few changes. He asked for me to check my email." Her voice had shifted from warm to professional in seconds.

She slid her laptop back on her legs and opened it, the blue glow washing over her face. Her gaze scanned back and forth, and with each passing second, more of their intimate moment slipped away. "Are you kidding me?"

He scooted closer, a knot forming in his stomach. "What?"

"His 'little change' is to change the entire color scheme for the second floor. And they're discussing possibly expanding the project to include the guest house."

His fingers tightened around his glass. The news settled over him like a weight, and tension crept into his shoulders. "That's . . . a lot of changes. And it would mean completely revamping your timeline."

She nodded, running a hand through her hair. "I know. I'll have to start from scratch on so many elements. And finishing it by the end of next week won't be possible."

"We can do this." He wrapped an arm around her. "We're a great team."

Their gazes met, and he could've melted into her soft, blue eyes. Then she looked away. "This doesn't affect your end much. Or really at all. It's all mine."

"I'll work on my stuff, then help you." He was nearly finished with his tasks for this visit. He could leave, catch up with his other clients, and not return to Traverse City until it was time for planting and system setup. But he couldn't. He had to wipe away the stress painting her beautiful face.

She briefly rested her head on his shoulder but straightened, putting a small but deliberate distance between them. "Thank you, Max, but even with your help, I won't be finished by the time we're supposed to leave."

"Then I'll stay and help." But could he? The weight of his workload was almost too heavy to hold.

As if reading his worries, she said, "What about your other projects at home? They need your attention."

"I'll have my second, Grace, help." If she wouldn't kill him at the suggestion.

She shook her head. "You mentioned the other day how your business is stretched thin because you took these projects with me."

He dug in his heels. Not sure why, but he was certain that going home without her wouldn't be good. "Well, that's why Grace is my second. She can handle it."

"But do you want her to? Tell me honestly."

He sighed. "No. I've already put so much on her."

"Then go home as we planned. And I'll meet you there."

That tightening in his chest, which he couldn't quite explain, squeezed him tighter. He wanted to argue, to insist on staying, but the rational part of his brain knew she was right. Still, the thought of leaving her behind twisted something inside him.

"I don't like it," he said, his voice low. "The idea of going back without you . . . it doesn't sit right."

She looked at him, her expression impossible to read. "I don't like it either, but it's the sensible thing to do."

He set his drink aside and pulled her into his embrace. "Sensible sucks."

She laughed. "I agree." Their gazes met, and that familiar tug pulled at him—the one growing stronger each day.

Another shrill ring cut between them. This time his damn phone rang. It was after ten. Don't people sleep? Grace's name flashed on the screen, a reminder of the real world waiting for them beyond this room.

He closed his eyes, and when he opened them again, Paloma was already reaching for her laptop, the professional mask slipping back into place. "You should get that," she said, not quite meeting his gaze. "I need to start replanning anyway."

He nodded, unable to shake the feeling that something pivotal had just slipped through his fingers. The bubble had burst, and reality was rushing in, bringing with it questions he wasn't ready to ask—or maybe wasn't ready to hear the answers to.

CHAPTER TWENTY-SIX

November 2nd, 3:30 p.m.

Max pulled into his driveway, easing his Harley beside Drake's Mercedes. It seemed his brother was back in town for the week. Max hit the kill switch, and the engine's rumble ceased, fading to a soft tick as it cooled. A twinge of melancholy struck him; this would probably be his last ride of the season. He'd gotten lucky with how long the fall weather held, but Old Man Winter was hiding around the corner.

The sound of a car pulling behind him banished thoughts of his bike and the impending winter. He removed the key and whipped off his helmet, his pulse quickening as he turned to see Paloma stepping out of her vehicle. The changes at the Sterling house had taken longer than expected, and it had been two weeks since he'd seen her in person.

With his overflowing work schedule, they'd rarely talked. His crew could only do so much, and there were a few projects he'd put off while in Traverse City that demanded his attention before the winter weather set in, leaving little time for anything else. Their brief text exchanges and hurried phone calls had only intensified his longing to see her again.

But she was back, and the rest of the day was theirs.

Paloma approached. The autumn breeze tousled her dark hair, and the fading sunlight brought out the vivid blue of her eyes, like a clear winter sky. Her fitted jacket and jeans accentuated her curves, reminding him of all he'd been missing these weeks.

The familiar comfort of her presence collided with a new, electric uncertainty. His fingers twitched, caught between the urge to reach for her and the sudden fear that his touch might not be welcome.

"Hey," Paloma said softly, stopping a few feet away. She fidgeted with the strap of her bag, betraying a nervousness that matched his.

"Hey yourself," he replied, aiming for casual, but his wide grin probably gave him away. "It's good to see you."

Her lips curved into a small smile, but her blue eyes held a question. "You too. It's been a while."

"Too long. I've missed you," he ventured.

Was that relief he saw in her eyes? Her gaze drifted from him to the motorcycle and the helmet dangling from his gloved hand. Her smile widened.

"Riding the bike today, huh?" she said, her voice low and sultry as she stepped closer. Her fingers trailed along the curve of the fuel tank. "You know what that does to me."

"Do I? I've forgotten. Why don't you show me?" he challenged.

Drawn closer to Paloma, heat coursed through his body. The small space between them crackled with electric desire, making the hair on his neck stand up. She pressed against him, and his breath hitched. Her warmth seeped through his clothes. His arms encircled her waist, pulling her closer. He reveled in the feel of her body against his. All the uncertainty of the past weeks melted away.

He removed his riding gloves and tossed them on his motorcycle. His thumbs brushed her cheekbones, and he cupped her face in his hands before crashing his lips against hers. The kiss was hungry and desperate; weeks of longing poured into a single, scorching moment.

She matched his hunger, her fingers tangling in his hair, pulling him closer. She arched into him, erasing any remaining space between their bodies. Max groaned softly against her mouth, one hand sliding down to her hip, gripping tightly.

They broke apart, panting. Her pretty lips were swollen, and her pupils were dilated. He rested his forehead against hers, unwilling to pull away completely.

"That was quite a welcome," he murmured.

Her lips curved into a playful smile. "Just showing you what your bike does to me," she teased, her breath warm against his skin.

"Damn, I need to ride more often. Maybe even in the winter."

"Right now, I'd rather you ride me," she said bluntly.

Her words bypassed his brain, striking deep in his gut, unfurling into a swarm of hungry butterflies. He swallowed hard, tasting anticipation on his tongue.

She nodded toward Drake's Mercedes. "Is the fancy car merely keeping watch, or is your brother playing sentinel inside?"

"I'm not sure," he said. "You pulled in right behind me. I haven't been inside. But probably."

She winked. "Well, that puts a damper on my plans to ravish you on this bike."

Desire coursed through him. He leaned in, ready to throw caution to the wind until a flicker of movement in the kitchen window caught his eye. Reality crashed back like a bucket of ice water. Right. The house. His brother. He pulled back slightly, keeping a hand on Paloma's waist.

"As tempting as that sounds," he murmured, nodding toward the house, "we might have an audience."

"That's okay. It's just good to see you, Max. I've missed this." She kissed him. "Missed us."

Her words cleared away his shadows. He'd worried the spark might have fizzled with her during their time apart. But here she was, standing before him, her eyes bright with desire and something that looked a lot like affection.

He drank in the sight of her. Weeks of longing crashed over him, made worse by her tantalizing proximity. He curled his hands into fists at his sides, fighting the urge to pull her close again.

He'd spent the last week trying not to overthink what had happened in Traverse City, reminding himself they'd agreed to wait until the Sterling project was completed to talk about what they were to each other. And did they need to? The way she looked at him now, the way she'd practically melted into his arms, had to mean something. And what if putting a name to whatever was growing between them would change everything?

Playing it cool, he took her hand, and they walked to the house. "Come on, let's get inside. I'll make us something for dinner." He pulled her close at the door, running his lips along her neck, taking in her sweet, sexy scent. "Then we're going to my bedroom, and I'm having you for dessert."

"Oh, Max," she laughed, her eyes sparkling as they walked toward the house. "Such a gentleman, aren't you? Offering dinner first when we both know what you're really hungry for." She pressed into his back, and he fumbled with the lock, turning around and pushing his hungry mouth to her lips.

Breaking the kiss, he reached behind and opened the door. "What can I say? I'm a nice guy." Keeping her in his arms, he walked backward to the foyer. "And I believe in doing things properly."

"Nice and proper, hmm? I'll be sure to remember that later," she said before going on her tiptoes and nipping her earlobe. "But I prefer rough and thorough."

He cupped her ass, pressing her against him. Never mind. She was going to be his dinner and dessert.

"I was beginning to think you'd set up camp in the driveway," said Drake.

Max's head snapped toward his brother's voice. His eyes narrowed at Drake, leaning against the kitchen sink. Paloma's hold slid from around him, her cheeks flushing red.

"I thought I saw you spying like a creep," Max said, resting a hand on her back and leading her to the kitchen.

"I'm the creep?" A sardonic smirk played on his brother's lips. "You were the one trying to crawl inside Paloma through her mouth."

Max laughed-groaned. "Shut the f—"

"Maximilian! Language!" His mother's voice rang out as she strode from the great room into the kitchen.

He jolted, his elbow knocking against a mug on the counter. It clattered with a thud into the sink. "Mom, what are you doing here?"

"Is that any way to greet your mother? I haven't seen either of my sons in weeks, so I came to you guys." His mom's gaze moved from him to Drake and then locked onto Paloma. She tilted her head, eyebrows rising a fraction.

His tongue was sandpaper in his mouth. He glanced at Paloma, then at his mom. How did he introduce her? Work partner? No, too formal after Traverse City. The memory of their time there flickered through his mind, and his cheeks burned hotter. *But are they dating?* They hadn't talked about it yet.

"Mom, this is Paloma—"

She stepped forward, extending her hand. "I work with Max."

His mom's lips thinned, and her eyes narrowed, settling coldly on Max. A crease formed between her brows. "Works for you?"

He shook his head. "No, with me. She owns an interior design business."

"Oh, decorates homes?"

Max winced. His mom, who'd redecorated their house six times in the past decade, would love chatting design. But he knew how much it irked Paloma when people confused design and decorating.

"I design them," she said, her voice carefully neutral.

His mom's brows furrowed. "So, an interior decorator?"

"Uh . . . Mom." He fought the urge to clamp his hand over his mother's mouth.

Paloma drew in a measured breath. "That's a different profession." Her fingers drummed against her thigh, the only visible sign of irritation.

His mom's gaze darted between them, her lips compressing further. "Well, lunch is ready if you'd like to join us," she said with brittle brightness.

An inexplicable tension settled over the room. Something was off, but he couldn't pinpoint what or why. His mother's smile was strained, but was it directed at him or Paloma? The uncertainty made his stomach churn.

Paloma looked at Max, then quickly away before she turned to his mother. "No, thank you. I actually have a . . . client meeting I forgot about," she said, her words coming out a touch too quickly. "I should really get going."

He stepped closer, the floorboards creaking beneath him. "We cleared our schedules," he murmured, unable to keep the edge from his voice. That had been the plan. He'd been up since dawn, racing through his work to have this time with her.

A flicker of something—guilt? Regret?—passed over her face before she schooled her features. "I know, and I'm sorry," she said, not quite meeting his eyes. "It came up suddenly. You know how demanding some clients can be."

His shoulders sagged, the fight draining out of him. "Right," he said, bitter disappointment coating his tongue. "At least let me walk you to your car."

She shook her head, offering a small, apologetic smile. "No, that's okay. Spend time with your mom." She turned to his mother, her posture stiffening slightly. "It was nice to meet you, Mrs. London. Thank you for the lunch invitation."

His mother's left eye twitched, a tell Max recognized from countless childhood confrontations. "Of course," she said, her tone clipped. "Another time, perhaps."

Paloma gave Max one last look, a mix of apology and something else he couldn't quite read—maybe defeat—before heading toward the door. The sound of her heels on the hardwood seemed to echo in the tense silence as she left.

"What the hell was that about? What's your issue with Paloma?" he demanded. Each word was measured and deliberate, but he pressed his hands flat against his thighs, fingers splayed, needing to ground himself.

"Don't take that tone with me. And I'm upset with you, not her." Her lips pressed into a thin line. "It has to do with what you were doing before you walked through the door."

Drake, who'd been slouched at the table like a bored teenager, sprang to life. He slinked toward the stove with all the subtlety of a cartoon burglar. Cupping his hand to his mouth, he stage-whispered loud enough for the neighbors to hear, "Psst! I wasn't the only one at the window like a creeper."

Their mom smacked his shoulder with the back of her hand. "I'm not a creeper. I was just excited to see my son."

"Yet you weren't after you saw your son had company." Drake's grin widened, and he tapped their mom's cheek. "Aw, you blush as bright as Max."

"Quiet, son." She ducked her head, suddenly very focused on checking on the delicious-smelling stew on the stove. Placing the lid back on the Dutch Oven, she looked at Max. "Think about the consequences."

His jaw clenched, the tension radiating down his neck. The kitchen was suddenly too small, too warm, the smell of his mother's stew cloying and suffocating. "I told you, Paloma doesn't work for me."

"I heard. But you are business partners, correct?"

He nodded, still not understanding. Yet, a familiar weight settled in his gut, that old feeling of disappointment he could never seem to shake around his mother.

"How well do you think you'll work together if things fall apart?"

"Wow, way to be a pessimistic Peggy."

Drake chuckled, earning a withering glare from their mom. "What?" he protested. "It's funny because your name's Peggy."

She rolled her eyes. I know why it's funny. But it's not. I'm realistic, not pessimistic. And you, Max, are impulsive." She left out the phrase, "as usual" but he heard it.

"Even if that happened, it wouldn't end either of our careers," he argued, but the words were hollow.

A familiar weight settled in his gut, that old burning weight of disappointment he could never seem to shake around his mother. He wasn't that reckless teenager anymore, the one who'd made impulsive decisions that had rippled out, affecting his life and others'. He'd worked so hard to become someone his mother could be proud of, someone responsible and trustworthy.

But now, looking at the concern etched on her face, Max was right back in high school. Or standing over his father's hospital bed, making promises to any deity who'd listen to his prayers.

"I'm not being impulsive," he insisted, hating how defensive he sounded. "Paloma and I, we've thought this through." But even as he said it, doubt crept in. Maybe she'd already considered all this, and that's why she'd hesitated to have anything more with his impulsive ass than sex.

"What you two are working on isn't profitable?" his mom asked, halting his spiral.

"No, it is."

"One project is with the Thompsons who own all those yoga studios," Drake said, butting it. "And an even bigger one for the Sterlings. That's why they were in Traverse City."

"The Sterlings?" his mom exclaimed, her eyes widening. 'You mean the obscenely wealthy Sterlings who own that top-selling home design magazine AND the hit TV show? Those Sterlings?"

He nodded again. "Yeah, so?"

"That's huge, Max. Think of the contacts." Her brows rose. "And the possible fallout if things didn't work out."

"We're professionals," Max argued, but even as the words left his mouth, a flicker of doubt chased after him. Images flashed through his mind: awkward client meetings, strained conversations, the spark between them fading to cold ashes. He swallowed hard, pushing the thoughts away. "Even if things didn't work out and, worst-case scenario, we ended up hating each other, we'd finish the project."

"And when their friends and colleagues wanted to hire you as a team. Then what?"

Good question. His certainty wavered. His mother's words wormed their way into his mind, planting seeds of doubt. Was he being impulsive? Was he risking everything he'd worked for? The possibilities he hadn't considered loomed large, threatening to overwhelm him.

Then there was Paloma's hasty retreat, the way she'd tensed at his mother's questions. Maybe she'd already considered all these complications. Their time in Traverse City had been perfect—away from expectations, just the two of them exploring whatever was growing between them. But now, watching her practically sprint from his house, he worried if trying to define things would only make her run faster.

They were good together, weren't they? The easy flow of their work partnership, the electric chemistry between them, the way she made him laugh. Did they really need to slap a label on it? But leaving things undefined, of pretending their connection was casual when it felt anything but, sat like a stone in his gut.

His mom sighed, "Oh, Max, when are you going to learn to be less impulsive?"

He wanted to argue that she was wrong. But was she?

What had started as something thrilling but complicated had become precarious, balanced on the knife-edge between professional success and personal happiness. And now, with the phantom warmth of her kiss still on his lips and the sting of her hasty exit fresh in his mind, he wasn't sure which way it would fall.

Chapter Twenty-Seven

November 6th, 4:30 p.m.

Paloma stepped back after ringing the doorbell of the Thompson house, her gaze drawn to the pineapple door knocker. The sight deepened her already somber mood, not because of what it implied about her clients' lifestyle, but because it reminded her of Max. Four days had passed since she'd last seen him—four days of replaying her hasty exit from his family home, of battling the guilt that gnawed at her insides.

The sudden introduction to his mom and her obvious dislike shattered the bubble of stolen moments and passionate encounters, making everything too real and serious.

Staring unseeing at the door, she worked to shake off the memory of Max's disappointed expression as she'd fled. He'd been kind but distant since then, and she couldn't blame him.

The door clicked, then opened, snapping her out of her reverie. The Thompsons stood before her. She smiled at them, forcing her professional mask back into place. She had a job to do, and clients to impress. She couldn't let her drama interfere with her work.

"Good afternoon," she said. "Are you ready for the final walk-through?"

"Are you sure Max can't join us?" Bill asked. "There was another matter we'd like to discuss with him now that we've reached the end of this project."

Her heart skipped. Did they have more work for them? Or maybe they'd recommend them to others.

She shook her head. "He's in court today testifying as an expert witness. The judge rescheduled at the last minute and couldn't get out of it. But we could reschedule for next week."

After the disastrous run-in with his mom, she didn't mind the break but understood why the Thompsons would want him here. And she wanted to keep them happy. Their satisfaction could lead to a flood of high-end clients. Her pulse fluttered. Maybe that's what they wanted to discuss.

Elodie rested her hand on her husband's arm. "Honey, I think we'll get all we need from Paloma. She can pass it along to Max."

There was a silent exchange between them that snagged at Paloma's attention like a burr catching on silk. Bill's lips curved in a way that made his usual friendly smile something else entirely.

They moved to the sweeping staircase where Max's masterpiece unfolded—a cascade of native Michigan plants in tiered planters. Wild columbine nodded their delicate heads, achingly reminiscent of his thoughtful tilts, while ferns unfurled in shadier spots, their movement mirroring his animated gestures during their brainstorming session. Pineapple plants, the Thompsons' quirky request, peeked out among the flora, evoking bittersweet memories of the theories she and Max had shared about their clients' lifestyle. The garden and how it matched her design were a living testament to their perfect partnership. It should have filled her with pride, but instead, it intensified the hollowness in her chest. She'd run out on him when they had plans, and the choice haunted her. Their relationship defied easy labels, but his feelings deserved more than her hasty retreat.

She followed the Thompsons through their newly designed home, cataloging details on autopilot. She had a job to finish, even as her heart longed to return to Max and make things right.

Elodie gestured to the living room. "The color palette you chose is perfect. It reminds me of a certain . . . exclusive venue in Chicago. I believe Max might be familiar with the scene there."

Her pulse picked up. The name was unfamiliar, but the mention of Chicago and Max wasn't good. Was it her imagination, or was there an odd tension in the air? Elodie's smile seemed a touch too wide while Bill's gaze lingered a moment longer than usual.

"I'm not sure," Paloma replied. "We focused on creating a sense of flow—"

"Oh, you've certainly done that." Bill moved closer. "You know, we've heard whispers about Max's . . . diverse experiences from his time in Chicago. It seems he has quite an interesting background."

Her hands grew clammy. How much did they know? And more importantly, why did they care? She swallowed hard, and her mouth suddenly dried. "I'm not privy to Max's history," she lied.

The Thompsons exchanged a look that seemed to carry an entire conversation, but Bill merely nodded and said, "Well, the color works. It is beautiful."

"Thank you, Mr. Thompson—"

"Oh, no, why so formal now, Paloma? Bill is fine. We're all friends here." He nodded at his wife. "Right, Elodie?"

"Yes, definitely," she replied. "And I congratulate you both. Your partnership with Max seems very . . . effective." Her hand brushed against Paloma's arm as they moved deeper into the living room.

They stopped at the table Max had laid her on and made her come so hard she'd nearly blacked out. Had Elodie picked this exact spot on purpose? And if so, why? Paloma forced a professional smile. "We do make a great team."

Bill looked at her from the other side of the custom coffee table. "A little birdie told us your teamwork extends far beyond the office."

Her mind raced. Who could have told them? She and Max weren't from Brighton or Woodland Lake. And, more importantly, what the hell was she supposed to do about it now?

"Excuse me, I'm not sure . . ." How did she finish that sentence? Her personal life wasn't their business, but she couldn't afford to alienate an important client.

Bill chuckled, moving around the table. "No need to be coy, dear. Word gets around in our little community. It made us wonder about the day we stopped by unannounced."

Elodie bent and traced her fingertip along the edge of the walnut coffee table, her dark eyes never leaving Paloma's face. Panic rose in her throat, strangling her.

"This table is truly a focal point." Elodie's voice dropped to a honeyed whisper. "I bet it's witnessed some . . . interesting discussions during your consultations."

Memories of Max between her legs on that table flashed through her mind. She struggled to maintain her composure. "Yes, it's . . . it's a focal point for sure."

Elodie glanced toward the fireplace mantle at an ornate, almost sensual statue. "Did we ever mention our home is equipped with cameras?" Her gaze moved to Paloma. "Outside and inside."

Paloma stared at Elodie, her mind struggling to process the words "cameras" and "inside." The room spun, and her heart hammered. The table. Max. That afternoon, they had seen everything.

Heat blazed across her face and neck. Her legs went weak, and she gripped the back of a nearby chair to keep herself upright. "Oh God," she whispered. The memory of what she and Max had done—his hands on her body, her cries of pleasure echoing through this very room—now made her want to sink through the floor and disappear forever.

"I am so sorry," she managed to choke out. "That was completely unprofessional. I never—we shouldn't have—"

"Darling." Elodie's voice was surprisingly gentle. "There's no need to be embarrassed. We were . . . impressed."

Paloma's head snapped up, certain she'd misheard. Bill had moved closer, and his expression didn't match her expectations of an angry client.

"You see," Elodie continued, exchanging a look with her husband, "we recognize passion when we see it. And you two have incredible chemistry."

Paloma swallowed, and there was an audible click from her now dry throat. "I don't understand." A new kind of nervousness replaced her mortification.

Bill cleared his throat. "What my wife is trying to say is that we're part of a very exclusive, very discreet community. Given Max's history and what happened here, we hoped you two might be open to new experiences."

Her embarrassment transformed into shock of a different kind as their meaning became clear. The pineapple door knocker, the oblique references to Chicago, the lingering touches—everything shifted into a new context. She and Max were right! The Thompsons were swingers.

"You're suggesting . . ." She couldn't finish the sentence.

"Only if you're interested," Elodie said, brushing Paloma's arm. "No pressure. Though based on what we observed, you two certainly know how to enjoy yourselves."

The weight of her mistake crushed against her chest like a physical force. She'd let all those careful boundaries she'd drawn dissolve in the heat of Max's touch. Now those dissolved lines had reformed into a noose around her reputation, business, everything she'd worked to rebuild.

Needing distance from the Thompsons and the situation, she stepped away and bumped into a side table, knocking over a frame. "I'm flattered by your offer," she began, choosing her words carefully. "But I think it's best to separate work and my personal life."

She set the photo down and took another step back, her mind whirling. How had a simple final walkthrough turned into this? More importantly, how could she salvage the situation?

Elodie tilted her head, and her blonde bob brushed against her shoulder. "You didn't with Max." Her tone sounded neutral, but who knew what was happening beneath the surface.

"That was a temporary lapse. One time," she lied. "We decided it was best to keep things strictly professional. We want to stay focused on our clients and our work. That's what's most important to both of us."

Elodie raised a brow, her smile thinning. "Is that so?"

"Absolutely," Paloma replied, her voice firmer now. "We make a great team because we prioritize our work, and that's how we plan to continue."

Bill chuckled softly as if amused by the whole exchange. "Fair enough, but I've seen you two together." He glanced at the table again, then put an arm around his wife's waist. "We respect your boundaries, Paloma. Just thought we'd put it out there."

She forced a polite smile though her stomach churned. "I appreciate your understanding." She glanced at the clock on the wall. "Now, if you don't mind, I've got another meeting soon, so we should finish our final walk-through."

"Of course, darling," Elodie said smoothly, a light laugh escaping her perfectly painted mouth. "No harm in asking, right?"

"Right," Paloma agreed, though she wasn't sure if that was true. It might have harmed what was growing between her and Max.

She quickly completed the walk-through, keeping her voice even and professional despite her heart pounding and her mind racing. When she finished, she handed them the last bit of paperwork. "If you have any further questions, please call." She hoped they didn't have any questions.

Bill clasped Paloma's hand a little too warmly. "Thank you for everything. And don't worry—we won't mention this to anyone. You'll do the same, right?"

"Of course," Paloma managed, withdrawing her hand as quickly as possible without appearing rude.

Stepping out of the house and into the cool air, the door closed behind her. She sucked in what air she could manage. They had a recording of her and Max. She might be royally fucked. Tears pressed in behind her eyes.

She got into her car, and her hands trembled as she gripped the steering wheel. The reality of what had happened didn't wash over her so much as detonate. Each erratic heartbeat whispered, "They saw. They know. They saw. They know."

Her phone buzzed. Max's name flashed on the screen.

Her heart lurched. What would she tell him? That their clients had just propositioned them? She took a deep breath and answered the call.

CHAPTER TWENTY-EIGHT

November 6th, 6:10 p.m.

Max sat in his office, gazing at the setting sun through the window, his phone ringing. He didn't expect Paloma to answer. She'd been avoiding him since she'd run from his house.

He'd given her space, but that ended today. There was a fine line between understanding and patient and accepting the role as her rainy-day entertainment.

The call answered, and when he jolted upright, the springs of his favorite ancient chair whined. "Hello," she said, her voice as hollow as a long-abandoned echo.

All this anger and demand fell away, replaced with worry. "Is everything okay?"

"I'm not sure," she replied. "Can we meet today? We might have an issue."

He glanced at his computer screen. It was after six. "With what?

"The Thompsons. They propositioned me. Well, us."

"What the fuck," he choked. It was a damn good thing he was sitting in his father's monstrous antique office chair. It was probably the only thing keeping him from keeling over onto the floor in shock.

She laughed, but there wasn't humor in it. "That's what screamed through my head the whole walk-through."

Rage boiled inside him. From what little he knew, people in that lifestyle were usually protective of their community and respectful of boundaries. Yet these two had the audacity to proposition her before the ink was even dry on their contract. And when she was alone in their home.

"Did they seriously think that was appropriate?" He kept his voice low, fighting the urge to shout." He should have been with her. "Why in the hell would they think you'd be interested?"

"They knew about your adventure in Chicago."

Her words punch him in the stomach. Why did his impulsive choices cause others so much collateral damage? "It was one damn time," he groaned, rubbing a hand down his face, pulling his beard until it stung. "I'm so sorry, Paloma."

"It's not your fault," she said, but he disagreed. She sighed, and his guilt was heavy. "That was only one tiny part. I think it's how we acted around each other had them looking through security footage."

He froze. Cold and heavy regret settled in his gut. "Security footage?" he echoed.

"Security cameras. Max," Her voice dropped so low he had to strain to hear it. "They have footage of us. On their coffee table."

"Christ," he choked. The phone nearly slipped from his numb fingers.

He shouldn't have been so reckless. His mother's words from their last conversation shouted at him, asking when he'd stop being so impulsive.

"Paloma," he finally said, his voice low and rough. "I . . ." He didn't know how to finish the sentence.

"Can we meet today?" she repeated. "Discuss damage control."

"Damage? Are we talking blackmail? Coercion?" His mouth went dry, his fingers drumming a nervous rhythm against his desk.

His ex had told him the swinging community protected their own, valued consent and boundaries. But the Thompsons had propositioned Paloma during their final business meeting. The timing couldn't be coincidental. A power play? Or did they think a nearly-sealed contract made it fair game?

"So far, neither," she said. "They seemed fine with me turning them down. I'll give you the full story when we're together. See what you think."

He stilled his restless, nervous tapping and checked the time. His eyeballs burned from exhaustion, but he needed to help her. "I'm still at the office and need to discuss a few loose ends with Grace. It might take a while. Would tomorrow morning be better?"

"No. I'm leaving for the Sterlings' first thing in the morning."

"Tomorrow? I thought we were going together next week?" The last of his selected plants were due to arrive the following Wednesday.

"There's a few big things arriving tomorrow afternoon. I need to be there and ensure the installation is correct," she replied. "It's a quick overnight before we return for the final phase together."

It was ridiculous that her going without him bothered him. He ignored his worthless reaction and asked, "Where do you want to meet?"

"Do you mind coming to my place?"

Grace walked into his office. He held up his index finger. She nodded, taking the seat across from his desk. "Yeah," he told Paloma. "I shouldn't be more than an hour or two."

They hung up, and he focused on Grace. "Ready to go over those reports?" he asked, rubbing the sleepiness from his eyes.

"Are you?" She tilted her head, meaning she'd already figured out more than he wanted her to know. "We can do this tomorrow if you need to. You've got that thousand-yard stare going."

"No, some of this can't wait." He shuffled the papers on his desk, trying to gather his scattered thoughts. "But if possible, let's focus on the urgent stuff now. I need to head out after to see Paloma. There's an . . . issue."

"Work or personal?"

His pen clattered against the desk. "Why would you assume personal?"

Grace settled into the chair and gave him a come-on look that made his neck heat. "I'm not blind. I've seen you two when she stops by." She leaned forward, lowering her voice. "The way you look at each other and gravitate toward one another in meetings. It's nice, actually. You smile more."

Her words, meant to be supportive, only intensified the acid churning in his gut. His impulsiveness could hurt not just him and Paloma but the company's reputation. "Grace—"

She held up a hand. "Don't overthink it, Max."

He wanted to laugh, but his sense of humor was buried under his stress. "Do you even know me?"

She smiled. "Whatever's going on, you'll figure it out. You always do." Opening her tablet, she asked, "Now, shall we tackle these reports?"

He nodded, forcing himself to compartmentalize. "Let's get started," he said.

The meeting stretched on, each topic bleeding into the next. His eyes grew heavy, his responses becoming more automatic as fatigue set in. By the time Grace gathered her things to leave, they were the only two left. Even the cleaning person had come and gone, the lemon-scented disinfectant hanging in the air.

Grace paused at the door. "Text me when you get home? You look exhausted."

He managed a tired smile. "Yes, Mom."

But she wasn't wrong, and with leaden feet, he made his way through the now-quiet office. In the break room, the coffee maker sputtered to life, filling the air with the aroma of fresh brew. He leaned against the counter and waited for his much-needed caffeine fix. His mind was a fog of exhaustion and unresolved worries about the impending conversation.

Coffee in hand, he shuffled toward the exit. In the parking lot, his footsteps dragged in the broken concrete. Sliding into the driver's seat of his truck, he took a long slug from his to-go mug, wincing at the scalding heat.

The gentle hum of the truck's engine and the passing landscape, shrouded in darkness, did little to keep his attention. He drifted to the Thompsons, their cleverness in extracting information, and the complications this could cause him and Paloma.

His body ached from the long hours and stress of the past few days. His eyelids grew heavier with each passing mile, exhaustion pressing down on him. The road ahead blurred slightly, and he blinked hard, clearing his vision.

He shook his head like a wet dog, attempting to jolt himself awake. He cranked up the radio volume, letting the pulsing beat of the music fill the cab. But even as the chorus reached its peak, his focus slipped again.

He needed a better distraction and told the car's Bluetooth, "Call Jackson."

The phone rang once, twice, three times. His fingers drummed on the steering wheel. After the fourth ring, Jackson's voicemail picked up. He disconnected the call.

He considered ringing Asher or Wyatt, but he was less than ten minutes from Paloma's house. He could power through the last little bit.

The road stretched before him, a dark ribbon cutting through the night. Streetlights flashed by in a hypnotic rhythm, their glow blurring into streaks of amber. His eyelids grew heavier, each blink lasting a fraction longer than the last.

He shook his head again, trying to clear the fog that seemed to be settling over his mind. The radio continued to play, but the music had become a distant, muffled sound as if coming from underwater. He rolled down the window, cold air cutting through the muddle.

Images flashed through his mind—the Thompsons' knowing smiles, Paloma's voice laced with tension. Each thought pulled at him, dragging him further into a fog of worry and fatigue.

His chin dipped toward his chest. He jerked upright, his heart racing, and forced his heavy eyelids open. The road swam before him, yellow lines twisting like snakes. He blinked hard, but his eyelids were weighted, and each lift was a monumental effort.

Paloma's house was right around the corner. Five minutes away, tops. He could make it. He had to make it.

His eyes slid shut, the darkness a welcome respite. Just for a moment, he thought. Just one more blink.

CHAPTER TWENTY-NINE

November 6th, 11:47 p.m.

Paloma's gaze darted to her phone resting on her dresser. She tapped the screen for what felt like the thousandth time. The harsh glow mocked her with each passing minute. She paced the length of her bedroom, her bare feet alternating between the cool hardwood and the textured loops of the braided rug.

She snatched her cell, thumb hovering over Max's contact. Her chest tightened as she calculated the hours—no, lifetimes—since he should have arrived. The knot of irritation growing in her stomach twisted into something darker, colder.

Sinking onto the edge of her bed, a silk blouse she'd carefully chosen hours ago slithered to the floor, a pool of midnight blue at her feet. She bent to retrieve it, her other hand still clutching the phone. Muscle memory took over as she hit redial, pressing the device to her ear. Each unanswered ring tightened the knot in her stomach.

"Hel-lo?" Max's voice crackled through the speaker, unusually slow and slightly slurred.

"Max!" She said in a breathless rush, pressing the phone closer, straining to hear. Beeps and mumbles filled this silence of his reply. "Where are you? What's happening?" she asked.

"I'm . . . I'm in the hospital," he mumbled, his words barely audible over the din of bustling activity in the background.

"Hospital?" She shot up from the bed, stepping toward her door, her foot catching on the forgotten blouse. "What happened?"

A muffled voice in the background cut through: "Mr. London, we need to check your pupils again."

His voice faded, and all she could make out was people talking but not what they were saying. "Max!" she called out, gripping her phone tighter. "Talk to me!"

"I . . . I think I fell asleep," his voice returned, thick with confusion. "The car . . . I don't remember."

Another voice, clearer this time: "BP's 110 over 70, heart rate elevated but stable."

She choked, unable to breathe. The room was suddenly too warm, too small. She pressed her palm against her forehead, fingers trembling.

"Max, I . . ." Her voice cracked. She swallowed, but her heart was lodged in her throat. "You told me you were tired."

"Still tired," he muttered.

"Are you okay?" she asked. The question was barely audible as guilt constricted her voice.

"I'm gooood. Like really gooood," he drawled, his words stretching and blending. There was a pause, filled with machine beeping and a background discussion. "They gave me something that makes me feel almost as goooood as when your mouth is around my cock," he announced to the entire ward.

A startled laugh erupted nearby, followed by a muffled snort and shuffling feet. She grinned despite the worry gnawing at her. "You're really flying high, aren't you?"

"Definitely," he laughed, then grunted as if in pain.

That sobered her, and she grabbed her shoes and keys. "What hospital are you at? I'm on my way."

"No. No." he repeated something like ten times. "Don't worry about it. It's late. I know you gotta go tomorrow. We don't want you driving tired. Believe me, it fuckkkking hurts."

"I'm fine, Max, but I need to make sure that you're okay."

"Aw, you do like me."

She choked out a laugh that sounded a bit like a sob. "Of course I like you. Now, where are you?"

He told her the name of the hospital. She heard the echo of the ER's chaos ringing in her ears even after hanging up. Grabbing her keys, she raced outside. The night air was cold against her flushed skin, but she wouldn't waste the time returning for a jacket and jumped into her car.

Streets usually bustling were now eerily quiet, lit only by the yellow glow of streetlamps. She sped through empty intersections. The clock on her dashboard mocked her with each passing minute. Her only companions were the soft whir of her engine and the occasional flicker of a traffic light.

She arrived in record time, barreling through the hospital entrance, nearly colliding with the sliding doors. Her chest heaved as she skidded to a stop at the nurse's station, her handbag swinging wildly at her side. Going by the grin the nurse was trying to hold in she was probably the one who'd been in Max's room when he'd commented on Paloma's oral skills.

After checking the woman's name tag, she said, "Hi, Kathy, I'm here to see Max London."

The nurse nodded, fighting a grin. "Are you—"

"Yes, I'm the one that gives the excellent blowjobs," Paloma blurted, her fingers drumming an impatient rhythm on the counter. "Can I see him?"

A choking sound erupted to her left. It was another nurse, wide-eyed and spluttering, dabbing at the coffee stain spreading across his scrubs.

Kathy bit her lip, a chuckle escaping despite her closed mouth. "Actually," she said, her voice thick with suppressed laughter, "I was going to say, 'Are you Paloma Wagner?'"

A warmth infused her cheeks, but she shrugged it off. "Well, that's me too," she said, her gaze already shifting to the room numbers.

"He's in room thirty-nine," the nurse said, then added, "And you'll be glad to know he's been cleared to go home. However, he does have a concussion, so he'll need some care over the next few days."

Her stomach dropped. "A concussion? Is it serious?"

"It's mild, but all concussions require careful monitoring. I assume you'll be staying with him?" Kathy asked, her tone matter-of-fact.

Paloma stilled her hand that was fidgeting with the strap of her purse. Her gaze darted to the calendar hanging behind the nurse's station. Tomorrow's date was circled in bold red. She was supposed to be in Traverse City tomorrow. Yet, the thought of leaving Max physically hurt. She'd stay, at least through the night. "Yes, of course," she told the nurse.

Kathy nodded. "Good. I'll give you detailed care instructions before you leave. For now, you can see him. He's probably eager to get out of here."

Relief filled her, but anxiety gnawed at her edges. "Thank you," she managed, already moving toward Max's room.

The rubber soles of her sneakers squeaked against the linoleum as she strode down the hall. She slowed at his room. Her fingers trembled as they brushed the cold metal of the door's handle. The acrid scent of disinfectant permeated the air, a stark reminder of where she was and why. She pushed the door open with a soft click.

Her gaze fell on Max. He was sitting up in bed, and the sight hit her like a discordant note in a familiar melody—recognizable yet jarringly wrong. His face was a canvas of scrapes and bruises, stark against his paler-than-usual skin. A nasty gash ran along his hairline, held together by a row of neat stitches. A deep purple bruise bloomed across his left cheekbone.

He wore a hospital gown, but his clothes were folded neatly on a nearby chair, ready for him to change. A small bandage on his arm marked where an IV had likely been earlier. His usually meticulous hair was messy, with a small patch shaved near the stitches.

"Hey," he said, his voice rough but stronger than she'd expected. He attempted a smile, but it turned into a wince.

"Oh, Max," she whispered as if speaking too loudly might shatter this surreal moment.

"It looks worse than it is, I promise. Doc says I can go home tonight." He glanced at the clock opposite his bed. "Well, this morning, I guess. You shouldn't have come. I'm sure you have an early start for Traverse City. I could've called my mom or one of the guys."

She brushed aside his objections, her gaze darting between Max and the discharge papers on the bedside table. "Are you . . . Are you sure you're ready to leave?"

"Yeah, doc says I'm good to go." He reached for his clothes and grimaced.

"Let me help," she said, snatching the pile before he could protest. She clutched it to her chest like a shield.

"Thanks." He frowned. "You okay?"

She nodded, not meeting his gaze, and busied herself with his clothes. "You told me you were tired," she said to the shirt she was unfolding, her voice barely audible.

"What was that?" he asked, leaning forward slightly.

"Nothing, I just . . ." she exhaled. "Do you need anything else? Water for the ride home? I could ask the nurse—"

"Paloma, I'm okay."

She nodded, still unable to meet his concerned eyes. Her bottom lip trembled, and she caught it between her teeth. She stilled, his shirt clutched tightly against her.

"What's wrong?" he asked.

"I demanded you come by my house. You'd told me you were tired," she whispered, swiping at a falling tear.

"Come here. Please." He patted the spot on the bed next to him.

She perched on the edge, her gaze fixed on the linoleum floor. The harsh hospital lighting cast shadows that danced across her vision, mirroring the chaotic swirl inside her. He put his arm around her, and she leaned into him. "This is on me. I chose to drive."

"When you didn't show up—"

"You were pissed?" he teased.

A watery laugh escaped her. "Yes," she admitted. "But then I heard you were in the hospital, I . . . God, Max. I don't even know what I'm trying to say." Her hands stilled, and she forced herself to look at him. "I guess I'm just . . . I'm glad you're okay."

"Hey." He cupped her cheeks and kissed her softly. "I'm okay. Really. And I'm glad you're here."

"Me too." She leaned away, looking into his eyes, heavy-lidded from the medication.

He smiled, but it came out lopsided. "Let's get out of here. You should get some rest. Big day tomorrow, right?"

The remainder of her impending departure was a physical weight pressing on her chest. She averted her gaze, focusing on their intertwined hands instead. "Right," she murmured, her voice barely above a whisper. "Big day."

The looming departure seemed to suck all the air from the room. Her gaze drifted to the window, where the inky night was slipping away.

Her chest tightened, and a feeling akin to homesickness washed over her. But that didn't make sense; traveling had never bothered her. In fact, she usually considered it a perk.

Unless . . .

The realization hit her like a sucker punch, leaving her winded. Home wasn't a place anymore. It was a person. It was Max.

No. That wasn't supposed to happen. The last time it had was with her fiancé, who had left her heart homeless.

Panic clawed at her throat, threatening to choke her. This wasn't part of the plan. She didn't do deep. She didn't do vulnerable. Not anymore.

But as her eyes traced the lines of Max's battered face, she feared it was too late. She was already in freefall, and the ground was rushing to meet her. Fight or flight warred within her, leaving her paralyzed between opposing impulses—to flee from these dangerous emotions or to burrow deeper into them.

"I should . . ." Do what? Leave? "You should rest," she finally managed, gently disentangling from him and standing. "Let's get out of here."

She helped him get dressed and discharged. The squeak of wheelchair wheels echoed through the hospital's endless corridor as she pushed Max toward the exit. Fluorescent lights cast long shadows ahead of them, stretching his silhouette into a distorted shape on the polished floor. From behind, she saw the slight slouch of his shoulders and the tilt of his head as he leaned it against the chair's headrest. Even without seeing his face, she could sense his exhaustion, his vulnerability.

"You doing okay?" she asked.

"Yeah," he twisted around, a flicker of pain crossing his features before he masked it with a wan smile. "I feel ridiculous being rolled out."

"Hospital rules." His frustration was palpable, and she wanted to ease it. "Think of it as your chariot, Your Majesty. Complete with your chauffeur."

He chuckled softly and winced. "Well, if I'm royalty," he said, his voice rough but warm, "does that make you my knight in shining . . . Chucks?"

"It does," she said, pushing through the hospital doors.

The drive home was a blur of streetlights and silence. Every few minutes, her eyes were drawn to his form slumped in the passenger seat, his features softened by medication-induced sleep. Each time, something in her chest tightened so intense it bordered on pain.

She pulled into her driveway and rested a hand on his knee, gently shaking him awake. "We're home."

His eyes fluttered open, a small smile forming on his lips. "Home," he repeated, the word carrying a weight she wasn't ready to examine.

Getting him inside was a slow process. Each wince, each sharp intake of breath as he moved, had her tightening her grip on him, torn between the desire to pull him closer and the instinct to run.

Finally, they reached her bedroom. She helped him sit on the edge of the bed and kneeled to remove his shoes.

"Thank you," Max said, his voice barely above a whisper. He reached out, his fingers brushing along her cheek and jaw. "For everything."

"We should get some sleep," she managed to say through all the emotions lodged in her throat.

He nodded, and she helped him get under the covers. She walked to the other side of the bed, her movements mechanical as she slipped under the sheets. The small distance between them was both too vast and not nearly enough.

She lay on her back, staring at the ceiling, acutely aware of his presence beside her. The steady rhythm of his breathing filled the quiet room. She should be comforted by it, relieved that he was safe and here. Instead, each breath seemed to chip away at the walls she'd so carefully built around her heart.

The blankets shuffled, and then his fingers found hers. He sighed as if he'd found all he needed. Almost immediately, his breathing evened out in sleep.

Her self-protection started repeating its mantra: pull away, protect yourself. She knew how this story ended—with heartbreak and abandonment. Instead, she held his hand tight and scooted closer.

The night deepened around them, yet she lay awake, Max's hand warm in hers, facing a truth she could no longer deny: she was falling for him, hard and fast. And she had no idea what to do about it.

Chapter Thirty

November 7th, 8:30 a.m.

A searing bolt shot through Max's shoulder, ripping a gasp from his throat. His eyes flew open, then squeezed shut, blocking the sun's blinding rays. Waves of pain radiated outward, ebbing and flowing like a relentless tide. He forced his eyes open again, squinting against the glare until unfamiliar shapes emerged.

This wasn't his bedroom. The last wisps of sleep clinging to his mind evaporated. His senses sharpened, and a sweet aroma enveloped him—wildflowers mingling with hints of coconut. His fingers brushed against soft, light blue fabric.

Paloma's house. He was at Paloma's house.

"Paloma?" The sheets rustled as he shifted his weight onto one elbow and rolled. White-hot pain flared across his upper back and down his arm. A strangled gasp escaped him as the spasm seized his muscles, freezing him mid-motion. He straightened, sucking a lungful of air and glancing at his shoulder. What the hell had happened?

A large, angry bruise dominated his shoulder and chest. The discoloration spread in an almost circular pattern but with irregular edges. At its center was an intense purplish-black blotch about the size of a grapefruit. Spidering out from the main area, lighter red and pink splotches extended toward the neck and down the upper arm.

He ran his fingers along a thin, parallel stripe of deep bruises from his shoulder to his upper chest. Flashes assaulted his mind: blinding headlights, a sickening crunch, the acrid smell of deployed airbags.

There'd been a car accident. He'd fallen asleep at the wheel. Oh God. His heart hammered against his ribs. Paloma had been there, hadn't she? He vaguely recalled her voice, soft and worried . . . No, that was after. She kept waking him during the night, her words blurring together.

Shit. Had he hit another person on the road? The thought sucker punched him in the gut. His lungs seized. Each breath came shorter, faster, scraping his throat raw. The room tilted and swayed, the walls closing in. He blinked rapidly, but the world blurred, darkening at the edges.

The door creaked open, and Paloma appeared, balancing two steaming mugs of coffee. "You're awake," she said, a small smile on her lips. "How are you feeling?"

"Did I hit someone?" His voice cracked, high, and strangled, each word clawing its way out.

She rushed forward, kneeling in front of him, her hands cool against his clammy cheeks. "No, Max. No," she said, her voice cutting through the roaring in his ears. "You hit the traffic median."

Her cool hands anchored him, and he focused on her face, on the gentle pressure of her fingers against his cheeks. He drew in a shaky breath, then another, each coming a little easier than the last.

"Traffic median," he repeated, the words still unsteady. The room's spinning slowed, the edges of his vision sharpening. His shoulders dropped a fraction, some of the tension uncoiling.

He closed his eyes, breathing in her calm and exhaling his relief. In, out. In, out. He opened them again after a count of five or maybe five hundred. The world seemed more solid, more real.

"Okay," he murmured, his voice low but no longer strangled. "Okay. Just the median. No one else." His hand, now a little steadier, covered hers.

She stood, her warmth and comfort leaving him. Picking up the mugs from the dresser, she handed one to him and perched on the edge of the bed, her posture oddly stiff. There was a distance in her eyes that hadn't been there before, and it made his heart sink.

"I'm sorry," he said.

The corner of her mouth dipped down. "For what?"

Where to start? For doing exactly what she feared would happen if they were more than business partners—complicating her life, messing with her career. He settled for, "Calling you. Keeping you up half the night. Missing your morning appointment."

"I'm just glad you're okay." Her tone was almost flat. That hurt as much as the bruises from the accident.

He could fix this. Get his shit together and help more than hinder her. "What time are you leaving for Traverse City? Don't worry about dropping me off at home. I'll call Jackson. See if he can pick me up."

"I'm not going. At least, not today."

He paused, the mug halfway to his mouth. He returned it to his lap. "What? Why not?"

"The delivery people were due to arrive at the Sterling house early. I wouldn't have made it on time."

Because of *him*. Because she'd come to the hospital for *him*.

Bits and pieces from last night came back. She'd watched over him during the night. He rubbed the spot over his heart, ignoring the tender bruises. He loved and hated that she'd done both.

"Felix is covering for me. I told him we'd be there tomorrow or the next."

That caught his attention, pausing his spiral. He couldn't leave for Traverse City in the next day or so. "I can't go. I have to call the insurance company. I was driving a work truck. Shit. I'm going to be late for—"

"I've already spoken to Grace. She's going to take care of the truck stuff. She also called in someone named Greg to cover your appointments today. In fact, she said you're good for the rest of the week. Heading up to finish the Sterling house won't be an issue."

His chest tightened. She'd done so much and rearranged her entire schedule all because of his carelessness. And what had he given her in return? Nothing but complications and setbacks. First, he's the catalyst for the situation with the Thompsons, and now this accident. He'd forced her to miss an important appointment and burden herself with his care. The familiar ache of self-loathing settled in his gut. Once a fuck-up, always a fuck-up.

"I'm so sorry for all of this. You shouldn't have had to—"

"Don't." Her tone was gentle but still distant. "It's fine. Really."

The tightness around her eyes and the slight downward tilt of her mouth told a different story. But he didn't want to push or make things worse than they already were. Instead, he'd make it up to her the only way he knew how: by fixing his mistakes.

Gritting his teeth, Max turned, his bare feet hitting the bedroom rug. A hiss of pain escaped him, and every bruised muscle protested the movement. His forgotten coffee sloshed over the mug, dripping onto his boxer briefs and leg.

"Max," she gasped, reaching for his mug, her fingers brushing against his. Instead of pulling away, he gently trapped her hand against the ceramic, his thumb tracing a small circle on her skin.

The bruising . . ." she murmured, her gaze fixed on the angry purple splotches marring his chest. Her free hand hovered inches from his skin, not quite touching.

He held his breath, torn. "It's not as bad as it looks," he lied.

Her eyes snapped to his, a flash of something—concern or frustration—crossing her face. "Don't." She shook her head. "Don't pretend with me."

The air was heavy with unspoken words and restrained impulses. He loosened his grip on her hand, allowing her to pull away. She didn't.

She let out a slow breath and let her fingers ghost over the edge of the bruise. He couldn't hold back a sharp inhale at the contact. She immediately withdrew.

"I'm sorry, I shouldn't have touched you," she said.

"No, it's okay," He replied, missing her warmth. "It's just . . . sore."

"Let me get your pain meds."

"No," he said firmly. Medicine would fog up his thinking. "We need to talk about what happened with the Thompsons. I'm so sorry you had to deal with that situation."

She stood and took a sip of her coffee. He couldn't help but notice the way her t-shirt clung to her curves as she moved. He shouldn't notice at a time like this, but she was so beautiful.

Her back was ramrod straight, but a little humor danced in her eyes. "It was so awkward, but I think we're okay. Maybe. Plus, there's nothing we can do."

"First, tell me everything they said. Then we can decide if there's anything we can do."

Pacing, she told him the whole story. It had him drowning in guilt. That one fucking night with his ex was following him like a damn curse. And he shouldn't have let his dick rule him that incredible afternoon.

"I agree," he said. "Let's wait and see. Them having a recording of us gives me an ulcer, but it seems like they want to keep their lifestyle quiet and won't risk talking or upsetting us so that we talk. If they call you, let it go to voicemail. I'll deal with them."

"I don't need to hide behind a man," she snapped.

He made to stand to stop her pacing, but a wave of dizziness hit him. He stumbled, and Paloma reached to steady him. Her hands gripped his bare arms, and they were face to face, barely inches apart.

Her gaze dropped to his lips, then quickly back to his eyes. She swallowed and stepped away, her hands falling to her sides. "Careful," she murmured.

He was tempted to pull her close, but something told him that'd be a mistake. So, he focused on the conversation. "I know you can take care of yourself, but you had to handle them in person, where they blindsided you. It's my turn to deal with any more awkwardness."

"Fine," she conceded.

"I say, we shelve them for now and put all our focus on wowing the Sterlings. They're bigger fish anyway."

She nodded. "I agree."

He saw a flicker of something in her eyes—a spark of the usual light returning. It kindled a small flame of hope in his chest. Maybe he could still salvage this situation.

Yes, he'd messed up, but he wouldn't let that define him or their partnership. One step at a time, he'd make things right. And maybe, just maybe, he could prove to Paloma—to everyone—that he wasn't the perpetual screw-up.

"Rest. I'm going to take a shower. Then we can go to your house to pack. Are you sure you don't want some pain meds?"

He nodded, and she turned to leave. He caught her hand. "Wait," he said, his pulse picking up. "I know I've complicated things between us. But I want you to know . . . you're the best thing that's happened to me in a long time."

Her breath caught. She squeezed his hand, her eyes shimmering. "Max, I—I can't do this right now. We can't."

She pulled away, leaving him with the ghost of her touch and a heart full of unspoken words. The door closed behind her. "I'm falling in love with you, and I don't know how to stop," he told the empty room.

CHAPTER THIRTY-ONE

November 24th, 8:30 p.m.

Paloma raised her glass of riesling, the local wine cool against her palm. Around her, the restaurant buzzed with Friday night energy, but her focus remained on the small circle at their table.

"To the Sterling house," she said, her voice carrying over the ambient chatter. She raised her wine, the golden liquid catching the light. Her gaze locked with Max's, and she loved the way his eyes sparkled with their shared triumph.

Her wine flute met his glass. The soft clink sent a shimmer of energy through her, and the sound seemed to amplify their collective joy.

Felix leaned in, his glass joining the toast with a crystalline chime. "Congratulations to you both," he said.

Abigail nodded and completed the circle, her stemware ringing out as it connected with the others. The four glasses formed a shimmering diamond in the air, but Paloma barely noticed the others. She and Max remained connected by an invisible thread of shared accomplishment.

Paloma sipped her wine, the crisp riesling dancing on her tongue. Setting her glass on the table, she couldn't contain her joy. "I still can't believe how well the final walk-through went."

Max shook his head slowly. "Right! I don't think I've seen Roy smile once in all the time we've met with the Sterlings. Today, it never left his face."

Abigail took a sip of her red wine. "That is impressive. I met him at a gala last year. He spent twenty minutes critiquing the canapés."

Paloma laughed. "I believe it. I had redesigned his balcony from scratch two weeks in. The same went for the bedroom layout. He had something to say about everything."

"And I had at least a dozen re-designs for the living wall," Max added. "But today made the aggravation worth it. They couldn't stop complimenting our work."

"Best of all," she paused dramatically to bask in the moment. "They've asked us to meet with their brand publicist. They want to feature us in their magazine's Christmas special?"

"What?" Felix exclaimed. "That's huge!"

She nodded, bouncing in her chair. "It'll be in their top-selling magazines and all over their social media."

This was the break she'd been waiting for. Her business had grown steadily over the past year, but this would change everything. It could mean bigger projects, like hotels and condos. A familiar determination settled in her chest as she looked around the table at her small circle of support. With this deal, she wasn't only rebuilding her business but burying the whispers that had called her a fool.

"To new horizons," Max said softly, raising his bourbon.

"What will you two do next?" asked Felix.

Max shrugged. "Now that the weather's turning colder, things are slowing down a little for me, but there's enough to keep everyone from getting too bored. We're focusing on design work for spring installations, using the downtime to upgrade our skills and plan for the busy season ahead." He looked at Paloma. "What about you?"

"With this project being extensive and out-of-town, I was careful not to take on anything else substantial. So, I only have two quick projects. One is for a home remodel, and the other is an ongoing project with a custom home in Ann Arbor." She sucked in her lips and then released them. "I've also had a colleague of Mrs. Thompson reach out to me. But I haven't decided if I'll do it."

Max nodded, saying without words that he understood her hesitation. There might even be a little guilt in his eyes, not that she blamed him. The Thompsons discovering his past was unfortunate but not his fault. And they were both to blame for losing themselves that afternoon on the infamous walnut coffee table.

And so far, there'd been no fallout. All invoices had been paid, no negative reviews had been posted, and it seemed they'd been recommending them—and only their work. There wasn't a hint of anything unprofessional from Elodie's colleague.

"Honestly, I want to keep my options open," she said. "I'm hoping for some bigger projects once the article prints and the Sterlings talk about their home and on social media. I might even put in a bid for small hotels and condos. I'd love to expand my portfolio."

"They'd be lucky to have your talent." Max clinked his glass against hers, his grin as warm as his eyes. She could melt in either.

"You two are so cute together," Abigail gushed.

Felix scoffed. "Not as cute as us."

Max dropped his gaze to his drink, his smile slipping for a second. Then he pasted it back on, but it had lost most of its luster. "Paloma mentioned you're coming back with us," he said.

"Yeah, it's our monthly family dinner. And I'm driving back a Blower Bentley for a client. You don't mind, do you?" Felix asked.

"Of course not."

The conversation continued around her, but her gaze and mind drifted to the window, to the people passing by and fading into the growing darkness. They were heading home the next day, leaving behind the magic of their professional triumph. And maybe something else too. Despite sleeping next to each other for two weeks, they might as well have been oceans apart. Her excuses had seemed so reasonable at first. He was working while recovering, so he needed to rest between. But his bruises faded, and still, the distance remained.

She took another sip of her riesling, the crisp wine doing nothing to wash away the nagging suspicion that she was running from something impossible to outrun.

Chapter Thirty-Two

November 24th, 9:00 p.m.

The restaurant door swung shut behind them. The cool November air was a sharp contrast to the warmth inside. Paloma shivered slightly. Max shrugged out of his jacket, offering it to her. She shook her head, not wanting him to freeze because she'd forgotten hers.

He moved behind her and draped the jacket over her shoulders. She put her arms in the sleeves, her hands lost in its large size, and she heated from his scent of cedar.

After saying goodbye to her brother and Abigail, he asked, "Should I call for an Uber?"

"I don't mind walking, but you might want a ride since I've confiscated your coat," she joked.

"I'm fine. Let's walk."

"It is a beautiful night," she mused, looking at the stars peeking through the city's glow.

Max hummed as if in agreement. They moved down the street, and with each block they passed, she became hyperaware of every point of contact, from the brush of his shoulder against hers to the warmth of the back of his hand, close enough for her to hold.

"I still can't believe how well today went," Max said, breaking the comfortable silence.

She grinned. "I know. When Mrs. Sterling hugged me, I thought I was dreaming." The perfumed embrace was still fresh—the way the perfectly made-up woman's eyes welled as she'd stepped from the conservatory into the living room. "It's exactly what I imagined, but better," Linda had said, her voice thick with emotion. Even now, hours later, the pure joy in her client's face made Paloma's chest tight with pride.

They rounded a corner, and the condo came into view, and a flutter of melancholy flipped in her stomach. This was their last night in Traverse City. Reality was waiting for them. They had no other job lined up. They were certain to get more offers, but that didn't mean he wanted to work with her.

Opening the door for her, they walked to the elevator. Inside, they stood on opposite sides, the small space suddenly vast with the distance they'd placed between them. The soft hum of machinery filled the silence but couldn't mask the weight of everything unsaid.

His fingers twitched at his side before he took a step forward. "I miss you."

Her breath caught, and she reached for the collar of his jacket draped over her shoulders. "I'm right here," she said softly, knowing what he meant—physical proximity wasn't the same as true presence.

"But you're not. Not really." There was no accusation in his voice, only sadness. "You're here, but you're running."

Instead of confronting the truth, she stepped in front of him. "Is that better?"

Reaching up, he tucked her hair behind her ears with an intimacy that made the lock on her heart stutter. "A little," he murmured, but his eyes held so much more—desire, yes, but also patience, understanding, and something deeper that she was afraid to name.

His touch was gentle, asking rather than demanding. She was afraid to listen to what it asked of her. Because listening meant admitting he'd already slipped past her defenses. He could shatter her in ways no one else could. The feelings she'd desperately hoped to contain had escaped their cage, and soon they'd trample her when he inevitably found her to be too much.

His gaze dipped to her lips, and desire sparked in her. She leaned into needing a distraction from her worries. "Will you kiss me?" she asked.

He nodded and leaned in. Before their lips met, the elevator dinged, followed by the doors sliding open. They didn't move apart until two staring teenage boys entered. Max stepped away, but the chasm didn't feel as wide.

"We're going up," he told the boys, nodding with his chin.

"That's what we get for paying more attention to the old people making out," one kid whispered to the other.

"Whatever, the girl's hot," the other replied, not nearly as quietly as he probably imagined.

Paloma snort-laughed. "We can hear you."

Their faces turned brighter than a clown nose. She peeked up at Max. He was biting on his bottom lip, silent laughter shaking his shoulders.

The elevator dinged its arrival to the top floor. The teenagers shuffled out of the way. Max wrapped his arm around Paloma as they left, pulling her to his side.

After the door shut, she asked, "Do you like me close, or are you jealous of my male admirers?"

"I definitely like you close." He tickled her waist. "But I'm also reminding them that while I may be an old decrepit man, I'm leaving with the hot girl."

She laughed while unlocking the condo. Once inside, she pulled him close, wanting their interrupted kiss. He went willingly, but when she tried to deepen it, to take it to the point where they were ripping off each other's clothes, he pulled back and said against her lips, "Slow down, sweetheart. We've got all night."

Then he kissed her like he cared about her. Like she was the only one falling. But she had to remember that good chemistry did not equal love. Just because she was feeling too much didn't mean he felt anything.

Focus on the pleasure and worry about the rest later.

She reached for his belt and unbuckled him. He put his hand over hers and repeated, "Slow down. Let me savor you."

He slid his hand through hers and guided them toward the bedroom. He took her purse and set it on the nightstand before sitting on the bed. Pulling her sideways onto his lap, he cupped her cheeks and pressed his lips to her. The kiss was slow and sensual as if he was savoring each moment.

Standing, he set her on the bed. Then he went down on his knees, unzipped her black leather boots, and removed them, followed by her socks. He circled the pad of his thumb over her ankle, eliciting a quiet moan from her.

"You like that?" he asked.

"Apparently. Though it's new news to me."

He bit gently on the spot and then soothed it with his tongue. Heat shot up her, pooling between her legs. "Max," she moaned, unsure what she was asking for.

Standing, he came around. The mattress dipped as he settled behind her. Removing her sweater, he kissed her shoulders before his lips trailed down her spine. At her bra strap, he unhooked it and slid his hand under the lace and over her breast. "Your skin is as soft as lisianthus."

She jerked away, her stomach clenching. "Who's that?" The question sliced through the air, razor-sharp. Was he comparing her to another woman? The asshole.

His chuckle rumbled against her skin as he pulled her close again. Warmth and irritation warred within her—how dare he laugh.

"It's a flower," he murmured, his breath warm on her neck.

"Oh." Embarrassment flooded her cheeks where jealousy had roared. She ducked her head, grateful he couldn't see her face. "That's really sweet," she admitted, smiling despite herself.

"And the truth," he said, his hands gliding down her stomach and between her legs.

She pressed against his palm, twisting around and inhaling his intoxicating scent. "Please, Max. I need you close."

He rolled to his side, and she met him in the center of the bed, tugging on his sweater. This time, he didn't deny her and removed it. Followed by his slacks and boxer briefs, then socks. A naked Max was a glorious sight. And not all of it was merely his tight muscles and heated eyes, but this moment of true closeness between them.

Reaching for her purse, she got a condom and put it on him. "Come here," he said. "I've missed your beautiful body against mine."

She pressed her front against his side, and his arm wrapped around her, bringing her on top of him. That sensation of being home filled her again. Even more so when she looked into his eyes, dilated with lust but also touched with something more.

Too afraid to ask what that something could be, she focused on what she could have and took him inside her. "You're so fucking perfect for me," he said.

She blinked back sudden tears and nestled into his neck. Her throat constricted, chest tight with emotions she refused to name. It wasn't the word 'perfect' that got her. All alone, it was trite, but added with, 'for me' as if she was perfect for him, that got her.

He rolled them but kept her wrapped in his arms as close as she had been when on top. It seemed she wasn't the only one who needed skin-to-skin comfort. "Why do you feel this good?" he asked rhetorically, then groaned, "Fucking amazing."

His thrusts were deep, and the pressure heady as his kisses. "Keep doing that. Don't stop," she begged.

"For you, anything," he said, kissing her and giving her exactly what she needed. Her orgasm coiled, then released. He brought her leg up, hitting a spot that had her seeing heaven.

"Oh, Go—Max," she gasped.

"Are you okay?" he asked.

She nodded, unable to speak. His rough pace and breathing told her he was close. She ran her short nails down his back, giving him a bite of pain he liked. He groaned her name as his body stiffened with his release.

Minutes or hours later, entangled in each other, her heartbeat returned to normal. She lay still, treasuring the warmth of his body pressed against hers, his steady breath tickling her neck. She traced absent patterns on his chest before catching herself and stilling them.

These tender moments after sex were more dangerous than the act itself. They made her want to confess things she couldn't take back, words and feelings pressing against her teeth and heart like prisoners testing their bars.

"I'll be right back," he said, disentangling himself and kissing her temple.

She reached for his pillow, then stopped halfway. No. She wouldn't be that girl who surrounded herself with his scent, who let herself need too much. Instead, she rolled, facing the wall, pulling her arms tight against her chest, letting reality crash over her like the roof of a house with a weak foundation.

The Sterling project was finished. Beautifully, perfectly finished.

There were no more projects to hide behind or excuses to keep this carefully constructed distance. There was nothing to buffer the inevitable moment when he'd want more—want things she wasn't, want the person he thought she was rather than who she was.

The bathroom water shut off, and she quickly rolled on her side, facing the wall. Soon he'd realize what everyone else had—that she wasn't worth the effort, that beneath her carefully crafted exterior lay someone too difficult to love.

The mattress dipped as he slid next to her. She kept her breathing steady, feigning sleep. The warmth of his hand hovered over her shoulder. Her fingers twitched to reach for him, but she curled them into her palm instead. After three heartbeats, he withdrew.

"Sweet dreams, Paloma," he whispered, settling beside her without touching.

The space between them was a preview of what was coming. She lay rigid, each second of this night feeling precious and painful. Tomorrow they'd drive home, and the fantasy would begin to unravel.

So she stayed still, listening to his breathing deepen into sleep, clinging to these last moments before reality demanded its due.

Chapter
Thirty-Three

November 25th, 6:00 p.m.

The traffic inched forward at a snail's pace, cars stretching endlessly ahead on the highway. Paloma drummed her fingers on the steering wheel, glancing at the clock on the dashboard for the hundredth time. They'd been stuck on their last stretch of I-96 for over an hour, and her schedule was backing up like the endless line of brake lights ahead of her.

"Any movement up there?" Felix's voice drifted from the back, slightly slurred with sleep.

She looked at him in the review mirror curled awkwardly across the backseat, his head pillowed on Abigail's lap. Her fingers combed through his hair as she stared out the window, her breath fogging the glass.

Paloma sighed. "We've covered maybe ten feet in the last fifteen minutes."

Beside her, Max shifted, the leather seat creaking. He reached over, his warm hand covering hers on the gear shift. "Hey, we have no major project to stress, so we've got time." He grinned, and his eyes crinkled at the corners. "Which is good because at this rate, we might make it back by Christmas."

A reluctant smile tugged at her lips, and some tension left her shoulders when she met his gaze. She loved how he was so mellow, willing to go with the flow, yet not passive. It was a rare combination that made their work, play, and even unexpected traffic jams enjoyable.

"Christmas," Felix groaned. "But I'm starving."

"I told you we should have taken my family's Cessna," Abigail groused good-natured.

"I was thinking about the carbon footprint," Felix replied.

"I'm not sure we're saving much sitting in this traffic."

"And I had to bring my truck back," Max reasoned, patting the dashboard.

Paloma's phone buzzed. She glanced at the screen on the car's Bluetooth and saw her mother's name flashing. "Uh-oh," Felix sat up. "We're going to be late for dinner. I'm glad you're telling her."

She quirked her brow at him in the rearview mirror, letting the phone continue to ring. Felix's eyes widened. "You wouldn't," he gasped.

She smirked and nodded.

"So mean," he muttered.

Her cell stopped ringing, and Max said, "What—"

Felix's phone began to sing, "Your Momma Don't Dance." He groaned and said, "I'm taking you down with me, Drunk Decision." He answered, saying. "Hi, Mom."

"Felix, darling!" Their mom said through the speaker call. "Are you all still coming for dinner tonight?"

"Nah, we decided to stop at Gino's for a pizza."

"That's not even funny," their mom scolded, but there was affection in her voice. When will you arrive? Is Paloma with you?"

"Yes, she is, and that's why we're late. She drives like a hundred-year-old granny."

"Oh, good, so she's with you. I wasn't sure; she's avoiding my calls again."

"I don't avoid your calls," Paloma lied.

"Felix! Why didn't you warn me that I'm on speaker?"

"I was about to tell you." His grin said the opposite. Paloma rolled her eyes, unable to hold in a grin. Her brother loved to wind up the family.

"We are on our way but will probably be late," she told her mom. "We're stuck in hellish traffic. And I'll be even later because after I drop off Felix and Abigail, I need to drop off Max at his house and pick up my car."

"He's that man you're working on the big project with, right?"

"That ain't all they're doing," Felix muttered.

Max made a choking sound and twisted around, his eyes wide. Paloma's pulse jumped, and she reached into the back seat and pinched her brother; at the same time, Abigail swatted him on the shoulder.

"What was that, Felix?" their mom asked.

"I said they're having a ball," Felix replied. "They make a great team."

"Ah, okay. Well, bring him along. There's plenty of food, and I'd love to meet him properly."

A slight tremor rippled through her fingertips, spreading like wild-fire up her arms. The idea of Max meeting her parents—especially her father with his razor-sharp judgments—amplified the jitters until she hummed with nervous energy. She glanced at him. He raised an eyebrow in question. His easy demeanor only intensified her worry; this might be a casual invite for him, but not her. She didn't bring men to meet her family. The only other man had been her ex-fiancé.

"I don't know, Mom," Paloma hedged. "It's kind of last minute, and I'm sure Max has other plans." She didn't want him to feel obligated, but a small part hoped he'd want to come, even if her father would be there.

"Nonsense!" her mother declared. "Max? Hi, are you there?"

"I am," he replied.

"Do you have plans this evening?"

"Um, no."

"Perfect. Would you please join us for dinner?"

He looked at Paloma, but she couldn't read his expression. She shrugged and mouthed, "Up to you."

In a neutral tone that gave away nothing, he said, "I'd love to. Thank you, Mrs. Wagner."

She continued to search his face but couldn't decipher if his acceptance was mere politeness or genuine interest. His gaze met hers, and all he offered was a slight smile.

"Wonderful. I'll let Clifton know. He'll be thrilled to meet you."

Paloma barely suppressed a snort. Her father, thrilled? It's more like he'd be sharpening his verbal knives, ready to grill Max about his business, plans, and life story. Then, her dad would move on to her.

After hanging up, Max asked, "Is Clifton your dad?"

She nodded.

"I thought he was designing a beachfront resort in California?"

"He is, but it's mid-project, so he's visiting before things pick up closer to the opening." After a pause, she said, "You don't have to come. It's short notice, and my family can be . . . a lot."

"No, shit," Max laughed, twisting around, giving Felix the stink eye.

"What?" her brother said, all false innocence.

"I'm going so I can poison your potatoes," he told Felix.

Paloma narrowed her eyes at the rearview mirror. "Don't worry. I was already planning on it."

"What! Hey, I'm just spicing up the family dinner! We don't want things as bland as Dad's desserts."

Max laughed, but she caught a glimmer of apprehension in his eyes. He was probably second-guessing his decision to join this family chaos.

"Well, next time serve a dish from your life, Flea," Paloma shot back, trying to sound mad but failing. It was difficult when Max was pushing his seat back, squishing Felix. Their laughter and Abigail's giggles filled the car, momentarily drowning out the frustration of being stuck in traffic.

Her gaze flicked between the road ahead and Max. His grin was wide, eyes twinkling with mischief, and her chest tightened. He looked so at ease, joking with her brother and Abigail—Paloma's two favorite people. It was like Max had always been and would be a part of their little group.

The car gradually quieted, with occasional chuckles from the back seat breaking the silence. Max turned slightly in his seat, angling toward her. His voice was low when he spoke. "Hey, about the dinner . . ."

He didn't want to go, and she couldn't blame him. She should be relieved, not disappointed. They weren't even dating, not really, so why would he want to meet her parents?

"My mom kind of pressured you into it. Don't feel like you have to go," she said.

He took her hand. "I'll come if you want me there."

"I . . ." Her heart did a little flip. She wanted him there. Desperately. The thought of him charming her mother and holding his own against her father's interrogation warmed her insides. But she was jittery. Max, at her family table, would make what was happening between them real.

Felix leaned forward between them. "I want you there. Now that Lotte's divorced, there's too much estrogen at these monthly dinners. Help!"

Paloma laughed, grateful for her brother's interruption of the heavy moment. "Last I checked, you and Dad manage just fine."

"Sure, until you all start talking about your periods."

"Oh, shut up. That's not what we talk about at every dinner," Paloma huffed.

"Yeah, we only do when we're on them," Abigail called from the back seat, her grin in her voice.

"And we can't help that our times are all in sync," Paloma finished, laughing.

"See what I'm dealing with?" Felix pleaded. "I need reinforcements."

Max glanced at Paloma, and she saw his unspoken question. She nodded at him. "I'd like you there."

"Good, glad that's settled," her brother said, clapping his hands once. "Because we might get there before midnight." He pointed out the windshield at the moving traffic. She turned to the road, where cars were moving forward with more purpose.

"About time," Max said, giving her hand one last squeeze before letting go.

They picked up speed. Conversation flowed easily, punctuated by laughter and the occasional grumble about the delay. The sun had long since set, casting the suburban landscape into darkness as they finally exited the freeway. She glanced at the dashboard clock—already past eight. No wonder her stomach was growling at her. But, damn, her parents would be annoyed, especially her dad. She hoped he wouldn't make the evening unpleasant and tense.

"Hey," Max said, his voice cutting through her worry. "That pizza place you mentioned earlier—think it's still open?"

"Gino's?" She clicked her tongue, considering. "Probably, why?"

"I was thinking we could grab a couple of pies," he said. "You know, as a peace offering for being late."

Felix leaned into the front seat. "Oh man, Dad would flip if we showed up with Gino's. Remember when he tried to ban it because he thought it was 'corrupting Italian cuisine'?"

"And then Mom caught him sneaking a slice at 2 a.m," Paloma added, laughing. The knot of tension in her shoulders loosened a fraction. "You know what? Let's do it."

Instead of turning right, she made a left, and less than ten minutes later, they were pulling into Gino's parking lot. She caught Max watching her, a soft smile playing at the corners of his mouth. "What?" she asked, suddenly self-conscious.

He shook his head. "Nothing. Just . . . I like seeing you happy."

His simple honesty made her pulse flip. Before she could overthink it, she leaned over and kissed him. It was chaste, but it was the first time she'd done it in front of anyone. "Thanks," she murmured, not quite meeting his eyes.

Felix made a gagging noise from the backseat. "No PDA."

"Shut up," she laughed, opening her car door. "Like I haven't seen plenty from you and Abigail last summer when I visited. Now let's get some food. I'm starving."

They piled out of the car and into the restaurant. They entered Gino's and were greeted with the warm, yeasty smell of pizza. The sizzle of cheese and the rhythmic thump of dough being kneaded created a comforting symphony. Max's hand rested on the small of her back, a gentle comfort guiding her through the crowded pizzeria.

Fifteen minutes later, they were back on the road, the car filled with the mouthwatering aroma of garlic and melted cheese. They turned onto her parents' street, and her grip on the steering wheel tightened.

Max reached over and took her hand, giving it a gentle squeeze. "What's wrong?"

"I love my parents, but they can sometimes be a bit much." And him, at their table, makes her scary feeling for him all the more real.

"I get it. Believe me," he said softly, "And don't forget, whatever happens, we've got pizza. And each other."

Her heart dipped. For now, they had each other.

Parking in front of her childhood home, she took a deep breath. The scent of Gino's famous garlic knots mingled with the faint trace of Max's cologne—each equally enticing. "Let's do this," she said, injecting a carefree lilt into her voice.

Everyone climbed out of the car, arms laden with pizza boxes. The cool evening air raised goosebumps on her arms as they walked to the door. Max's warmth beside her was a stark contrast, his presence solid and reassuring. The porch light cast a soft glow, highlighting his straight spine and a slight lift of his chin. She recognized the posture as one he adopted before important business meetings. But the soft smile he gave her when their gazes met revealed the nerves behind his confident façade.

Before they reached the porch, the front door swung open. Her father's frame filled the doorway, his expression unreadable in the gathering dusk. But then he lifted his chin and sniffed. His stern facade cracked.

"Is that . . . Gino's?" he asked, a note of longing in his voice.

Paloma exchanged a quick glance with Max, a silent laugh passing between them. Maybe tonight wouldn't be the weighty, relationship-defining dinner she'd feared. Maybe it could just be pizza and family and Max's warm presence beside her—uncomplicated, for now, at least.

Chapter Thirty-Four

November 25th, 8:30 p.m.

Max stepped over the threshold and into Paloma's childhood home. The warmth of the house was a stark contrast to the cool evening air outside. His grip tightened on the pizza boxes as he followed her inside, acutely aware of her father's evaluating gaze.

In the entryway that opened into a spacious living room, Mr. Wagner offered his hand to Max. "I'm Clifton Wagner and you're Max…"

"London," Max filled in, "I, um," he glanced at Paloma for help.

"Remember, Dad. I told you about him. He's the Landscape Architect I've been working with."

Max had hoped he'd also be introduced as more than a work partner, but they had just returned home and hadn't had a chance to talk. He shook off his disappointment and glanced around the home. He noted the soft, warm lighting from strategically placed lamps, casting a gentle glow on the cream-colored walls. A large, plush sofa dominated the room, adorned with various throw pillows in textures and complementary earth tones. Above it, his gaze lingered on the abstract art, recognizing the garden pattern immediately. Paloma nudged his arm softly, a silent acknowledgment that she'd known he'd appreciate that detail.

They smiled at each other. He turned to her father and said, "You have a lovely home, Mr. Wagner."

"Thank you," her father replied with a nod.

A flurry of movement from the kitchen caught his eye. A woman who had Paloma's eyes and smile emerged, wiping her hands on a dish towel. Her gaze landed on him, curiosity evident in her eyes.

"Oh, you must be Max," she said, approaching with a warm smile. "Thank you for joining us. I'm Sophia."

Max shifted the pizza boxes to one arm, extending his hand. "It's a pleasure to meet you."

"Paloma told us you two have been working together on some projects," Sophia continued. "You're a landscape architect, right?"

"That's right," he nodded.

"I've heard the Sterling home was a success," Clifton said.

"Who did you hear that from?" Paloma asked, glancing between her father and Max.

Clifton's lips curved into a small smile. "From a few colleagues. It seems the Sterlings are very happy."

Max looked at Paloma. Her eyes widened, sparkling with an unmistakable gleam of triumph. The corners of her mouth twitched upward, and she stood straighter, her shoulders squaring almost imperceptibly.

His chest expanded, filled with admiration for Paloma's talent and the shared joy in their success. He caught himself leaning toward her, drawn by the triumph blazing in her eyes.

Her father gave his full attention to his daughter. "Which brings me to—"

The patter of small feet coming down the hallway captured everyone's attention. A moment later, a blond toddler appeared in the doorway, his eyes widening at the sight of Paloma."Aunt Oma!" he squealed, launching himself toward her.

Paloma's face lit up as she caught the little boy, swinging him into her arms. "Max! What are you doing up, mister?"

Emmaline appeared in the doorway, slightly out of breath. "I'm sorry," she said, brushing a strand of hair from her face. "He heard voices and insisted on saying hello."

Her gaze swept the room, landing on Max. A flicker of recognition passed over her features, followed quickly by a carefully composed smile. It was clear she remembered him from high school and equally clear, she hadn't expected to see him here. And why did she almost look guilty?

Paloma turned to Max, with the toddler settled comfortably on her hip. "This is my nephew, Maxwell, and you know my sister, Emmaline."

Max smiled, offering his hand to the little boy. "Nice to meet you, buddy. I'm Max too."

Still clinging to Paloma, the little boy turned to look at Max. His dark brown eyes, wide with curiosity, traveled over Max's face, taking in every detail. "But, I'm Max," he said.

"That's right. You're both Max!" Paloma laughed, bouncing the toddler gently. "Isn't that fun?"

"Little Maxwell's brow furrowed as he processed this new information, his small fingers playing with the collar of Paloma's shirt. Then his face brightened. "Two Max!" he declared triumphantly, holding up two fingers.

"Smart kid," Max said, grinning. He was still holding out his hand, and this time the toddler reached for it, tiny fingers wrapping around two of Max's larger ones in an adorable approximation of a handshake.

Paloma's mom clapped her hands together, drawing everyone's attention.

"Well, why don't we move this to the dining room? The pizza smells delicious, and the roast is now overcooked and slightly eaten." She glanced at Emmaline, whose cheeks pinkened.

"Sorry. I was hungry and have to leave in half an hour. I'd made plans to meet up with an old friend after Max's bedtime."

"Oh, who?" asked Paloma.

Emmaline pulled in her bottom lip, then let it out. "Kim."

Paloma smiled as if that were the best news ever. The corner of Felix's mouth twitched, and he looked away, saying, "That's great! Have fun."

"Well, you can visit with your brother and sister before you leave," their mom motioned to a large dining room with a formal Cherry-wood table.

"I'll meet you there," Emmaline reached for her son, who was dozing on Paloma's shoulder. His eyelids fluttered, fighting a losing battle against sleep. "I'll put him down and join you in a minute."

She disappeared down the hallway with the sleeping toddler, and the rest of the family went to the dining room. Max leaned into Paloma and asked, "What's with Kim?"

"Old code," she whispered, her breath warm against his ear. "It means she's up to something our parents wouldn't approve of." He returned her conspiratorial smile, feeling momentarily like he was part of the secret.

He chuckled, recalling his teenage antics with his brother. "That takes me back. Drake and I had our codes too. We thought we were so slick." His voice lowered, curiosity piqued. "Any idea who the mystery person might be? Or is that strictly need-to-know basis among siblings?"

Stepping inside the dining room, she said, "Not sure. But I'll find out."

Felix leaned between them. "And you'll let me know?"

"Please, you're the nosiest one out of all of us. You'll get it out of her well before me."

"No lie there," Abigale said before kissing Felix on the cheek.

He grinned and pulled out a chair for her. "You know me, love."

Clifton took the seat at the head of the table. Sophia went to the kitchen and returned with a roast that, in Max's opinion, looked great for warming in the oven well past its time.

"Max, sit here," Paloma said, patting the chair beside her.

He sat, his hand resting on the table, inches from hers. His fingers twitched to take hers, but the space could have been miles for all that was between them.

Until her pinky grazed his knuckle. The touch was featherlight but electric, sending a current up his arm. He glanced at her from the corner of his eye, catching the hint of a smile playing at her mouth.

He turned his hand ever so slightly, palm up, an invitation. Her fingertips traced the lines of his palm, the gesture hidden from view by the table's edge. The rest of the room seemed to fade away, leaving only the whisper of her touch against his skin.

"So, Max, indoor gardens," Clifton said, setting down his napkin. "That's an interesting evolution from commercial landscaping. What drew you away from traditional exterior work?"

Paloma's hand withdrew, but the warmth of her touch lingered. He straightened in his chair, shifting into professional mode. Beneath the table, he pressed his knee against hers—a silent promise that their moment wasn't over, merely postponed.

"Your daughter," he replied. "I had designed a few indoor gardens for businesses, but she presented me with the challenge of working in a home and with a designer. I was too intrigued to pass up the opportunity."

"Ah yes, seeing possibilities," her father said, a slight edge beneath his pleasant tone. "The Sterling project certainly proves your instincts were right this time."

"Clifton," his wife chastised quietly.

Wow, that was shitty. Max opened his mouth to defend Paloma, but she rested a hand on his thigh and shook her head once before turning to her dad. "I've learned from my mistakes. I hope one day you'll notice."

"I have noticed. How could I not? The Sterlings have been showing off and talking about their home to anyone who'll listen. They've been recommending your services to all of their friends and colleagues."

Max glanced at Paloma, noting the spark of excitement in her eyes. Her father seemed harsh, hard to please, so this level of praise from him was probably rare and significant.

"That's . . . that's wonderful to hear," she said, her voice steady but with an undercurrent of delight. "We put a lot of work into that project. I was in charge of the home and guest house. Max designed their conservatory and the landscaping for their deck and the surrounding gardens. The way he integrated those spaces with my interior changes elevated and brought the entire project together."

Her words settled over him like a warm blanket, easing the knot of anxiety he hadn't realized was there. Her acknowledgment of their partnership meant more to him than he cared to admit, especially here with her family.

Clifton raised his eyebrows slightly, his gaze shifting between Paloma and Max. He seemed to be considering the new information, his expression thoughtful. Then he nodded and said, "I see. Well, as I was saying, the hospitality sector could be a great opportunity for you. Your ability to create cohesive spaces inside and out would be highly valued. And I have the perfect project for you."

Her brows pulled together. "You do? For me?"

"Yes, you. Two boutique hotels in Louisiana." Clifton continued, reaching for a slice of garlic bread. "One in New Orleans and the other in Baton Rouge. A hotel flag bought them and wants them redesigned. They want to see how these flagship projects go before doing this to more."

The room grew impossibly hot, thick with Clifton's offer. The formerly appetizing aroma of pizza now turned Max's stomach. His water glass was slick with condensation under his fingers, giving him something to focus on besides the sudden roaring in his ears. Paloma's chair creaked as she shifted away from him.

"Why now?" she asked.

"Because I think it'll be a good fit for you. I've been watching you. You're finally focusing on your career. And you've proven yourself with the Sterling project."

His stomach dropped, and the warm feeling from moments ago began to cool. Not because of the project itself—he'd support her career in a heartbeat—but because he knew Paloma. When things got complicated or personal, work became her refuge. And this opportunity was coming right when they needed to figure out what they meant to each other.

Clifton took a sip of his wine. "Would you be interested?"

She looked from her father to Max. He couldn't read her expression, but he recognized the slight tension in her shoulders—the same tension she'd get right before stepping back, keeping things profes-sional.

"Why are you looking at Max?" her father asked. "Does he have a say in your business?"

His face burned. Yesterday, wrapped in the success of completing the Sterling house and the intimacy of working together, everything had seemed possible. But sitting here now, an outsider at her family table, he suspected he'd been seeing what he wanted to see rather than what was really there.

Chapter Thirty-Five

November 25th, 9:30 p.m.

Paloma's gaze drifted to the mishmash dinner of pizza and roast, the steam rising from the dishes. Her stomach churned, a stark contrast to the usually comforting aroma of her mother's cooking and her favorite pizzeria. The job offer and her father's suspicion that there might be more than work between her and Max hung in the air, mixing with the garlic and tomato sauce.

The Louisiana project could be the stepping stone she needed to establish herself as a versatile, in-demand professional. A business-woman who seamlessly transitioned from residential to commercial spaces, from cozy homes to bustling hotels—she could master both. It was also an opportunity to show the world—and herself—that she wasn't the same naïve woman who almost lost her business and heart.

But what about her and Max? Then again, this could work in her favor with him as well.

"What do you think?" her father asked.

Always the pressure with him. He demanded and wanted every-thing immediately. That would be another issue if she took the job. She'd constantly be drawing boundaries.

"I don't know, Dad. I need more details," she replied. "There are a couple of small projects I've committed to. I'd need to make sure they don't conflict."

"I'm sure you could juggle it," her father said dismissively.

"And it sounds like an amazing opportunity," her mother added.

There was no doubt it'd be good for her career. And while she'd never admit it to Max, the timing of this opportunity was perfect. The thought of staying, of letting their relationship run its course saddened her. Her past had taught her the same lesson: once men got to know her, they left. Hell, even her father was nearly a stranger. But losing Max would damage her heart. A slow withdrawal will be better, safer. The fall wouldn't hurt as much when he inevitably walked away.

"When does it start?" she asked.

"After the holidays, in mid-February," her father said. "But I'm leaving tomorrow to check out the sites, and you'll need to go with me if you're interested."

"Tomorrow! Why would you wait until now to tell me? Do you think I don't have other projects?"

Her father took a bite of roast, taking his time. After swallowing, he said, "I had to see how the Sterling project went. And you'll have time. After this trip, you'll have a few months until it starts."

She pushed away her plate. Eating was impossible. "And you didn't consider that I might have other things to do," she snapped.

He waved a hand. "When we talked a few weeks back, you told me you didn't have anything big after Sterling. So, do you?"

She shook her head. "No, but—"

"But nothing. This is big. Could be bigger than what even the Sterlings could do for your career."

She wanted to look at Max, but by doing so again, her dad would return them to the spotlight. And admitting she and Max were more than business partners would take away all credibility in her father's eyes. Plus, everything her father said was true. Having experience in the home and hospitality sector would be amazing for her career.

"I need to think about it." She took a sip of her wine.

"Then think about it while in New Orleans. Tell me at the end of the trip," her father said. "It's only three days."

She nodded, her fingers tightening around the smooth glass, fighting to keep her expression neutral. To her left, Max shifted in his chair, drawing her attention. She resisted the urge to look at him, acutely aware of her father's scrutinizing gaze.

Felix cleared his throat. "Hey, Max, how'd that bid go for the winter festival at that ski resort opening up?"

"The one that's opening in the next town over?" her mom asked.

Max nodded. "Yup. They want a grand opening party with snow and ice sculptures, live music, and games."

Grateful for the change in subject, she quickly glanced at Max. Their gazes met briefly, and she saw all the questions he wanted to ask, but she wasn't ready to answer.

"I think we'll get it," he replied. It'll be something slightly different from our usual projects, but it will be fun."

Her father leaned forward, interest in his eyes. "What exactly is your role as a landscape architect in this?"

"My role . . ." Max began, then paused, clearly distracted. "Sorry. My role is designing the outdoor spaces for the festival."

Max reached for his drink, taking a quick sip before continuing. "I'll design temporary and permanent landscape elements for a winter wonderland setting. This includes planning spaces for ice sculptures, creating a layout for a snow maze, and designing an area for an outdoor ice bar."

Her mother's eyes widened. "That sounds lovely! But how does landscaping work in winter conditions?"

"We'll focus on creating spaces that will showcase winter features." Max rolled his fork between his fingers. He glanced her way, offering a quick smile, a flash of connection she knew better than to trust. "For instance, we'll incorporate evergreen plantings that look beautiful under snow. The lighting schemes will highlight ice formations and snow-covered areas. But everything will work double-duty in the summer, creating shaded retreats for the hikers."

Her father nodded slowly, his expression thoughtful. "And how does this tie into the existing resort architecture?"

The dinner dragged on. She pushed food around her plate, appetite long gone. And when her mom asked if anyone wanted coffee, Paloma seized her chance.

"It's been a long day, and I still need to take Max home," she said, rising quickly.

"And possibly pack?" her father asked. "I'm heading out at six in the evening."

"I'll call you in the morning," she replied.

He nodded. "Fine."

"Thank you for dinner; it was delicious," Max said, and his too-quick movements told her he was as anxious to get out of there as her.

They made their hasty goodbyes, exchanging quick hugs and promises to get together soon. The cool night air hit her face as they stepped outside, offering sweet relief from the stuffy dining room.

Once settled in the truck, Max's cologne, a scent she'd grown to associate with comfort, filled the small space. For a brief moment, she was tempted to take his hand, to accept the reassuring warmth of his skin against hers. The urge to lean over and kiss him, to forget about New Orleans and her father's expectations—her ambitions, her fears—was overwhelming.

Before she could do either, he put the truck in reverse and drove toward his home. The engine's hum filled the tense silence, punctuated only by the rhythmic click of the turn signal. Streetlights cast alternating patterns of light and shadow across Max's face, highlighting his slight frown. Her mind was too full to figure out what to say, and it seemed Max had nothing to say.

He finally spoke when they were a few miles from his house. "So . . . New Orleans, huh?"

She glanced out the side window. "Yes. It's a great opportunity."

"And us?" he asked, parking in his driveway.

"Max." She pulled her car keys from her purse. His house was dark and lonely—just like her future would be if she had let him in completely. "Can we hold off on this conversation until I get back? I should only be gone a few days." That was all she needed, a few days to think alone, without Max's summer blue eyes and perfect smile.

His jaw tightened. "No. You said we talk about us when we returned. We're back."

"And I have a lot on my mind."

"Except me," he snapped.

"That isn't fair. This isn't about you. It's about my career."

"Yeah, yeah, I know. You'll always pick it over me."

"I didn't realize I had to pick."

He sighed, looking at his house, then back at her. "You don't. But I need to know where I stand with you."

"Fine, do you want me to lie to you? Tell you everything will work out even though accepting the job will change things between us."

"The change doesn't have to be bad. We can make it work." He took her hand, his thumb circling her palm. "I could fall for you."

Her heart soared, then deflated like a knife twisting in her chest. Because "could fall" meant he hadn't—and he wouldn't. Distance would creep in. He'd meet someone else, someone less complicated, less afraid. She'd seen this movie before.

She slid her hand from his. "Could we please put this on hold until I get back?"

"Fine," He sighed, opening his door, the interior light blinding her. "Goodbye, Paloma. Enjoy Louisiana."

He paused with his hand on the door. His gaze was heavy, and it took every ounce of her self-discipline not to turn and meet those eyes she was growing to love. She held her breath, her heart pounding. But the moment passed, and she heard the soft click of the truck door closing.

He walked away, not looking back.

Chapter Thirty-Six

November 26th, 9 a.m.

Sunlight slanted through Max's bedroom blinds, and he watched the shadows creep across his ceiling. The morning stretched before him like an endless void, punctuated only by the promise he'd made last week—breakfast at his mother's house.

He should be in his kitchen making his mom's favorite berry muffins. Instead, he lay in lethargic limbo replaying last night's dinner at Paloma's parents' house. She was probably there right now, planning and packing with her dad—a scenario notably absent of him.

He should get up. Stop being an asshole. His mom had been fretting over him constantly since the car accident, bringing over food, calling, and stopping by. She was yet another person he'd managed to burden with his jackass decisions. The thought of facing her today, of watching her eyes track his movements for signs of pain or distress, had his chest tightening. She'd see right through any attempt to pretend he was fine. He'd end up worrying her more if he visited.

Rolling over, he patted blindly at his nightstand for his phone, intent on making the call that would disappoint her again. His fingers brushed against the cool metal as his doorbell chimed, the sound jarring in the morning quiet.

"What the fuck?" he muttered, dragging himself upright.

The last thing he needed was company. It meant admitting the day had to start and that life was moving forward whether he was ready or not. He crossed to his front door in quick, angry strides. He yanked it open and found Drake on the porch, looking far too alert for the early hour.

"What are you doing here?" Max demanded.

His brother grinned. "Good morning, Grumpy McGrump. I'm making sure you don't make our mom cry by bailing on breakfast."

Max blinked. "How the hell did you know I was thinking about bailing?"

Drake shrugged. "I've heard from a friend that Paloma's heading to Louisiana. Are you going to let me in, or should we have this conversation on your porch?"

He stepped back, and his brother came inside. "How in the world do you even know? Didn't you drive in this morning?" Max asked.

"Last night," his brother replied. "Do you have coffee?" He made his way toward the kitchen.

Hadn't Emmaline left early to meet someone? Max's spine straightened as the dots formed and connected. "Who do you know that would even know about the Louisiana job, let alone so quickly?"

"Like I said, a friend." Drake suddenly seemed way too focused on the coffee machine.

Max leaned against the counter, crossing his legs at the ankles. "Who did you spend last night with?"

"I don't kiss and tell."

"You're not gonna be able to kiss anybody after I punch you in the mouth," Max grumbled.

"Temper, temper," his brother laughed.

"Are you seeing Paloma's sister?" Max asked.

"Define seeing."

"Great," Max muttered, pinching the bridge of his nose. Emmaline deserved better than his brother's usual hit-and-run routine, especially fresh off her divorce. "Try not to be yourself with this one, okay?"

Drake's eyes flashed, his easy smile hardening at the edges. "Don't worry about me, or I should say, her. She's working some stuff out of her system. We're enjoying each other." He grabbed two insulated mugs, handing one to Max. "Focus on yourself. And Paloma."

He filled his coffee and said, "There's nothing to focus on. She's in Louisiana. We'll talk when she gets back." If she has the time. Damn, that thought was bitter as the brewing coffee.

Drake opened a cupboard, closed it, and opened another. "What are you looking for?" Max asked.

"Ingredients for the muffins. It's too late to make them here. We'll take the stuff over and make them at Mom's."

A laugh huffed out of Max despite himself. "By 'we'll' you mean me, right?"

"Yup."

"Get changed. We'll drive over there together. We can talk."

"I don't need to talk."

Drake rolled his eyes. "Don't be that dude."

"What dude?"

"The one who won't talk about his feelings, but will drown in them, making himself and everybody around him miserable."

"Then don't be around me, asshole," Max replied without any heat.

"No can do. I kinda like you. And—"

Max raised his brows. "Kinda?"

"I'm still pissed about my Lego city you destroyed."

"Dude, I was eight."

"Time doesn't heal all wounds," Drake sighed theatrically. "Tell me what we need to bring. I'll gather them while you get dressed."

Max did both, and they were in his brother's Mercedes twenty minutes later. Drake pulled onto the main road, his usual lead foot noticeably gentler on the gas. Great. Even his brother was treating him like he might break.

"Just say whatever you're thinking," Max grumbled, watching suburban houses blur past. "The silence is worse than your usual smartass comments."

Drake clicked his tongue. "You're not gonna like it."

"When has that ever stopped you?"

"Fair point." His brother turned down their old street, muscle memory making them lean into the curve by the Montgomery's house. "I think you're making a big deal out of Paloma taking the job."

Max snorted. "How? You act like I begged her to stay. Or shouted at her, threatening to break up if she took the job." Like that was even an option. They had to be a couple to break up. And she wasn't interested in anything beyond sex.

Drake pulled into their mom's driveway, killing the engine. "I know you, brother. I saw it in your face when you opened the door. You're giving up." Before Max could respond, he grabbed the bag of ingredients and headed to the front door.

Was he? Maybe it was time.

He followed his brother up the familiar brick path and nudged him aside to unlock the front door. "Mom," Drake called. "Your favorite son is here!"

The moment Max stepped inside, it hit him: the aroma of freshly baked quiche, warm butter-kissed pastry, savory roasted leeks, smoky bacon, and the rich perfume of eggs and gruyère melting together in perfect harmony. His stomach growled, betraying how ready it was for something other than the sad bowl of cereal he'd been planning to eat while wallowing in his house.

"Oh, didn't know you knew about my other son, James," she joked.

"Haha, Mom," Drake said, entering the kitchen with Max behind him.

Their mom stood in her favorite apron, the blue one with tiny cats all over it. A smudge of flour was on her cheek. "I thought it was funny," she said before pulling what looked like quiche from the oven. I was about to call you two."

She set the pan down and wrapped them both in a hug that somehow managed to encompass them despite their height difference. The counter was cluttered with cooling racks and mixing bowls, and the morning sun streamed through the window over the sink, catching the steam that rose from everything fresh-baked. Drake was sneaking pieces of French toast when their mom turned back to the oven. Max had to admit that his brother had been right to drag him here. The familiarity of their mom's kitchen and the constant stream of questions and commentary would leave no room for brooding. It was exactly what he needed, even if he'd never say it out loud.

"How'd the Sterling house go?" His mom asked.

Had that project ended a few days ago? It felt so much longer. "It was good."

"It was good," his mom repeated, one brow raising. "That's it. That's all I get? A morose, 'it was good.' Were they happy? I mean, of course, they were; my incredibly talented son was working for them.

Do you think that it'll lead to more of these types of projects with Paloma?"

He emptied the contents of his bag on the counter and grabbed a large bowl from the cupboard. "Doubtful."

The sound of the metal whisk hitting the pan silenced, and his mom turned to him. "Why? Did something happen? Were they not satisfied?

"No, all of that is great. They were incredibly happy. Better than we had hoped." He told her about the positive feedback and the upcoming magazine interview. However, the glow and excitement that had surrounded him had faded.

His mom took the same stance he had earlier with Drake. She leaned against the counter, crossing her legs at the ankles. "What's the problem?"

"Paloma's taking on a large project in Louisiana, so she won't be able to take on new ones here for a while," he said flatly.

"Aw, well, maybe that's for the best. You're pretty busy without another business venture." She picked back up the whisk. "And visiting Paloma will be fun. Louisiana has so much to do."

"We'll see." He busied himself mixing the muffin ingredients.

His mom rested a hand on his arm, stilling him. "Why? Did she break up with you?"

"No." He stepped away from her comfort. "We weren't even in an actual, official relationship, so I doubt she'll think long-distance is worth the effort."

"Why not? You're a catch."

His mother's earnest expression and vote of confidence only made his chest tighter. He shot her a "yeah, right" look—the one that pulled at a corner of his mouth and had his eyebrows climbing toward his hairline. It was the same expression he'd been giving her since he was a teenager who thought he knew everything.

The whisk returned to the counter with a light smack. "What was that look for?"

"Come on, Mom, you know it, and I know it. I'm an impulsive fuck up. Why get entangled with me?"

"Max, you have a successful business and a great circle of friends. A home. And it seems working with you has benefitted her a great deal. I don't see where this belief you're a screw up is coming from."

His title as a landscape architect might have gotten them clients, but his impulsiveness nearly cost them both jobs. He shouldn't have come on to Paloma at the Thompson house. He shouldn't have fallen asleep at the wheel. Hell, he shouldn't have let his curiosity lead to that night with his ex in Chicago. Had he thought through the consequences of his actions, they wouldn't be haunting him. Maybe Paloma would be more interested in him.

He couldn't tell his mother about any of this, so he said, "Aren't you the one who always says I'm impulsive?"

"Yes, you are on the impulsive side, but not wild. And while you may have been reckless at one point, that was a long time ago. And I'm sorry if I made you think I viewed you as reckless."

"I still am. I change my mind constantly. I go back and forth. When we first met at The Hill, I turned Paloma down."

"You turned her down?" Drake said. "Why in the hell would you do that?"

Max startled, forgetting his brother was there. "Long story, but yes, I did. Then, I almost immediately changed my mind once we started working together, even though she made it clear she thought a professional relationship was better. I made everything more difficult."

"Did you push something she didn't want?" his brother asked. "Did you wear her down? Or did you only make your feelings known?"

"I'm not an asshole, or desperate," Max huffed. "I'm not gonna force myself on someone not interested."

"Then let yourself off the damn hook," Drake said. "Paloma isn't going to do anything she doesn't want to do."

He had a point. Paloma's strong will and assertiveness were two of the things he loved about her. And yes, he could admit he was falling for her.

"True," he said. "But the fact remains that my impulsiveness had made our working relationship more difficult. And in turn, she's probably happy to get rid of me. From the start, she'd said she wanted things simple. That wasn't us."

"If you care about her, you should make sure she knows," his mom said.

"This comes from the woman who told me not to pursue someone I'm working with."

"Well, son. It's too late for that. You did, and it is obvious you care about her. Impulsiveness is one thing, but are you also afraid to go after what you want? I see how you hold back, waiting for others to decide if you're worth choosing." His mom wiped her hands on her apron and moved closer, placing a palm on his cheek. "And Max, you are worth choosing. The question is, are you brave enough to let Paloma make that choice for herself instead of deciding for her?"

His brother stole a spoonful of the muffin mix and said around it, "And this isn't about you, asshole."

"Drake," their mom chastised him.

At the same time, Max asked, "What the hell are you talking about?"

"Lotte mentioned Paloma was engaged—"

"Who's Lotte?" Their mom looked between them. "How—"

"A friend," Drake said, probably hoping to cut off more questions.

"Yea. The guy screwed her over. What's that to do with me?" Max asked.

"Don't you think her trust in men, in commitment, would be all kinds of fu—" He glanced at their mom. "All kind of screwed up?"

He turned to his bowl, dumped in the frozen berries, and mechanically folded them in the muffin mix. Drake had a point. And her ex-fiancé wasn't the only one who'd hurt her.

And Max was no better. He hadn't stolen from her, then tried to make her feel like it was her fault, but he hadn't shown her that he was willing to fight for her, for them. Instead of talking to her, he'd been ready to let them fade away.

"Earth to Max," his mom's voice cut through his thoughts. "You're going to crush those berries into juice if you keep stirring like that."

"Sorry," he muttered, setting the bowl down. "I am an idiot."

His brother snorted. "Only now realizing this?"

"Drake," their mother chided him, then turned to Max. "Care to elaborate?"

"I've been so caught up in my head, thinking about all the ways this could go wrong, that I almost . . ." He ran his hand down his jeans. "Listen, I'm sorry, but I have to bail on breakfast."

"Are you planning on running over to Paloma's right now?" Drake asked.

"Um yeah, how'd you—"

"Really, weren't you bitching like five minutes ago about being impulsive?"

Max grinned. "Piss off. I've decided being impulsive isn't always a bad thing. Like when I need to talk to someone important before they leave the damn state." He kissed his mom's cheek and headed for the door.

"They took an early flight," Drake called after him.

Max halted, but only for a second, then headed for his car. He was about to take impulsiveness to a whole new level.

CHAPTER THIRTY-SEVEN

November 26th, 4:00 p.m.

Paloma leaned against the iron railing of her balcony. The metal was warm from the New Orleans sun. Below, tourists weaved between locals on Bourbon Street, some clutching orange to-go cups from Café du Monde, many other sporting plastic beads, and hurricane glasses. Their laughter floated up to her like music from a party she wasn't invited to.

Her fingers traced the hollow beneath her collarbone, pressing against the ache. Her phone sat heavy in her pocket. She should have called Max before leaving. But wasn't this exactly what she'd wanted? Space. Distance. A chance to protect her heart.

Ceramic clinked against the mosaic table. "What do you think of the two hotels?" her dad asked.

She turned to him, grateful for the distraction of work. Historic buildings differed from the residential renovations she was used to, but the challenge kept her mind busy—at least until tonight, in quiet hours when her regret would visit. She wrapped her hands around a tall glass of lemonade. "The structure and history within the walls are amazing. I've got so many ideas."

"The site has an unusually generous lot size for a boutique property in an urban context," her father said. "However, the current outdoor dining terrace layout doesn't optimize the guest experience or operational efficiency. It needs a complete redesign to better integrate with the building's flow."

"Did you see the skeletal remains of a garden?" She stared, unfocused, at her drink. Max's face swam into view—that contemplative look he'd get when studying a space, seeing past what was, to what could be. His shoulders would square slightly, his head tilting as if measuring angles only he could see, and his eyes alive with the quiet passion he had brought to every design. He took that same careful attention to everything: how sunlight fell across a courtyard, how people naturally moved through a space, the secret language of roots and soil.

He'd looked at her that way too, studying her like she was a garden worth tending, worth the patience of seasons. Her chest tightened. She'd run from that look, from the weight of possibility it carried.

The irony wasn't lost on her—she'd taken this job to keep things casual, to prevent herself from falling too deep, and now here she was, missing him with an intensity that made it hard to breathe. Maybe running hadn't protected her heart at all. Maybe it had just given her new ways to break it.

"Are you dating Max?" her father asked.

Her hand jerked, the slice of lemon hit the side of the glass. The liquid settled, but the ripples in her chest didn't.

"Why are you asking—" The words caught in her throat, too thin to carry the weight of denial. She swallowed and tried again, aiming for professional detachment.

"The garden you mentioned. I like the idea of bringing it back," her father said. "And the Baton Rouge hotel sits on three acres. The outside should be as impressive as the changes we have planned. I looked up his landscape business and his designs. He has a great eye. I wouldn't mind getting a bid from him."

Her pathetic heart jumped and clapped at the chance to see Max. "You should," she replied. "Max and everyone who works for him are incredibly talented."

"Good to know. But you didn't answer my question. Are you seeing him?"

"Why does it matter?" Each syllable landed like a small stone between them. Her father rarely asked about her personal life—why start now, and why about Max?

"For this job, it doesn't. As my daughter it does."

She traced the mosaic pattern on the table with her fingertip, gathering her thoughts. "Why does it matter 'as your daughter?'" she asked, keeping her voice carefully neutral. The question had an odd texture in her mouth, like tasting a familiar food prepared by unfamiliar hands. Where was this sudden fatherly concern coming from? Mom was usually the one who noticed these things. Dad just . . . worked.

"Because this one seems worth knowing." He covered his mouth and muttered, "unlike that asshole ex-fiancé. The leech."

A smile tugged on her lips. "You hated him from the start, didn't you?"

"Richard was a shifty shit. The kind of guy waiting for everyone to take care of him." Her father wasn't wrong. "But Max seems like a good man."

"He's the best," she admitted softly. "But no, we aren't seeing each other." It wasn't a lie. They were never a couple. Though he'd felt like hers.

"Huh, I read that wrong. I was certain—" A knock had them turning toward the sound. Her father stood. "It's probably Tim with the old blueprints of this place."

When he disappeared into her room, Paloma leaned forward, resting her elbows on the ornate balcony railing. The crowd ebbed and flowed like a tipsy tide—tourists with their to-go cups and flashing cameras weaving between locals who navigated the street with practiced ease. They celebrated below while her heart ached above. Had she sabotaged something beautiful out of fear?

She closed her eyes, letting the weak winter sun caress her skin. Everything about him had felt so right. The way he'd match her impulsive ideas with his wild schemes, feeding off each other's energy until they were breathless with laughter or passion or both. His kindness, that crooked smile that made her heart stutter . . .

And sweet Jesus, the things that man could do with his hands.

What was the point of running from how he made her feel when her thoughts always circled back to him? She was certain that distance wouldn't dim him; nothing would.

She pulled out her phone with trembling fingers, her thumb hovering over Max's name in her contacts. With a deep breath, she pressed his call and lifted the phone to her ear, ready to stop running from what mattered.

A throat cleared, and she turned from the street. Her dad's frame filled the doorway. He gave her a look she'd never seen before—softer than his usual business exterior, almost awkward in its tenderness. It was strange and touching all at once, this glimpse of the dad he might have been if they'd spent more time talking about life instead of work.

"The man you said you aren't seeing is here to see you," he said, stepping onto the balcony and to the right.

Her heart stuttered. Max stood in the arch of the door, clutching a huge bouquet of dark purple flowers mixed with beautiful white ones. His phone rang from inside his jacket. She hit "end call," setting her phone on the table. The noise from his pocket silenced.

Those summer blues she'd tried so hard not to think about crinkled at the corners, his eyes dancing with a warmth that had haunted her dreams. The blooms trembled slightly in his grip, betraying a nervousness that matched her own.

"What are you doing here?" Her heart raced, hardly daring to believe he was there on her balcony, holding flowers and wearing that sunshine smile she loved.

"Could we talk?" His gaze bounced from her to her dad and back to her. Yeah, she'd rather have this conversation without her dad watching them.

But he seemed too amused to retreat quietly. His lip twitched, and he asked, "About work? And only work?"

She chuckled. Who knew her dad had a sense of humor? It was as dry as dirt, but there. A warm glow bloomed in her chest, discovering that her father wasn't only blueprints and business plans. These unexpected moments of fatherly concern showed her that New Orleans might offer more than a fantastic work opportunity.

"No, Dad," she said, grinning.

He nodded, then looked at Max. "It's nice to see you again."

"You as well," he replied. He and her father continued talking, but she didn't catch it because of the unique design of the fuchsia flower. "Is that the clitoris flower?" she asked.

Her dad coughed. "The what?"

"It's a butterfly pea. The other is lisianthus," Max replied, sounding a little strangled.

Lisianthus? Her heart melted. It was the flower he'd used to describe her skin. That he'd not only come to New Orleans but brought these specific blooms spread warmth through her chest like honey. It was perfectly Max: turning even small gestures profound through careful attention to detail. He hadn't grabbed just any pretty flowers, but chosen ones that told their story. Without words, he was telling her those quiet moments had mattered to him too.

"Well," her father said, checking his watch with exaggerated interest, "I have that call with the contractors about the foundation work." He pushed away from the wall, his shoes clicking against the weathered tiles. At the doorway, he paused, looking between them with that same unfamiliar softness. "The terrace plans can wait until tomorrow, Paloma."

She nodded, grateful for his discretion even as her stomach fluttered with nervous energy. Just before stepping inside, her father turned back to Max. "Those are beautiful flowers. My mother used to grow lisianthus in her garden." He smiled a real smile that made him look years younger. "She always said the best gardens grow from patience and care."

Her father's gaze met hers, gentle and knowing in a way she'd never seen before, then he disappeared into the cool darkness of the room beyond, leaving her with Max and only the sounds of Bourbon Street rising between them like a tide.

Max held out the flowers. "I should have been clearer last night. I said I could fall for you. That's a lie."

Her heart died in his pause.

"I'm already falling for you."

And then it revived.

She stared at the offered bouquet, her hands remaining firmly on the railing. The metal had cooled beneath her palms, or maybe all the warmth had moved to her heart. His words struck at the soul of what she'd been trying to avoid by taking this job. Because she was falling too—had been falling for months.

"I . . . then why did you walk away?"

Below, a jazz band started playing, the mournful wail of a trumpet climbing up to wrap around them like Spanish moss. "I wasn't sure what you wanted," he said. "Everything you did seemed designed to keep me at a distance."

She had, and it had been cruel. "You're right," she admitted softly, the words catching in her throat. "I kept one foot out the door, didn't I? Always ready to run." She gave a quiet, rueful laugh. "And then I got mad at you for not chasing me."

The corner of his mouth twitched, an almost-smile that always made her heart skip. "We're quite a pair, aren't we? Me waiting for a sign, you waiting for me just to know."

She stepped toward him, close enough to catch his scent of cedar and possibility. "So where does that leave us?"

"That depends," he said, offering the bouquet again. This time, she took it, her fingers brushing his. "Are you still running?"

The flowers were cool and damp against her palms, their fragrance rising like a promise. "No," she said finally, meeting his eyes. "I'm ready to grow roots."

He cupped her cheek, kissing her gently. Her skin heated at the intimacy of his touch, at the rightness of being here with him.

"Max," she said. "I'm falling for you too."

He bracketed her in the corner of the balcony, his arms on each side of her, close enough that their bodies touched. "Then let's grow something beautiful together." He pulled her closer, claiming her mouth in a kiss that tasted of promise and possibility, of gardens yet to bloom.

He drew her closer, his kiss deep and sweet as chicory coffee. She melted into him, the world narrowing to this moment, to only them. Running his hands up her back and into her hair, tilting his head, he whispered against her mouth, "I know it's only been a day." He laughed. "Not even a full day, but damn, I've missed you."

"I don't deserve you," she sighed.

"Don't say that." He leaned back and then kissed her nose, followed by her forehead. "We're perfect for each other. We deserve each other."

He angled his head, and their kiss went from sweet to heat in a heartbeat. His closeness wasn't enough, and she pressed tighter, moaning into his mouth.

A sharp whistle pierced the air, followed by the distinctive clatter of plastic beads hitting the balcony tiles. Paloma broke away with a laugh, glancing down at the strand of purple beads now coiled near their feet. Below, a group of tourists raised their hurricane glasses in a cheerful salute. "Keep it going," someone shouted, and another hollered, "That's hot!" followed by wolf whistles and a, "Take it off, baby!"

Laughing, Paloma turned slightly from Max and looked at their feet. A tangle of purple and green beads dangled from the balcony's black and rust bars. She nudged the beads at her feet until they fell. "Show's over, I'm not showing you my boobs," she said.

A woman shouted, "What about him?"

"He's not showing anything either." She winked at the blonde below. "At least not to you."

The woman placed two fingers in her mouth and let out an impressive whistle, followed by two thumbs up. Paloma laughed harder, in love with this city, the day, and the man holding her hand.

She led him inside her room, not bothering to close the balcony and twisting around to kiss him. "Show me how much you've missed me," she breathed, nuzzling the warm spot beneath his ear where his cologne mixed with something distinctly him—like sun-warmed cedar and fresh earth after a rain.

"I'll start with a kiss." His lips brushed her temple. "Then with your shiver when I touch you here." His fingers traced her collarbone, that hollow that had ached for him. "Followed by the soft sounds you make . . ." He pressed his mouth to her throat. "Then how perfectly you fit against me, and me inside you."

They'd reached the bed, and he sat; she straddled him. "I know you like to go slow," she said, removing his shirt. "But I need you like I need to breathe."

He hiked her dress to the tops of her thighs. "We've got our whole lives to savor each other. Let's indulge now."

"Thank all the gods in the world." She rose to her knees, lifted her arms, and allowed him to remove her dress.

"Okay, maybe I need a moment to savor this sight." His hands run up her sides, stopping at her breasts. There, he ran his fingers along the lace of her red bra, leaving a trail of fire where he touched.

"God, Paloma. This color on you . . ." His busy hands moved down her stomach to her matching panties. "More red. More lace. All perfection," he muttered, pressing his thumb against her clit. She gasped, rocking against his jean-clad erection.

Scooting back, she unbuttoned and unzipped him. She gripped the waist of his jeans and boxer briefs, sliding them and herself down his body. Craving his taste as much as the feel of his body, she stopped to lick his pre-cum before taking him deep into her mouth and throat. His groan could probably be heard down Bourbon Street.

He slid his hands into her hair, pulling slightly, turning her on even more. As if he couldn't help himself, his hips rocked. Unable to take all of him, she wrapped a hand around him and worked the rhythm and pace she knew he loved.

The curses and sounds from him were nearly feral. His tugs a little harder on her hair. She reveled in both. "Stop," he grunted, "You feel too fucking good. But this isn't going to end until I'm buried inside you, and you're coming apart around me."

One hundred percent in love with his plan, she gave him one final suck that ripped another guttural groan from him and then she kissed her way up his body. Laying on him, she traced the line of his jaw with trembling fingers, her heart racing from desire and a certainty thrumming through her veins. This was Max—her Max, who studied gardens with the same care he studied her, who chose flowers that told their story, who flew across states to fight for them.

"I have a condom, but I'm on birth control . . ." she whispered against his lips, the words carrying all the trust she'd found in his steady hands and patient heart.

He looked into her eyes. "I've never not used a condom." Rolling her onto her back, he settled between her legs and asked, "Why do you want to go without?"

"I've also never not used one, and it is probably too soon to tell you this, but I'm all in with you. I believe with all my heart you're the man I'll spend the rest of my life with, and because of that," she drew a finger down his chest, "I want to be as close to you as possible."

He thrust slowly and gently inside her. Then stilled, saying, "Magnificent mind, inside and outside of the bedroom. I'm the luckiest man."

Every inch of her body was alive where his gaze roamed over her. Desire darkened his eyes but softened them into something deeper that reached beyond hunger. He drew her close, wrapping her in his arms as his hands slid over her back, his fingers making her skin hum. Each touch was a promise, his breath against her neck igniting a heat that left her aching and restless. She pressed closer, craving the sensation of his heartbeat thrumming against hers.

Her need quickened as his hands moved over her with a reverence that took her breath away. He knew exactly where to linger, where to draw out her sighs and soft gasps, stoking her desire until it built like a slow, sweeping tide. She melted into the sensations, letting go of the guarded distance she'd held, surrendering fully to their love.

Their movements became a cascade of urgency, each kiss, each touch drawing her deeper into the steady rhythm they created together. She clung to him, solid and real beneath her hands, grounding her as her breaths grew shallower, in sync with his. Their heartbeats blurred, lost in each other as everything beyond them dissolved. Her release crested and broke, a wave that left her gasping, every nerve sparking alive in its wake, just as his own shuddered into being. Their bodies found a breathless symmetry.

They melted into each other like watercolors bleeding together in the velvet silence that followed. His palm found a home over her heart, his thumb painting drowsy patterns across her skin. She traced the familiar landscape of his jaw, marveling at how a simple touch could hold entire worlds within it.

"How did you find out where I was staying?" She indicated the room, where bright afternoon sunlight streamed through the open French doors, highlighting the faded pattern of the once-elegant wallpaper, its edges curling slightly near the crown molding.

"I called Felix. He told me."

"But why didn't you wait? My dad had said at dinner this would be a quick trip."

The mattress shifted as Max propped himself on one elbow, the antique bed frame creaking softly beneath them. "I've been to your house. I saw the bookshelf full of romance novels and figured you appreciate the 'grand gesture.'"

She rolled onto her side to face him, impressed and intrigued, as a burst of laughter from the street punctuated the moment. The gauzy curtains danced in the afternoon breeze, carrying the sweet, warm scent of pralines from the shop below. "How do you know about the 'grand gesture?' Your mom?"

"Wow, that's sexist." He pulled her closer, making her squeal as he tickled her ribs. The ceiling fan wobbled slightly as it spun, its chain tinkling against the dusty glass shade. "I'll have you know Jackson and Asher got me into them. His sister, your friend, Hope, dared them to read one. They did and liked them. Now, she's their book dealer with the best recommendations. They might have passed a few my way."

She kissed both his cheeks, relishing the taste of salt on his skin and the solid warmth of his body against hers. "I'll have to thank her."

Curled into each other, their heartbeats steady and sure, she smiled against his chest. She'd believed she was too much—too intense, demanding, and hungry for life and love. But Max didn't just handle her fire; he matched it, stoked it, and made it burn brighter. She wasn't too much at all. She was exactly enough, exactly right, for the one person who mattered.

Epilogue

May 20th, 4:30 p.m.

Max leaned in the booth at The Hill, the cracked vinyl-covered cushion releasing a leathery crackle-squeak. Paloma stole a french fry from his plate, and something soft and unfurled in his chest at its casual intimacy. His gaze drifted to the copper-topped bar where they'd first officially met—where she'd perched on that corner stool in that red dress that had nearly stopped his heart, though he'd been too proud then to admit it. The setting sun painted her skin in shades of gold through the window beside them, and his pulse did its familiar dance—the one it had been practicing since she'd first turned business into pleasure with a stolen old-fashioned and talk of indoor gardens.

The same band playing the night they'd first met was on stage, their sultry bass filling the air. Strange how much had changed since that evening, yet some things remained the same. Her light sweater fell off one shoulder, so different from the red dress she'd worn like armor that first night. But instead of her sharp, impatient fingernails tapping the bar top, they traced lazy patterns on his palm. The ice in their drinks clinked with the gentle melody of contentment rather than the nervous rhythm of his restless stirring.

"I still can't believe Lilith's brother bought this place," Paloma said, breaking into his thoughts. He followed her gaze to his friend chatting with a couple near the spot where they'd first shaken hands, pretending the touch didn't spark something deeper than a business arrangement.

"I can. The last time we all hung out, it was like his old life was slowly killing his soul. You should've seen his face when he told me he'd made an offer. Like a kid on Christmas morning," he replied, remembering how different things had been then: Tate trapped, Asher looking at Lilith, and Max stuck in a groove so deep he couldn't even see the edges. He glanced at the same dented and scuffed antique mirror behind the bar that had caught Paloma's reflection that night, her eyes bright with possibility as she pitched him the project that would change everything.

"That's great. He seems like a nice guy," she replied.

"Uh, oh," he teased. "I know you have a thing for nice guys."

Paloma turned from the crowded restaurant that was slowly becoming a bar as more tables were cleared away for dancing. "Only one certain nice guy," she said, her gaze falling to his few remaining fries. He pushed his plate closer, anticipating her next snack attack.

"Speaking of Christmas." She reached into her bag and pulled out a thick envelope, and she withdrew the latest issue of Sterling's magazine, Hearth & Haven. "Did you see? They reposted snippets of our interview."

He took the glossy pages, studying their photo. They stood in the conservatory, sunlight streaming through the glass ceiling, highlighting the blooming climbing roses. "We look good together," he said softly, meaning far more than the photograph.

"We are good together," she replied, covering his hand with hers. The gold band on her finger caught the light—not an engagement ring, not yet. They were too busy to plan a wedding, but he wanted to show his commitment. His hands had trembled as he'd given it to her. And she'd cried happy tears when he'd explained what it meant to him—a promise to grow together, like the homes and hotels they created.

The past few months hadn't been easy. Building a relationship while juggling projects in two states tested them. But where he'd once seen his impulsiveness as a flaw, it was a treasure to her. She loved his surprise visits. And when those weren't possible, they made the most of video calls.

The last part of the Louisiana project would be smooth sailing, a mix of pleasure and business. He and his team would arrive in another week to work on the gardens and grounds of the two hotels.

The bass notes from the band shifted into something slower, more intimate. He recognized the opening notes—their song, the one that had been playing that first night at the bar when she'd pitched him the Thompson project. He'd been too caught up in his doubts back then to notice how the melody suited them. Now, watching her sway unconsciously to the rhythm, he had to have her in his arms.

"Dance with me?" he asked.

She nodded, stealing one more fry before he helped her from the booth. Her palm slid into his, their fingers intertwining. Walking to the small dance floor across the room, away from the tables, she melted against him, her head finding that perfect spot between his neck and shoulder. The soft notes of her perfume made his breath catch and his body warm.

He rested his hand on the curve of her spine, right above her waist, recalling how he'd once denied himself even the briefest touch, convinced he'd only ever be her second choice. Every subtle shift of her body aligned with his now, like puzzle pieces clicking into place. She curved against him like a vine finding its trellis—fitting, given how their love had grown from that conversation about indoor gardens.

"Remember the first time here when we truly talked?" she murmured against his neck, her breath warm.

"Mm-hmm." He ran his hand up and down her fitted sweater, looking toward the bar where they'd sat. "You in that red dress, propositioning me." His chest rumbled with quiet laughter. "If I'd known then what I know now . . ."

She lifted her head, meeting his eyes. "That I'm worth the trouble?"

"That you're worth everything." He brushed a kiss against her temple, breathing in the familiar scent that now meant home instead of temptation. "The distance, the complicated schedules, my mom's constant hints about grandchildren . . ."

"Your mom does love to hint. Although, we should've known that would happen once I moved into your place." Paloma laughed, and the sound filled his heart. "Last week, she sent me a Pinterest board full of nursery designs."

He grinned. "Sorry."

"I don't mind, not really. It's good ideas for our someday."

He held her close. The way she'd said 'our someday' about kids, so casually certain of their future together, tightened his chest with joy.

The pressure of her hand increased against his shoulder, her body subtly pushing against the direction he was moving. Her steps quickened ahead of his own. He pulled back enough to see her face. "You're leading again," he murmured.

"Because you're doing it wrong," she whispered, and he heard her smile. Her fingers pressed into his palm, steering them toward the center of the floor. "The tempo's faster."

He chuckled, pulling her close. "I love you. Even when you're impossible."

"Especially then," she corrected, rising on her toes and kissing him. "And I love you. Even when you're being stubborn."

"I wasn't being stubborn about the jasmine wall. I was right," he said, guessing she was referring to their disagreement about the Baton Rouge garden.

"You were." She settled back against his chest. "But I was right about where it should go."

He held her closer. "That's why we work so well together."

Around them, the restaurant buzzed, laughter and excited voices ringing. Through the window, stars were beginning to appear in the deepening twilight. He closed his eyes and smiled. Everything he'd ever wanted was right here in his arms, and soon, this moment wouldn't be just another evening out—it would be every evening of their lives.

"What are you thinking about?" she asked, her fingers playing with the hair at the nape of his neck. That simple touch still sent shivers down his spine, as it had since the first time she'd touched him.

He smiled against her temple, savoring how perfectly she fit in his arms. "I'm thinking about how good you look in red," he murmured, his hand sliding over her crimson cashmere sweater until his palm rested right above her ass. "And how much better you'll look out of it when we get home."

She pressed closer, her lips brushing his ear, nearly making him forget they were in the middle of a crowded restaurant. "Let's go home. I want your hands on me more than I want to dance."

"Even more than my fries?" he joked.

"Yes." She tilted her head. "But maybe we take them home. For later."

"Done." He handed her the keys to the motorcycle. "I'll get a to-go box and meet you outside."

She kissed him thoroughly before they returned to their table—him for the food, her for the helmets. But he didn't head for the counter to pay. He enjoyed the view of her walking to the door, his body humming with desire and love.

The first time she'd walked into this bar, they'd both been ready to walk away. He'd held back, believing his impulsiveness would only lead to more mistakes, more disappointments. And she'd only wanted a night, too afraid letting him close would only end in heartbreak.

Now, she wasn't walking away from him but toward their future. What had started with a proposition at a bar had, like their best designs, grown into something far more beautiful than either could have created alone.

BONUS

Love this story? There's more where that came from. Join my newsletter for exclusive insights, writing updates, behind-the-scenes peeks at my creative process, and a free short story that you won't find anywhere else. Sign up at DKMARIE.COM and let's keep the story going.

Dear Reader

Thank you for joining me on this journey! If you enjoyed Paloma and Max's story, I'd be incredibly grateful if you'd share your thoughts in a review. Even a single sentence on Goodreads or your preferred book platform helps keep their story alive for other romance readers.

Looking for your next read? Choose between two worlds: stay in our charming Michigan town with my *Lake House Love series*, or venture into the city with my urban romance series *Opposites Attract*. Keep reading for more details about each book.

Want to find out all the reasons Tate left behind his life in the city? Keep reading for the opening chapter of Tate and Eden's story, in *Stormy Waters*.

Happy reading!

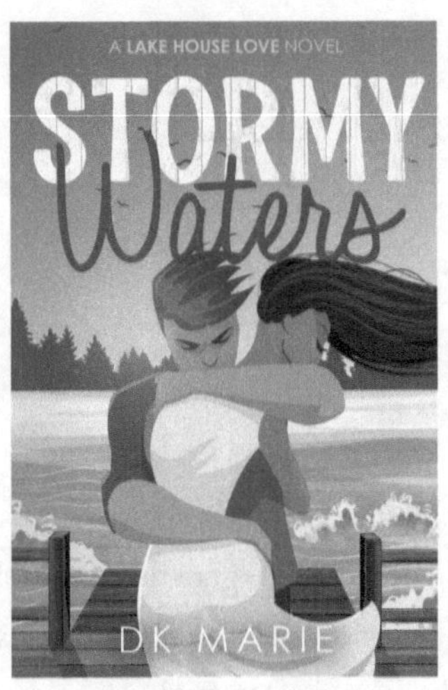

Chapter One

Eden Perez shifted her Mustang into reverse. The engine revved, and the tires spun, yet it remained stubbornly in place.

"What's wrong?" her daughter asked from the car's Bluetooth.

"I think I'm stuck." She shifted into park, opened the door, and groaned.

Her tires sat on—no, had sunk into—her muddy lawn instead of the gravel driveway. "Raven, I need to hang up. Figure out what to do."

"Okay, but you're still going to my basketball game tonight, right? We're playing against our rival."

The way her eleven-year-old daughter always double-checked their plans said she didn't believe Eden would show up. It made her heart ache. "Of course. Watching you crush the other team will be the highlight of my day. Te amo mi nieta."

Raven giggled. "What did you say?"

The last sentence had slipped from Eden's lips without a thought. She said it every time she ended a call with the only other person she loved—her abuela. But she and Raven didn't have a touchy-feely type of relationship. That was what happened when the mother spent most of her daughter's life over two thousand miles away.

But Eden was here now and would stay...as long as her fellowship went well, and Motts Children's Hospital hired her.

She cleared her throat. "I said, 'I love you' in Spanish."

There was a tick of silence, and in it time stopped as she waited for Raven's reply.

"That's so cool. I love when you speak Spanish. Will you teach me?"

Eden pressed a hand below her collarbone, near her wilting heart. "Yes, but your bisabuela—your great-grandma—would be a better teacher. I speak more Spanglish than Spanish."

"But she lives in New Mexico."

"I hope that'll change..."

If I get hired at the hospital, maybe I'll convince her to move to Michigan. Eden hated all the uncertainties.

Raven's dad, Asher, said something in the background, then Raven sighed. "I gotta go. Time for school."

They said their goodbyes and hung up. Eden grabbed her umbrella from the passenger seat and stepped from her car. The heels of her favorite leather ankle boots sank into squishy grass, and the scent of wet earth filled her nose. "April showers bring May flowers, my ass. In Michigan, it brings mud. Lots of mud."

How had she managed to forget the state's temperamental springs? Since returning in May, she'd once again experienced all the seasons, getting a crash-course reminder in the 'Great Lakes State' moody weather.

She tiptoed around puddles to the car's rear. *Dammit.* The tires were buried in muck up to the rims. There wasn't time for this delay. She had a million errands before picking up Raven from school. And skipping an afternoon with her daughter wasn't going to happen.

"How is it I'm able to operate on infants with perfect precision but can't back out of my driveway without ending up in my front yard?"

After a few calming breaths, she walked to the passenger's side since it was still on the gravel driveway. She retrieved her phone from the center console, hoping the only repair shop in this tiny town also had a tow truck because she had no one to call.

Her elbow smacked into the door's window, and she cursed as her ancient cell phone tumbled from her hand. It landed in a shallow puddle with an ominous crack.

"No, no, no. Please, no."

Grabbing it, she groaned. The screen was shattered and black. She wiped it on her jeans, then held the power button. Nothing.

She sucked in a lungful of rain-soaked air and stared at the reason she'd rented this house—the lake in front of her. It wasn't large, but most of the surrounding land was owned by the government, so there weren't many homes. The patter of the light rainfall hitting the water was usually soothing. This morning, it mocked her.

Sighing, she looked at the only other house on the dead-end road. The family was kind but basically strangers. She couldn't bang on their door. It wasn't even seven in the morning.

She craned her neck toward the large restaurant atop the hill, aptly named The Hill. Its massive patio jutted like a stubborn chin from the steep bluff. She could walk there and borrow someone's phone. Maybe she'd get lucky, and one of the college kids would be opening the restaurant. They were nicer to her than the older ones who re-membered the first time she'd lived in this small town.

Pressing her lips together, she pushed off from the car. Bemoaning her luck wouldn't check items off her to-do list. She could deal with whoever was there if it meant getting her hands on a working phone.

Making her way up the steep incline toward the restaurant, she toed around the nastiest potholes, wishing for a sidewalk. A gravel road combined with last night's storm wasn't ideal in a stiletto heel. She should've chosen a more reasonable shoe, but after five days in clogs, she'd wanted something feminine.

Less than halfway up the hill, after countless near falls, she regretted her choices—from her footwear to waking her neighbor. In retrospect, they had two little kids and were more than likely awake and starting their day.

Oh well, no point in turning back. Eden was almost at the restaurant. And her jeans were already mud speckled, and her equally dirty boots were probably destroyed.

After too many more minutes of struggling up the muddy hill, she stepped onto the worn wooden floor of the massively long metal-covered porch of The Hill. She sighed. Mental and physical weariness tugged at her. She'd have to add changing out of her ruined clothes and getting a new phone to her already growing to-do list that wanted to eat up every moment of her day off from the hospital.

She pushed through the entrance, and a ding echoed through the large, empty restaurant. Well, empty except for one man. Tate Siren, the new owner of The Hill—and her landlord—stood behind the long bar with a laptop in front of him.

It had been easier dealing with the old married couple who used to own the restaurant and two homes at the bottom of the long gravel driveway she'd just walked and now despised. Her stomach never did an excited flip at seeing them, as it did now, looking at Tate. Nor did they sneak into her late-night fantasies.

And he was a handsome distraction that was one-hundred percent off-limits.

His beautiful mouth pulled into a smile. It always surprised her how genuine it appeared. She almost believed it.

However, Tate's sister, Lilith, was Asher's girlfriend. The very same Asher who was Eden's ex and the father of their daughter. And while her ex was a kind man, Eden had screwed up enough with her choices that she could only imagine the stories Lilith—or the town gossips, told Tate.

"I hope you aren't too hungry. The morning cook doesn't arrive for another hour." Tate pointed to a carafe. "But I have coffee. Want a cup?"

She shook her head even as her caffeine addiction screamed yes. "No, I was hoping to use your phone."

"Is everything okay?"

"No. My car's stuck in the mud." She held up her cracked cell. "And I just broke my phone. Could I use your phone to call a tow truck?"

"I'll do you one better." He closed his laptop. "I have some boards behind the restaurant that I've used to help a few customers who'd had the same problem."

She stepped to the bar, moving between two stools. "That's okay. Letting me use your phone is more than enough. I don't mind wait-ing." She did but hated being indebted to someone even more.

"The reason I started helping customers is because the single tow truck in town is owned by one of the slowest men in Michigan. I'd bet good money a sloth would beat him in a race."

Her chest tightened, and she crossed her arms over the pressure. There went her beast of a to-do list, but that was better than being beholden to Tate. "It's fine. I'll wait."

He squinted his gray eyes, but instead of calling her out, he said, "My morning is shit. I could use the fresh air."

"I—"

Holding up a hand, he shook his head. "Listen, it's partly my fault you're stuck. I didn't realize until the snow melted that I needed to have your driveway graded. Let me take a look. If your car's going the way of the poor horse from *The NeverEnding Story*, we'll call for professional help."

Surprised laughter bubbled from her, popping some of her stress. "Guess I wasn't the only kid in love with that old eighties movie," she said.

"Kid? I watched it last weekend with Chloe. Bawled like a baby during that scene," Tate joked.

A twinge of jealousy pinched Eden. Tate was closer to his niece than Eden was with her daughter.

His phone dinged, drawing her attention to where it lay on the bar between them. The name Katrina appeared on the screen. Tate flipped his cell, muttering, "Christ."

He didn't say more, but it seemed as if her cloud of stress had transferred to him. "Everything okay?" she asked.

"Fine. Great." His tone and frown told a different story.

But he wasn't any of her business and didn't give her time to pursue the topic, anyway. He came around the bar, walked through the dining area, and stepped toward the main doors. "Come on. Let's see if I can help you get unstuck."

She followed, relieved the rain had let up for the moment. Looking from the sky to Tate's back, she took in his faded black Henley. The way it showcased his broad shoulders and defined biceps was lovely. Her gaze fell to his butt. Perfection. *Stop. Look somewhere else. Think of something else.*

Her mind drifted to the missed phone call. The name Katrina was vaguely familiar. A face flashed in Eden's mind when they reached the long driveway. A pretty blonde with cupid lips and cornflower blue eyes that had a sharp edge to them, Tate's girlfriend, Katrina. Were they together, or had they broken up when he moved?

Again, it wasn't her business, yet she blurted, "Are you and Katrina still together?"

"No." He didn't turn around, but it was obvious in the stiffness of his reply and how his broad shoulders tensed that the question upset him.

She was such a thoughtless jerk to ask such a personal question. This was probably why she'd had very few friends. "I'm sorry. That was nosey and rude." The hill was progressively becoming steeper, and her calves burned with the effort of not tipping or sliding down the mud-slicked driveway.

He turned just as her right foot slid forward. She locked her leg muscles, barely managing not to fall. Though, she suspected, moving might change that.

"Shit, Eden." He dropped the boards he was holding and hustled forward, helping to get her into a standing position that didn't hurt. "Those heels are dangerous on this surface."

"Shit, Tate. Had I known how my morning would be, I'd have worn hiking boots. Scratch that. I wouldn't have gotten out of bed."

Ugh. She was being rude again. Looking up to apologize, she found him grinning. And so close. He really did have an exquisite mouth.

Keeping hold of one of her arms, he shuffled around until he was behind her. "Let's walk the rest of the way like this. Then I can catch you when you slip in those ridiculously high heels. I'll come back for the boards when you're at the car."

She wasn't a damn damsel in distress, but the fear of breaking an arm or fingers more than halfway through her fellowship, had her accepting his help. "My hero," she drawled, and began walking, his soft chuckle making her smile.

Not even two steps later, Tate grunted. Gravel shifted behind her, and she was on her back, looking at the gray sky in a blink. Her heart pounded, and she waited for the cold, wet, and pain to sink in. Instead, there was deep laughter from under her. Under her?

Oh. Tate was under her, his arm around her, his big hand splayed on her stomach, keeping her in place. "Are you okay?" he asked.

She took stock. Nothing hurt. In fact, his warm, firm body along her back felt rather nice. "I think so. You?"

He sat, adjusting her onto his lap. "Just my ego hurts."

But you smell wonderful, like an outdoor adventure.

She shook her head. The inexplicable reaction of desire for him was becoming a nuisance. Holding onto his firm thighs, she pushed up. He gripped her waist, giving her the boost she needed. Turning, she looked at his black Converse, smirked and offered her hand. "Let me help you the rest of the way down the hill. We don't want you falling in those ridiculous shoes."

"My hero," he drawled in the tone she had used moments ago. She laughed and it mixed with his.

Wiping his palms on his jeans, he stood. "Let's walk next to each other. Help whoever falls next."

"Good idea."

Her playful mood lasted until they reached her car a few minutes later. Tate stood next to Eden, staring at her Mustang. "Damn. It looks like the mud is trying to swallow your car whole."

"Told you." Suspecting he regretted his offer, she gave him an out. "Ready to loan me your phone?"

Tate retrieved the boards he'd brought from the restaurant and aligned them with the rear tires. "Nah. Let's try this first. Start your car and reverse really slowly. I'll get the boards tucked so the wheels will stop spinning, and then you can back out on them."

She got inside and did as instructed. Slowly pressing on the gas, the tires caught and crawled backward. After she'd moved a couple of inches, he hollered for her to stop and switch into drive with the wheel turned all the way to the left.

The direction was simple, but her follow-through was a disaster. Her mud-covered boot slipped while she pressed on the pedal. The car shot forward, and Tate's startled yell echoed across the lake.

She slammed on the brakes as her heart crashed into her throat. Had she hit him?

No, she was driving forward. But what if he'd somehow fallen under the rear wheels??

Shit. Shit. Of all the people to hit, it had to be Lilith's brother. *Like the woman needs another reason to dislike me.*

Jamming the car into park, she jumped out. Relief pressed into her. Tate stood a few feet from the back of her car. His jeans and black Henley were covered in slime and muck. His gorgeous auburn hair was more a, well, muddy brown. There were even flicks of dirt in his close-cropped beard.

Even more surprising, he was laughing. She rushed to him. "I am so sorry."

"Well, you know how to make a man forget his problems."

"What? By giving you new ones?"

He snorted. "Yup."

"Will you have to time to go home and shower before opening your restaurant?"

"Depends on when my cook arrives. If he arrives on time, I can get home and back before the early lunch rush."

"Does he normally show up late?"

Tate nodded, not looking the least bit annoyed.

"And that doesn't bother you?"

"He works as a security guard to make ends meet. Sometimes he oversleeps."

Eden scoffed but kept her negative comments to herself. He seemed to hear them anyway and said, "If he needs a few extra minutes of shut-eye to make it through the day, I don't mind."

"You give people an inch, they'll take a hundred miles."

Tate cocked a brow. "Isn't the saying, 'a mile'?"

"It's always more. A lot more."

He opened his mouth, then closed it, seeming to study her. She hoped he wouldn't try to change her mind. It wouldn't happen, and she didn't have time for a debate. Her to-do list was waiting.

To her relief, he only said, "Not always." Then he tapped his muddy shirt. "Thankfully. I have a change of clothes in my office. I'll wash up in the bathroom sink."

She glanced at her tires. They were no longer stuck. She could be on her way. Her gaze moved to Tate. He was looking up the steep hill toward his restaurant as a violent shiver shook him. Knowing she was the cause wrapped her in guilt. She couldn't leave him cold and covered in mud.

"How about I get your clothes while you can take a shower at my house? Then you won't have to open late or spend the morning finding mud in odd places."

Even though the offer had left her mouth, it surprised her. She needed to pay him back for his help, but her nearly neurotic need for privacy meant she didn't have company often. Her only regular visitor was Raven.

Yet, the thought of Tate inside her home didn't bother her in the slightest. Unlike most people, his presence soothed instead of agitated her.

"You sure?" he asked.

"Tate, you're covered in the worst parts of spring because of me. It's the least I can do."

"Since a clump of something just slid into my jeans and down my ass crack, I'm not going to refuse your offer."

Walking to the porch to unlock the door, she teased, "Please don't use my loofah to clean your behind."

"No way," he said, following her. "My ass is much too delicate and sensitive. I'll use your face towel instead. Those are much softer."

She snickered, pushing open the door. "Gross. I'm going to hide a few bathroom items before I get your clean clothes," she joked, removing her ruined boots. "There're fresh towels and washcloths in the linen closet."

"Is that a hint to stay away from the ones you're using?" His lips twitched, then broke into a smile that made her heart flutter.

She couldn't help returning it. "Maybe."

He told her where to find his clothes, and after driving to the restaurant to get them, Eden knocked on the bathroom door. "Where do you want me to leave your stuff?"

"Would you mind setting them on the sink?"

Heat crawled up her neck to her cheeks. "But you're in the shower."

"Would you rather me stroll out in only a towel? And I have the water so hot the glass in your living room is probably fogged. You won't see anything."

She took a deep breath and stepped inside, keeping her eyes fixed on the counter. Setting his stuff on it, she grabbed for his muddy ones. "I'll soak your clothes and wash them this evening with mine."

"Thanks. And, hey, what's with the control panel in here? I feel like I'm in a carwash."

"The previous landlord had approved the upgrades," she replied, a tad defensive.

She *had* gone overboard, but after a rough shift at the hospital, her sauna shower was worth every damn penny.

"Believe me, I'm not complaining. I'm scheming ideas of how to shower here every day."

Laughing, her gaze drifted in his direction, and she froze. His back was to her, and the glass was fogged, but she saw a massive, colorful tattoo through the steam. Tracing its outline on his broad shoulders and most of his back, she then moved to his wet, tapered waist. He was exquisite.

"Eden?" He glanced over his shoulder.

She jolted. "I'm sorry, um, I didn't know you had such a big tattoo on your back."

He smirked as if to say, "That's not the only big thing I have." *Don't think about his dick size. Look away, woman, look away!*

The hiss of water cut off. "I'm finished. But you're welcome to stay for the whole show."

She ripped her gaze from him. "Dios mío, sorry! Sorry! I'll give you privacy." Her pulse raced faster than her legs as she left a very fine naked and dripping Tate in her bathroom.

Want to discover if Eden can balance her second chance with her daughter, a demanding medical fellowship, and the irresistible distraction next door? Continue reading Eden and Tate's story, available now at Amazon, Barnes & Noble, Apple Books, and Kobo. For exclusive content and updates, visit dkmarie.com

About The Author

I love to indulge in all things hot. Men, writing, reading, and coffee. The order of importance depends on the day.

Like characters in my books, I live in Michigan, enjoying her happily ever after with my husband, kids, and cat. When not writing, I love to visit the theater, concerts, and travel.

I adore hearing from readers. dkmarieromanceauthor@dkmarie.com

Acknowledgements

There are so many people to thank. First is my family, who've supported me, even while they may not always understand my need to disappear with my characters for days, weeks, and months on end. They also remind me to join the real world, and though I grumble sometimes, I appreciate the balance. Love you.

Next to my writer friends, I'd be truly lost without your guidance and chats. They keep me sane. Thank you, Shanna V., Tanna Jenkins, Margaret E. I love talking shop, crafting ideas, and falling down rabbit holes together.

There's also my talented editor, Dani Galliaro. Your insight and humor are priceless.

Also, I must send a shout-out to my fantastic cover designer, Avery Kingston. Your eye for making covers fun and artful amazes me.

And to you. With readers, these stories would be only musings in my mind. Thank you for letting me share them with you.